THE GOD IN THE SEA

An Aristotle "Soc" Socarides Novel

PAUL KEMPRECOS

Thalassa Imprints

Published by Thalassa Imprints
Cover Designer: David Berens
Print ISBN: 979-8-218-33219-8

This is a work of fiction. Names, characters, places, brands, media, and incidents are either the product of the author's imagination or are used fictitiously. Any resemblance to similarly named places or to persons living or deceased is unintentional.

Also by Paul Kemprecos

Aristotle "Soc" Socarides series
Cool Blue Tomb
Neptune's Eye
Death in Deep Water
Feeding Frenzy
The Mayflower Murder
Bluefin Blues
Grey Lady
Shark Bait

❧❧❧

Matinicus "Matt" Hawkins books
The Emerald Scepter
The Minoan Cipher

❧❧❧

Killing Icarus
"The Sixth Decoy," Best Mystery Stories of the Year, 2021

"Do not seek evil gains; evil gains are the equivalent of disaster."

—Hesiod 700 B.C.

Prologue

New York City, April, 1897

WITH A CAREER AT sea that spanned decades, Captain Ian MacNab had lost count of the close brushes he'd had with disaster. But he never would have dreamed that when fate finally caught up with him it would be in the form of a stable full of hungry horses.

The horses were eating their hay at a rate faster than the stable owner had calculated when he agreed to deliver dozens of bales to the yacht under the captain's command. The bales transported to the waterfront fell far short of the number the captain had ordered as a buffer for the yacht's only cargo, a wooden crate around eight feet tall and six feet square.

The bill of lading described the contents of the crate as dry goods. Whatever the box contained was extremely heavy. The crane strained to lift the crate from the dock and lower it into the hold. If there had been time, another supplier could have filled the hay order. But the yacht was scheduled to depart within the hour on its voyage to Boston; delay was not an option.

Captain MacNab ordered his crew to place the bales between the crate and the insides of the hull. To prevent the cargo from shifting position fore and aft, where no hay cushioned its movement, he personally made sure the crate was tied down with a spider's web arrangement of hemp lines.

Satisfied he had done the best that could be expected, the captain made a last-minute inspection. The boat had been designed as a commercial yacht, light and fast, with low draft for coastal running. The boat's dual function was reflected in its expansive hold, and the oak hull was reinforced with steel ribs.

MacNab strode along the starboard deck for the length of the boat and back to the bow on the port side, squinting against the reflection of the sun off brightwork that had been polished to a mirror finish.

"Shipshape and Bristol fashion," he said to himself.

The captain's eye took in the single smokestack between two masts that could carry auxiliary sail but were mainly for show. Then he ordered his deck hands to cast off the dock lines and waved at the bridge, signaling his first mate to get under way.

As the yacht left the dock, the captain looked skyward. High above his probing gaze were two layers of clouds. The lower layer consisted of rippling white patches. Curling against the azure sky at higher elevations were whiskery white wisps that looked as if they had been brushed onto a canvas.

The sun's rays toasted the captain's ruddy face between his reddish-blond beard and intense blue eyes. The breeze was hardly strong enough to tousle the flags that hung from the rigging of the ships docked along the Manhattan waterfront.

The weather looked good. But the slight smile that had been dancing on his lips at the prospect of a pleasant voyage morphed into a frown as he recalled the old sailor's rhyme: *mare's tails and mackerel scales make ships carry low sails.*

After leaving New York, the yacht cruised along the coast of Connecticut and put into New London to refuel. By then, a metallic overcast the shader of pewter obscured the sun. The captain pondered his choices. The boat could sit out the impending changes in the weather in Connecticut, anchor in a Massachusetts or Rhode Island port if conditions deteriorated, or it could continue to its destination. After pondering his choices, the captain settled on a third option.

The yacht wasn't exactly a racehorse of the sea, but despite its utilitarian lines, the vessel's two coal-fired engines could drive it at a respectable speed. It could outrun the bad weather, the captain wagered, even though the decision to gamble ran counter to his life-long faith as a devout Presbyterian. His church didn't mind if a man took a tipple now and then to warm his innards. Yet any game of chance was seen as a sin. Even a devout old sea dog like the captain could be seduced into taking a toss of the dice, especially since the yacht's owner had promised a bonus for on-time delivery.

After putting out to sea again, MacNab ordered the engineer to keep the engines pounding at full speed. He told his helmsman to follow the original course around the elbow of Cape Cod, the peninsula that bends off the coast of Massachusetts like a curled arm.

The yacht cut a wake through Nantucket Sound and began its turn around the Cape into the Atlantic Ocean. By then, the sky had darkened to the color of ash and the wind had freshened. The greasy rollers under the yacht's hull were laced with veins of greenish-white foam. The barometer was showing a drop in air pressure, an indicator of dirty weather to come.

The captain bent over the chart table and penciled in a new course. His original plan was to make a dash along the coast, then head to Boston after rounding the Cape. He decided instead to delay the run to Boston and drop anchor in the protected waters of Provincetown Harbor.

The strategy might have worked if one of the yacht's twin engines had not broken down after the turn to the north. Without sufficient power to punch its way through the turbulent seas, the vessel dipped and rose like a seesaw. Waves frequently buried the bow.

In spite of the howling wind and the seas pounding the hull, on the bridge an uncanny calm prevailed. The helmsman was an experienced hand who had steered the boat through Atlantic gales before this one. Under the watchful gaze of the captain, who sat in a swivel chair, he stood wide-legged at the helm, hands gripping the spokes of the wheel. He could feel the forces swirling around the rudder, but his palms were unnaturally dry, and he held a steady course.

The yacht came up on the fist-like tip of the long, skinny peninsula, and the helmsman began the westerly turn that would take the vessel out of Atlantic waters into Cape Cod Bay. After rounding the Cape, he put the boat on a southerly course with the intention of heading east and into Provincetown Harbor.

The seas began striking the yacht broadside rather than head-on. The helmsman had stretched his fingers and relaxed his hold on the wheel. He had been expecting the waves to subside as the yacht made the lee of the Cape, and was surprised when the boat gave a sudden lurch, and rolled to starboard. There was a loud thud, the deck shuddered underfoot, then after a pause, the yacht rolled on its port side. The noise repeated, and the yacht again rolled violently to starboard. The helmsman widened his stance and tightened his grip, struggling to keep control of the wheel.

As the deck slanted to the right, the captain gripped the armrests to avoid being ejected from his chair. The thudding sound from below could only mean one thing. Somehow, even with the precautions he had taken, the cargo had broken loose and was sliding back and forth in the hold.

He guessed that the vessel's see-saw motion in the open ocean allowed the crate to break free of the lines holding it in place. The few bales that were supposed to offer protection would have shifted position. Without its grassy cushion, the cargo was free to slam into the interior hull. Untethered cargo in stormy seas was the most dangerous situation the captain could imagine.

MacNab barked an order to his first mate, who was holding onto the binnacle to keep his balance on the slanting deck.

"Get a crew below and secure the cargo!"

The captain knew as the words left his mouth that it was an impossible order to follow. Even if the mate were able to round up crew and get into the hold, the shifting cargo would be impossible to contain.

The mate took a couple of steps, staggered like a drunk after a night on the town, and grabbed onto the binnacle again as the yacht rolled to the port and the inner hull was subjected to another pounding. The cycle repeated on the starboard side after a few seconds.

With his mind's eye, the captain saw the crate pounding the inside of the wooden hull between the steel ribbing like a ram battering down a castle gate. He also saw a glimmer of hope. If they could change course, the seas would no longer strike the boat from the side. The crate would move fore and aft where it would be constrained by bulkheads and might not do as much hull damage. It could gain them a few minutes.

With preternatural calm, the captain ordered the helmsman to steer the yacht into the waves.

As the steerer went to comply, the yacht rolled sharply to starboard. There was another thud, this time accompanied by a loud cracking sound. It was the moment the captain had dreaded. Even the sturdy oak planking had its limits.

The end came quickly.

The sea poured into the hold through a splintered opening in the hull that quickly expanded in size. The yacht tilted at a sharp angle, and after a minute or so, it rolled over on its side, slid beneath the waves, and rapidly plunged to the bottom. The impact broke the hull in two around midships like a cracked egg.

The crate spilled out onto the floor of the sea along with the dying bodies of the crew, the yacht's officers, and Captain MacNab, who'd lost the only wager he'd ever made.

Chapter One

The Present

PROFESSOR EMORY BRADDOCK was a man of such precise habits it was unlikely he would have changed his routine even had he known this day was going to be his last.

He rose every morning with the sun. After the usual light breakfast of oatmeal and blueberries sprinkled with nuts and cinnamon, he checked the news, weather, and traffic reports, adjusting the departure from his colonial style house in Lexington to make sure he'd arrive at the Boston Museum of Fine Arts at his usual time.

At 7:45 AM he pulled his silver BMW into his reserved parking space behind the granite temple on Huntington Avenue. Minutes later, he strode through quiet, high-ceiling galleries populated with ancient statuary of gods and goddesses.

He was in his office no later than eight o'clock.

An express package sat on the desk in front of him. He decided it was a publicity kit and tossed the thick envelope onto the stack of mail to be opened in the afternoon.

Dr. Braddock spent the morning responding to emails and returning telephone calls, including one from his niece who was working on an archaeological dig in Central America. He took a break from his work at noon and strolled to the cafeteria in the sun washed I.M. Pei wing for a lunch date with a generous but boring benefactor.

Relieved to return to his desk after lunch, he picked up a miniature replica of a scimitar he'd found in an Istanbul souvenir shop and reached for the express package. Inside the envelope were two squares of cardboard tightly bound with heavy-duty packing tape.

As he sliced the tape, the stiff cardboard rectangles sprang apart slightly. The release of pressure closed a circuit powered by two AA Duracell batteries. The electronic pulse thus generated excited molecules in the thin layer of plastic explosive sandwiched between the cardboard squares.

Dr. Braddock's secretary heard a noise that she later described to the police as the sound of a refrigerator door slamming shut.

But the professor didn't have a refrigerator in his office. And a refrigerator could not have accomplished what was done to Dr. Braddock unless it had been dropped on his head.

The secretary knocked on his door to ask the professor if he had heard the noise. There was no answer, so she knocked again, then she opened the door and stepped into a haze of rancid smoke.

The Boston police bomb squad would later conclude that the force of the explosion had been small, but highly focused, meaning there was little collateral damage. Only when she walked around the desk to inspect what looked like a red and gray Pollock painting on the white wall did she find the professor. He lay with his back down in his overturned chair.

As the secretary realized the source of the spatter, a shriek started in her toes and worked its way up to her throat where it stopped, finally breaking from her mouth as she fled the office.

Before long, distant sirens began to wail.

Chapter Two

Six Weeks Later

TO GET TO CAPE COD from the Florida Keys, you head north from Islamorada and drive more than fifteen-hundred miles, through the sprawling East Coast Megalopolis of co-joined cities, towns, and suburbs. You try to time your travel to avoid the rush hour around Washington and New York, praying to the gods of the road that you won't get stuck in construction bottlenecks or bogged down in accident stoppages, eating fast but not very good food, and snoozing in the motel closest to the highway at the end of the day.

I had stayed the night in a discount motor inn outside of Baltimore and started the next morning with a free breakfast of powdered scrambled eggs, mystery meat sausage patties, and chewy wads that could have been English muffins or foam insulation disks. The thin brown liquid produced by the coffee machine paired well with the fake creamer in the little plastic cup and only curdled a little.

After hours of driving on the interstate highways, I could tell I was close to home. The breeze coming through the windows of the pickup truck smelled less like exhaust from an 18-wheeler and more like the breath of a mermaid. Patti Page was crooning in my head about sand dunes and lobster stew. Then the highway ended, angled up and changed into the on-ramp leading to a high bridge shaped like a bow. The Ford F-150 crested the bridge road, and I glanced down with red-rimmed eyes through the suicide fence at the wide canal that separates Cape Cod from the mainland. A fishing boat was headed for Buzzards Bay and a tug plowed through the swirling currents in the direction of Cape Cod Bay.

The truck's wheels rolled onto the tarmac and around the traffic circle at the other end of the Bourne bridge. I was officially on Cape Cod, the seventy-mile-long peninsula that curls off the east end of Massachusetts into the Atlantic Ocean.

I filled my lungs with fresh air, exhaled a long, slow breath, and said, "Home sweet home, pal."

"*Mrrrp.*"

The trilling sound issued from the pet carrier secured by the passenger side seat belt. My old Maine coon cat Kojak is losing his sight and hearing, but his sniffer must have picked up the salty tang in the air. Kojak is a couple of cans of Friskies short of a ticket to catnip heaven, but he's got gypsy in his soul as the old song goes. He had weathered the long drive like a seasoned traveler, although he snoozed most of the way.

It felt good to be back in New England. When you take away the alligators and the shirt-sticking humidity, Florida has a lot going for it, although gated retirement communities and strip malls aren't my style, with or without palm trees. But if I'd known what was waiting for me as I crossed over the canal that splendid June day, I might have turned around, headed back over the bridge to points south, and taken my chances with the gators.

The ancient Greeks believed that once you crossed the

mythological river Styx, you can never go back. Yeah, I know, the Cape Cod Canal is a far cry from the shadowy boundary between light and darkness. But crossing the canal that day changed my life, and almost ended it. If I hadn't gone over the ribbon of sparkling waters, maybe I wouldn't have met some strangers with guns, paid a long-overdue debt to an old comrade-in-arms, or encountered an ancient god with a bad temper and a score to settle.

All that lay ahead. At the time, I was preoccupied with a big decision I had to make. The charter boat owner I worked for in Florida had made me a tempting offer before I headed north. He would buy my charter boat, *Thalassa* II. I would run the boat in the summer on Cape Cod as a captain for hire. In the winter I'd head to Florida to run his southern boat.

It wasn't a bad deal. I'd have year-round employment and a few coins jingling around in my pocket. I wouldn't have the headaches that came with running a shaky business. Nor would I be living proof of the folly of borrowing money from relatives. On the other hand, *Thalassa* would no longer be mine. I'd be a hired hand on what had once been my boat.

The potential buyer was a rich guy named Jim. One day he might get bored with playing at being a captain and decide he didn't need the tax write-off. In that case I'd be stuck without a boat or a job.

Jim and I had hooked up the previous fall. My last charter of the season had been four jolly women from Billerica celebrating their high school reunion with a fishing trip. They knew how to catch fish, and we had a great day. I shot a bunch of photos of the classmates and their catch; we exchanged hugs all around and vowed to do it again. I washed down the deck of *Thalassa* then strolled over to Trader Ed's waterfront bistro to toast the end of the season with a cold beer.

Using the shortened version of my name, the bartender said, "Whatcha gonna do for the winter, Soc?"

I sipped my beer. "Don't have a clue."

"Maybe you should talk to Jim," he said. He jerked his thumb toward a booth where another charter boat captain was talking on his cell phone.

I waited until he ended his call, then went over and said, "The bartender suggested I talk to you."

"Have a seat. I've got something that might interest you."

Jim needed someone to crew on his second boat in the Florida Keys. The pay would be mostly tips on top of a small base salary. I'd have a place to stay and the use of his new Ford-150 four-by-four pickup truck. I could take my cat with me. We sealed the deal with a second round, which he bought. I went home to tell Kojak to slather on the sunscreen.

Chapter Three

THE DECISION WAS a no-brainer. When the fish leave the waters of Nantucket Sound in the fall my charter business goes with them. I get a small pension from the Boston Police Department, but I usually scratch a living from other sources of income. I'm a certified SCUBA diver and pick up a commercial diving job here and there. Small stuff like clearing boat props or scraping hulls. But that's mainly warm weather business.

Cop work sticks to you like Velcro, I guess. After I turned in my Boston cop uniform, I got a private detective license. I'm not exactly the Pinkerton Agency at its prime. Even when I do get a case, it might not cover expenses and usually doesn't. Cape Cod mostly shuts down once the tourists leave. A few lawyers have my name on file, and sometimes I get a job working with a legal team.

After signing up with Jim, I arranged for *Thalassa* to be hauled out of the water and wrapped with plastic against the elements. I locked the boathouse and Kojak and I hit the road. Three days later we pulled up in front of a one-story bungalow that had a screened-in Florida room where Kojak could nap safe from gators.

I was looking forward to getting away from the raw Atlantic winds, chilling rain, and wet snow that transform Cape Cod into a pneumonia factory. And I welcomed the chance to earn a few bucks doing something I liked.

Working as a mate was a cushy job. I made sandwiches, baited hooks, kept the gear in good shape, and took over the wheel for the captain. I made decent tips and tried not to throw money away in the waterfront bars, but most of my income went toward the boat loan for *Thalassa*.

The fact that the loan had come from my family made it even more of a worry after I fell behind on my payments.

Then my brother George called. It was a big surprise, because we rarely talk. George and I don't have the best brotherly relationship. He resents me for breaking away from the family business, while he'd been drawn into it. Parthenon Pizza has given him prosperity, a big house and big cars, a beautiful, intelligent wife and two amazing children. But it has also given him difficult dealings with my parents, who built a pizza shop into a company with a nationwide distributorship of frozen Greek foods.

George was the sole vote against a company loan to buy *Thalassa*. Sometimes I wish his *no* vote prevailed. He has used the deal as leverage against my sister Chloe in an ongoing powerplay to take control of the company.

"Hey Soc," he said. "When are you coming home?"

I suspected the worst. My father is in a nursing home with dementia, and his physical health isn't the best.

"Couple of weeks," I said. "Everything okay with Pop?"

"He's pretty much the same," George said.

With news of my father out of the way, I'd expected George to bring up the late loan payments. Instead, he said, "You hear about what Ma's been thinking?"

"Haven't talked to her in a while. No."

"She wants to put you on the board of directors of Parthenon. She's worried she won't be able to keep going at the bakery because of Pop."

"News to me, George. What do you and Chloe think of the idea?"

"I think it stinks. Chloe hasn't said what she wants, but you two are tight, so you know where she'd be coming from. You could out-vote me on everything, including the boat loan."

I thought about the photo of George and me in happier days that hangs on the bedroom wall of the boathouse. We're both standing in our backyard in Lowell in front of the basketball hoop attached to the garage. We've got our arms wrapped around each other's shoulders. Our basic appearance hasn't changed. We both have the same firm jaw and generous nose, although there is more salt than pepper in our thick manes of dark brown hair, and George has put on a few pounds. What's missing is the brotherly affection we had for each other back then.

I didn't like George saying I might try to sleaze my way out of repaying the boat loan. "I would never use my position in the company to do something like that, George."

"So that means you'll take the offer?"

"Nope. It means I will wait until I get an official invite to join the board before I decide."

"Guess I shouldn't expect you to do something for the family," George said. "You know what gets me? How quick you are to help perfect strangers, but when it comes to your own family you're nowhere to be seen."

"You can do better than play that card, George. I know I've disappointed Ma and Pop and laid everything on you and Chloe. I wish it had been different, but I'm the one who's carrying the guilt."

"Being guilty is easy," he said. "Dealing with family stuff is hard."

"No argument there, George. Maybe Ma's offer is the chance to set things right."

"Have fun in Florida," he said, implying that he was far too busy with the company to take a vacation.

Then he hung up. The call from George was all I needed to cut my stay short and head home to get *Thalassa* ready for another season. If I could schedule some early charters, maybe I could catch up on my loan payments.

I knew that it was a long shot, but a couple of days later I was driving north with my cat.

Chapter Four

RATHER THAN HEAD directly home, I got off at the Hyannis exit of the Mid-Cape Highway and detoured to the marina where *Thalassa* had been stored over the winter. The manager said things weren't looking good for getting the boat into the water. The fork-lift used to move boats around had broken down. A replacement part on order from a factory in the Mid-West might arrive the next day. Or not. He had no idea how long the installation would take. He'd call me when he knew for sure where things stood.

"That's okay," I said, even though it wasn't. The manager was doing his best. But the delay was bad news. I walked over to where *Thalassa* was up on its wooden staging and ran my fingers over the white plastic wrapped around the boat in a caress that would have thrilled Sigmund Freud. My mother named the boat after the Greek goddess of the sea as a condition of the loan. In the hissing consonants of the name, you can hear Odysseus's black ship cutting through Homer's wine-dark sea.

Jim was willing to pay a fair price for my boat. But to him, it was just a diversion. For me, *Thalassa* summed up all that was good in my life. Even if I ran the charters, *Thalassa* would be owned by Jim. He might even change the name to something catchy like *Fish n Chicks*. On the other hand, if I didn't sell the boat to pay off the loan, I'd be letting down the family. And that would be just as unbearable.

Jim had asked me to drop the Ford off at the marina. I reluctantly left the keys to the pickup with the manager in exchange for the set he'd been holding for me since the fall. The manager said he had started my truck once a week. I half-wished that it wouldn't start this time, so I'd have an excuse to squeeze out another day with the Ford, but when I put the key in the ignition the engine caught after a few gassy hiccups.

The high lift Chevy pickup has a raised body and over-sized tires. It was a gift from a client who gave it to me after my truck was torched by an arsonist. When I took ownership, it had a home-made camouflage job that might have been done by a color-blind painter. I got tired of people pointing at me and paid to have it painted Aegean blue. Printed in black letters on the doors were the words: Thalassa Fishing Charters. And under that line was my name, Captain Aristotle Socarides.

So much blue moving around on four wheels is an eye-catcher. As I drove out of the marina parking lot leaving a purple haze of exhaust emission, I glanced up at the deck of a waterfront restaurant. One of the diners was pointing at me. I waved and he waved back.

I guess there's some truth to that old saying, you can wrap a fish in pretty paper, but it's still going to stink.

Chapter Five

HALF AN HOUR AFTER leaving the marina, I drove the truck off the paved road onto a dirt and gravel driveway. The melting snow and spring rains had carved the potholes deeper and wider than they were when we headed south in the fall. My teeth clacked like castanets and the shock absorbers on the truck got a thumping workout for about a quarter of a mile before I pulled up to the boathouse that I'd converted into a bachelor pad for Kojak and me.

The house sits on a small rise overlooking a bay separated from the vast blue of the Atlantic Ocean by a grassy strip of sand a few hundred yards across. Like its name, Pleasant Bay is mostly placid in the warm months when the mainland blocks the prevailing southwest breeze. Winter is a different kettle of fish. The barrier beach that keeps the Atlantic from my doorstep is practically useless when it comes to slowing down the northeast winds that roar in from the ocean. True to form, the icy blasts had pried a scattering of shingles from the roof.

I got out of the truck, stretched my arms, and swiveled my head to work out the neck kinks. Then I carried Kojak into the house, poured senior cat nibbles into his bowl and filled his dish with fresh water. When I opened the carrier, Kojak hopped out like a frisky kitten, headed directly for his dish, and inhaled his snack as if he were coming off a hunger strike.

The house smelled like a penicillin lab. I opened the windows to flush away the moldy air. Then I stepped out the back door onto the deck and swept my eyes over the bay for the first time since last October. The water that had been navy blue when I headed south to Islamorada with Kojak was now tinged with green.

I flopped down in an Adirondack chair. The sun toasted my face, and I dozed off. When I woke up it was dusk. The lights around the bay shimmered in the gloaming. I filled my lungs with the scent of pine and marsh mud, so different from the rotting vegetation smell of Florida, and I knew I was home.

Then I went inside, found some pasta still in its package, put it together with canned tomato sauce, and added sugar and cinnamon that gave it a Greek touch. After dinner I watched TV sitcoms until my eyelids drooped. I had a good night's sleep and called the boatyard the next morning. Still no word on when the fork-lift part would arrive. Maybe tomorrow.

A day's delay might be a good thing. I had chores to do around the boathouse. I could climb up on the roof to replace the missing shingles, or I could slap a new coat of paint on my outboard skiff. I keep the skiff tied up at the dock below the house in the warmer months. During the winter it sits upside down on a couple of sawhorses in my back yard. I didn't feel like crawling around on the roof, and the skiff was ready and waiting, so I went to work scraping the bottom.

If all had gone as planned, I would have sanded the hull to a velvety smoothness and applied a coat of paint as carefully as Rembrandt in his prime, then tackled the roof job. I'd kept the phone with me, and when it rang, I thought the marina might be calling with news of *Thalassa*. It wasn't.

"Been trying to reach you," said the deep baritone voice of John Flagg.

Flagg and I met in the non-commissioned officers' club behind the walls of the Quang Tri citadel in Vietnam. The club was where dirty deals were put together to transport opium from Laos, only fifteen miles away. A fellow Marine would have knifed Flagg in an argument over a bar stool if I hadn't diverted his attention with a kick in the crotch. Flagg was part of an army intelligence agency that had a bad attitude and an even worse reputation, but we hit it off. We were both from Massachusetts. He was a Wampanoag Indian from the town of Aquinnah on Martha's Vineyard. I was born and bred in the Greek-American community of Lowell.

Now he works for a shadowy government agency that doesn't exist on paper. Months go by without me knowing if he's dead or alive. Our personalities clash, and we've had a rocky relationship through the years, but he's a good friend and sometimes we work together.

"Just got back from Florida," I said. "What's up?"

"Broke my leg."

"Ouch. What happened?"

Flagg saves words like a miser hoarding pennies. "Long story."

"Sorry to hear that. What's the favor?"

"I'm at my house on the Vineyard. Getting around on crutches. Don't need you now, but thought I'd give you a head's-up in case. You available?"

"Just call and I'll catch the next island ferry."

"Thanks. I'll let you know."

He hung up. I stared at the phone in my hand.

Wondering.

I placed the phone back on the cradle, went outside and picked up the scraper. The more I scraped the more I thought about Flagg.

Flagg's call was puzzling. He's bailed me out of some tight situations, but rarely asks for help. What was different this time? I put the scraper aside, went into the house and changed into clean shorts and a T-shirt. I plunked a beat-up old Red Sox cap on my head, gave Kojak a snack, got into my high lift pickup, and headed off to pay Flagg a surprise visit.

Chapter Six

IT TAKES AN HOUR or so to get to the Steamship Authority terminal in Woods Hole. I parked in the off-site lot and got a shuttle ride to the terminal where I bought a round-trip ticket to Martha's Vineyard. The car ferry plowed through the glassy waters of Vineyard Sound, docking forty-five minutes later at the Oak Bluffs pier. A car rental place a short walk from the ferry landing gave me an off-season deal on a Jeep Cherokee.

The road out of the island's bustling commercial hub ran past sheep farms and through quiet villages. Flagg lived on the southwest side of the island in a town that used to be called Gay Head before the Wampanoag tribe petitioned to have the name changed back to Aquinnah.

Flagg's house is off a narrow, winding road a couple of miles out of town. The mailbox has a number but no name. Years had passed since I'd last been in Aquinnah. After coming home from Vietnam, I paid a visit to Flagg's sister Annie to tell her I'd seen her brother, and he was well. She was an artist who made clever items for the craft shows around the island. She was attractive and fun. We hit it off and had a thing going for a while. We parted as friends, the kind of friendship that stands the test of time if you don't see much of each other.

A black Tahoe with Virginia plates blocked the driveway. I parked on the side of the road and walked around the SUV. I wondered who was paying Flagg a visit. Maybe it was someone from Langley where Flagg has an office. The SUV was parked facing out in position as if for a fast getaway, which is not as dumb as it sounds.

If you ask Flagg what he does for a living he'll say he works for the government, then he'll change the subject. If he knows you well enough, he'll wink and say he does sneaky stuff. With Flagg, even something slightly out of the ordinary like a parked vehicle raises tantalizing possibilities. That's why I decided not to make a big deal of my arrival. I left the driveway and walked through scrub oak and pine forest. When I came to the edge of the woods, I stopped and studied the low-slung, silver-shingled house. All seemed quiet. Flagg's World War II-era Jeep was in the driveway but there was no sign of its owner.

I watched and waited for a few minutes, then broke from the woods into the open and walked across the scraggly lawn. Half-way between the house and woods two hard-faced men burst out the front door. They were both dressed for a biker's wake. Black T-shirts and jeans. But it was my funeral they must have had in mind because they raised a couple of short-barreled automatic weapons to their shoulders.

Some people say that in moments of crisis, time stops or goes into slow motion. I can't say whether that's true or not, but things were happening far too fast. My choices were limited and unappealing. I could turn around and bolt for the woods. Or stand where I was and hope for the best. Either way, twin streams of hot lead could cut me in half like Ginsu knives through a pork loin.

A shout jerked me out of my dangerous lethargy.

"Hit the dirt!"

Chapter Seven

MY BODY GRABBED the controls from my sluggish brain and hurled itself forward, my arms spread like an owl on a mouse. My fingers grabbed empty handfuls of nothing, and I did a bellyflop that knocked the air out of my lungs.

I covered my head with my hands, as if it would do any good, and braced myself. Instead of the rattle of gunfire I heard two *thuts*, like the sound a gas station air hose makes filling a tire.

After an eternity or maybe longer, a resonant voice said, "Taking a nap, Soc?"

I uncovered my head, extracted my chin from the furrow it had plowed into the ground, and pushed myself onto my hands and knees. Fingers grabbed my arm in an iron grip and lifted me to my feet. I stood on shaky legs, pulling painful gulps into my lungs, and looked past the funhouse reflection of my face in the mirrored lenses of Flagg's aviator sunglasses. Two crumpled bodies lay like tossed rag dolls where, seconds earlier, a pair of men with guns had stood.

"You okay?" Flagg said.

I spat out blades of grass and brushed the dirt off my chest and knees. "Yeah. All that was injured was my dignity and I never had much of that."

"Looked like you were trying to dig a hole to China."

"Your friends wanted to send me a lot farther away than

Hong Kong."

"That reminds me. Wait here."

Flagg was holding a pistol equipped with a sound suppressor down by his thigh. He went over to the bodies, taking his time, moving his broad shoulders in a shambling walk that went with his short, powerful legs. He got down on his knee, felt for a pulse in the neck of one man, then the other. Flagg is extra careful, which may be why he is still alive. He kept the pistol aimed at the men's skulls while he performed his post-mortem.

Satisfied with the results of his deadly work, he got back to his feet and ambled back.

"We can relax. Nothing to worry about."

Relaxation was not in my immediate plans, but there was never a doubt in my mind that the gunmen were no longer a threat. Flagg could shoot the eye out of a flea at that range.

"From the looks of it, those two had plenty to worry about," I said.

"Not anymore. Wish I could say the same for the one that got away."

"There was a third guy?"

"He followed you through the woods. If you'd turned and run, he would have cut you down."

"I'm losing my edge," I groused. "Thanks for saving my butt."

"Any time. Now tell me what you're doing here."

"You don't remember? You said on the phone you had a broken leg. That you needed a hand."

"I said I *might* need a hand."

"Who *were* those guys?"

"Name isn't important. They're three brothers who run

an organization that doesn't like people poking into their business."

"What kind of business?"

"Every dirty thing you can think of, and then some. Drugs, human trafficking, weapons, assassinations, torture. You name it, they do it."

"You can fill me in on the details after you tell me what happened to the crutches and the broken leg."

His thin lips tightened. "I got careless, slipped up and blew my cover. They found out where I lived. Figured it was only a question of time before they paid me a visit. Didn't feel like hanging around 24/7 for them to pull an operation together. I knew they were tapping my phone. My idea was to let them think I was helpless and maybe they would come to me. The busted leg was a scam. I needed to call someone, so they'd overhear me."

"Let's see if I understand. You called me to lure them here?"

"That was the plan." He glanced at the bodies. "It worked."

"It almost didn't work for me," I said, putting an edge in my voice.

"Hell, Soc. This place is loaded with surveillance eyes and ears. I knew they were coming. Even left the door unlocked so I could set up an ambush while they were inside. I was waiting in the woods. You were never in any danger."

"What about the third guy?"

He thought about it. "Well, maybe a little danger. I had the situation mostly under control. More or less."

"Mostly or more or less?"

"Take your pick. Nothing's a sure thing in this

business."

"Speaking personally, I'm glad it all worked out. What next?"

He pulled a cell phone from his jeans pocket and walked a short distance away where he could talk in private. After talking on the phone for a minute, he strolled back.

"Cleaning crew is coming in," he said. "Going to be a while. Let's go for a ride."

Flagg squeezed his big body behind the wheel of the Army Jeep. I got in on the passenger side. We drove down a barely visible track through the woods behind his house. The corpses decorating Flagg's property could have been pink plastic flamingo lawn ornaments as far as he was concerned.

It was a short drive to the red brick Gay Head lighthouse. He parked near the Indian craft shops and cliffside restaurant. We joined a stream of camera-toting tourists. At the cliff-top overlook we found a spot off by ourselves where we could talk without being overheard.

"Got your charter boat in the water?" Flagg said.

"Not yet. Just came back yesterday from a job in Florida and there's been a delay at the marina. I was catching up with chores when you called."

He gazed out at the multi-colored clay cliffs that drop down to the sea from the lighthouse.

"Been thinking, Soc. Might be a good idea if you made yourself scarce for a few days 'til we mop up this operation. They've got your phone number from when I called. Might be able to track you down same as they did with me."

I nailed Flagg with a steely-eyed stare. "Wish you'd thought about that before you dragged me into this thing."

"Yeah, me too," he said, resignation in his voice. "Dumb thing to do, but I was getting sick and tired of those guys stalking me. Figured I'd better take control in case they got lucky. I needed help with the scam. My old buddy Soc was the first one who came to mind."

"Your old buddy Soc is truly honored."

"Don't blame you for being pissed. Third guy getting away complicates things. They're probably already working on who you are."

"I can't make myself scarce. I've got to get my boat ready. I'll be fine. I'm not that easy to find."

He shook his head. "This is a sophisticated outfit. They've got your phone number. That's like having a key to the front door of your life. Tell you what. I'll have a couple of guys keep an eye on you. You'll never see them."

I pictured Flagg's gun-toting pals skulking around the boathouse. On the other hand, he was trying to make amends for screwing up. I gave him half a loaf.

"What if your security detail only keeps watch at night? I can take care of myself during the day."

"Let's talk about it. I owe you lunch for your trouble."

"Not necessary, Flagg."

"My treat. How about a burger?"

It was hard to imagine sinking my teeth into a juicy burger without thinking about the blood-soaked dead men littering Flagg's lawn. I told him I had to catch the ferry.

He drove me back to my car and said he'd be in touch to talk about security arrangements.

"You have a cell phone yet?"

"I tried one for a while to keep in contact with charter clients, but I kept losing it."

He reached into his pocket and pulled out a phone.

Handing it to me, he said, "Burner won't leave a trail, and you can call me with one press of a key. I know you don't like these things. Humor me."

"Consider yourself humored."

"Good. One more thing."

"What's that, Flagg?"

"This is government property. Don't lose it."

I drove back to Oak Bluffs, returned the rental car, and waited for the ferry at a nearby watering hole. I tried to wash away the flashbacks to the shoot-out at Flagg's house from my memory. It didn't work but the beer tasted good.

Kojak was just inside the door of the boathouse waiting to ambush me. A leg block from a full-sized Maine coon cat, even a shrunk-down geezer like Kojak, is impossible to ignore. Which is just the point in cat logic. I poured some crunchies into his special dish with the kitten face on it. Like they say, dogs have an owner, cats have staff.

As I walked to the refrigerator to reward my labor with a cold beer, I noticed the light blinking on the call recorder. I pressed the play button and a voice like gravel sliding down a chute growled from the speaker: "Hey Soc. It's Joe. I need a diver. Call me."

The last time a 'Nam buddy called and asked for help I almost got used for target practice, but I owed Joe Bones a lot. My life, in fact. I picked up the phone and kept on going to the deck. I settled into an Adirondack chair, took a sip of cold brew, and pressed Reply. When Joe answered I said, "Okay. When and where?"

"Don't you want to know *what*?" Joe said.

"Sure. What?"

A raspy chuckle came from the other end of the line. "Not over the phone. I can tell you better in person. Any chance you can come to P'town? I'll buy you a beer."

"There's a very good chance. I'm just back from Florida. Still playing catch-up. How about tomorrow afternoon?"

"That works."

"Good. But I'm buying. I still owe you."

"Hell, Soc, I cashed in your IOU when you helped me nail the jerk poaching my lobster pots."

"Doesn't count. You paid me off in lobster meat. You can buy the second round. Usual place?"

"I'll be in my office. Thanks for doing this, Soc."

"No problem." I chuckled. "This must be old 'Nam vets day."

"Huh?"

"You're the second Vietnam vet who's called me."

"That's 'cause you're such a friendly guy."

"Yeah, that must be it, Joe. See you tomorrow."

I hung up, thinking Joe would be a refreshing change from Flagg. Shows how wrong you can be.

Chapter Eight

THE LIGHT FROM THE sun rising above the outer beach flooded my bedroom on the east side of the boathouse and woke me up like a natural alarm clock. I rolled out of bed, then groped my way into the kitchen where I gave Kojak a handful of kitty nibbles and brewed a pot of coffee. As I sat at the kitchen table and gave my jaws a workout on a stale bagel I had snagged from the motel my last night on the road, I remembered the missing roof shingles and thought I ought to do something in case of rain.

I got a ladder, a bundle of shingles left over from previous winters, and a nail gun. I climbed onto the roof and swept my eyes over the bay. A white-hulled boat was sitting a couple of hundred yards from the boathouse. It was in a fishing dead zone where I'd spent many an hour, waiting for a bite that never came.

I've always been a nosy type; and I was looking for any excuse to put off shingling. I climbed down from the roof, went into the boathouse for a pair of binoculars, then stepped out on the deck and pointed the binocs at the bay.

Adjusting the lenses, I saw that there were two men in the boat. The guy in the bow had a fishing rod resting easily on the gunwale. No big deal. But the man in the stern caught my eye. He was looking at me through his own pair of binoculars. He must have seen me checking him out because he suddenly lowered his binocs, picked up a fishing rod and made a bad cast. A few minutes later the bow man set his rod down and lifted anchor. The boat headed back toward land.

There could have been a perfectly good reason for their interest. The boathouse is sort of picturesque if you like weathered Cape Cod quaint. It was an odd episode, but I shrugged it off and went back to shingling. I had almost finished the job when the phone rang around midday. The marina manager was calling to tell me the fork-lift part had arrived, but he couldn't get *Thalassa* into the water until the next day. Or the day after that.

I said I'd call him in the morning, then went back onto the roof to gather my tools. I climbed down, changed into fresh shorts and a polo shirt with the logo for my fishing business, and set off to Provincetown to meet with Joe.

About forty-five minutes after I left the boathouse, the truck crested a hill on Route 6 where the wrist of the Cape's bent arm is squeezed between Cape Cod Bay and the Atlantic Ocean. Provincetown is where the clenched fist would be and the knuckles were the Province Lands, the high, tawny dunes on the Atlantic side. The tall granite spike known as Pilgrim Monument jutted from the top of a hill behind the old fishing village.

Leaving the highway, I drove onto Commercial Street, the one-way lane that runs along the curving shore of Provincetown Harbor. The Pilgrims who stopped here in 1620 would never recognize what they left behind. After they sailed the *Mayflower* across the bay to Plymouth to celebrate Thanksgiving, a rough crowd began moving in. Provincetown became a rummy stop-over for passing pirates, privateers, and thirsty mariners.

People started calling it Helltown. Then the Portuguese

fishermen arrived with their families, a few churches went up, and respectability began to creep into the narrow streets. Next came the artists who'd heard about the crystal light and the cheap rent, then the summer visitors including many attracted by its growing reputation as a gay seaside resort. The tourists came in droves to gawk at the unconventional folks and munch on foot-long hot dogs and fried clams.

Provincetown has mostly lost its naughty vibe, but it's still got an artsy reputation as a place where you can have a good time, drop a few coins, and act a little crazy, especially around Carnival time. Art galleries, restaurants, shops, guest houses and bars line both sides of the street. The business of taking folks out to spy on whales in their natural habitat started in Provincetown. The whale watch fleet operates from MacMillan Wharf, the long pier that extends from the center of town into the harbor. Every day, boatloads of camera-toting passengers are ferried out of the harbor on specialized boats to Stellwagen Bank to check out cavorting humpbacks and bluefin whales.

The town was waking up from the winter hibernation it slips into after the tourists leave in the fall. Some businesses were open, but the shops and restaurants weren't mobbed the way they'd be after Memorial Day launched the summer season. I parked in the public lot and walked past a massive anchor and some benches in a little park, across Commercial Street to the Governor Bradford bar. The door to the Bradford occupies a corner of the building. You step from the street and bump into the shorter section of the bar, which makes a right-angle jog before running pretty much the length of the room.

Joe Bonega was sitting on a stool just inside the entrance,

his body angled so he could see who came in the door. Nicknames are a Provincetown thing. Most people call him Joe Bones. I almost tripped over him, half-blinded by the transition from bright sunlight to the interior of the Bradford, whose walls are painted in various shades of brown that add to the cave-like atmosphere.

Joe doesn't wear an eye patch, but with his angular features, skin as weathered as a piece of driftwood, long gray hair, and spiky white beard, he looks like an aging pirate. The comparison to a sea rover wasn't far-fetched. He'd skirted the law more than a few times, although he's not even remotely in the same class as Blackbeard or Morgan.

He slid off the bar stool. His left arm was in a cast, but he used his right to give me a rib-crushing hug.

"Hey Soc. Great to see you, man," he said. "Thanks for coming."

His raspy voice was a souvenir he picked up in a rice paddy when he was hit by shrapnel from a well-placed mortar round. I know this, because I was there, and if Joe hadn't taken the hit, I wouldn't be talking about it today.

"Good seeing you too, Joe. Been much too long. We're not getting any younger."

"Speak for yourself, old man." He slid back onto his stool, and I took the seat beside him. "Coupla beers for me and my pal the Mad Greek," he said to the bartender, who drew two foaming mugs and set them down on the bar top. We clinked glasses, toasted the Marine Corps with a Semper Fi, and chugged down half the contents of the mugs. Joe pointed to the logo on my shirt. "That's your boat, *Thalassa*. Something to do with the sea."

"You're right. Since when do you speak Greek?"

"I don't. Friend of mine runs an art gallery that's got the same name."

"My mother named the boat as part of a business deal. She thinks the sea holds the answer to every problem."

He tapped the side of his head with a forefinger. "Your mother's right. *Thalassa* has the answers to *every*thing."

"Thanks for the advice," I said. "What's up with the busted wing? A jealous husband catch you going out the widow of his wife's boudoir?"

"Naw. Nothing that exciting," he said ruefully. "I was painting shutters and fell off a ladder."

"Hard to believe a woman wasn't involved."

"Never said that, Cap," he said, giving me a wink. "I was helping a lady."

"In that case, I hope the busted wing was worth it."

He grinned like a middle-aged Satan.

"Hell, Soc. "it's *always* worth it."

"Thanks for sharing, Romeo. Now I'm caught up with your love life, tell me why you called. You said on the phone that you need a diver."

"Big deal, Soc. Real big deal. Guess you didn't see the stories about me in the papers."

"Like I said when you called, I just got back from Florida."

"Oh yeah, you would have missed all the fuss. Goes back a few weeks. I was dragging for groundfish in the bay and my net snagged something on the bottom. Thought I might lose the net and the catch. Got an ax ready to use in case the boat got swamped. I gave the engine a touch more throttle and the net came free. Got ripped up some, but you won't believe what I landed."

"Try me."

A customer came and sat next to Joe's stool. He jerked his eyes toward the door. "Show is better than tell," he said. "C'mon."

Chapter Nine

I THREW SOME BILLS onto the bar, then we left the Bradford and walked across Commercial Street to the wharf. Joe's boat was tucked into a slip off a floating dock across from the whale watch ticket booths. Provincetown used to be one of the biggest fishing ports in New England. In the old days, the slips would have been filled with fishing boats. The fleet has shrunk over the decades and only about a half dozen boats are still working on a regular basis.

Joe's boat was one of the older ones. Battering seas and sun exposure had taken a toll. Joe had retouched the black hull, gray trim, and white captain's house, but it would have taken more than a layer of glossy paint to hide the dents, gouges and rot. The name painted in white letters on the stern was *Zora*. Joe had named his boat after Manny Zora, skipper of the *Sea Fox*, who was one of the town's big rumrunners during Prohibition.

Joe led the way down a ramp to the floating dock. He swung one leg over the rail of the boat, steadying himself with his good arm, and put the other leg over and onto the deck. I climbed on board, and we made our way through the clutter of plastic fish boxes, tubs and piles of netting to the wheelhouse.

Joe unlocked the padlock on the door. We stepped inside and he pointed down the companionway to the cabin.

"There's a package below, sitting on the bunk. Wondered if you could bring it up."

I climbed down the short stairway and saw something long on the bunk, wrapped in black plastic and tied with a couple of bungee cords. I picked it up and discovered it had some weight. I carried the package back up to the wheelhouse.

Joe poked his head out the wheelhouse door and checked to make sure no one was around. Then he asked me to unwrap the package.

I unhooked the bungees and unrolled the plastic from around a metal shaft around a yard long and an inch in diameter. The shaft was the color of spinach and was mottled with gray clusters of barnacles and marine growth. One end was jagged. The other end branched out into three barbed prongs.

Joe was watching my reaction. "Whaddya think it is, Soc?"

I lightly touched the tip of a prong. "It's a trident. An old fish spear. Ancient maybe. I'd guess it's bronze and it looks like it broke off from something."

Nodding, Joe said, "That's pretty much what I figured. And I want to find that something."

"Where did you snag it?"

Flashing me a crooked grin, he said, "Hell, Soc, how many fishermen you know would be dumb enough to tell you where to find their hot spot?"

"None that I can recall, but we're not talking fish."

"That's true. Okay, I'll tell you this much. I think we pulled it off an old wreck."

"And you need a diver because you're talking about possible salvage."

"Depends. For now, all I need is someone to go down and find out where this funny old pitchfork came from. Maybe shoot some pictures. Can you do it?"

"What kind of depth are we talking about?"

"Around sixty feet. Sandy bottom for the most part."

"Any wreck showing on the charts?"

"Nope. Not a danged thing."

"How much time are we talking?"

"Dunno. Two or three days. Depending on the weather. We'd move fast. Get in and out. Start tomorrow. Can't pay you a lot right now."

I held the trident over my head as if I were throwing a javelin. Maybe it was my imagination, but I could almost feel its ancient energy travel down my arm. I lowered the trident, thinking that I wasn't going to get *Thalassa* into the water as early as I'd hoped. Why not help an old comrade in arms?

"I wouldn't be doing this for money, Joe."

"We'll talk about that later. Sounds like you're on board, though."

"Maybe. We're talking about a major technical dive. The diver, which is me, might have to spend some time on the bottom. No offense, Joe, but even if I attempted the job, I'd need a two-armed dive tender working the deck while I'm below the surface."

"You've got the use of one of my arms. And you'll have Tink."

I wasn't sure I heard him right. "Who, or what is Tink?"

"Tinkerbell. Don't worry about his nickname. He's big, and strong as a couple of bulls."

"Experienced working as a dive tender?"

"No, but he's worked with me on the boat."

I shook my head and added a thumbs down to emphasize my objection.

"Doesn't cut it. Visibility at that depth stinks. I might have to fight strong currents, dodge rigging and avoid sharp edges that could ruin my day. Don't know if you noticed my gray hair, but I've added a few years since we served in 'Nam. Most of my commercial work these days involves shallow water dives."

"That sounds more like a no than a maybe."

"Let's say it's not a yes. Even if the dive doesn't get me killed, it might not accomplish what you want, which is to find out what's on the bottom and bring it up. Sorry."

"Kinda thought you'd say that, but I had to try. No problem. I got a diver who works for nothing and doesn't complain. I call it my dope on a rope."

"You're losing me, Joe."

He slapped me on the back using his good arm and pointed to a black plastic box tucked in a corner of the wheelhouse. "Open that and you'll see what I'm talking about."

The yellow plastic container was around three feet long and half that size in width. I got down on one knee, unsnapped the clasps and lifted the cover back on its hinges. Inside the box was a bright yellow plastic object about the shape and size of a cannister vacuum cleaner. At one end were two black cylinders and at the other, a clear plastic bubble.

"Nice little ROV," I said, using the abbreviation for a remotely operated vehicle, basically an underwater robot.

"Bought it from the guys who run the pirate museum on the wharf. They got a new model and sold me this baby for short money. You know how to operate one of these things?'

"Sure. I've used ROVs a number of times to scope out dives. Takes a knack, but it's no big deal."

He tapped the cast on his bum arm. "It's a big deal for me. Does this gadget change your answer?"

"As my fishing partner Sam used to say, 'Finestkind, Cap.'"

"I knew my old buddy would come through."

"Like I said, your old buddy just got back from Florida. I've got to take care of a few things. I'll see you tomorrow and we can plan the dive."

"Thanks, Soc! *Zora*'s ready when you are." We shook hands to seal the deal. "Got another favor to ask. Keep this under your hat. Don't tell anyone we talked. Safer for everyone that way."

Joe was tougher than an old horseshoe crab, but I thought I saw a flicker of fear in his brown eyes.

I made a zipper motion across my mouth. "Quiet as the grave."

He gave me a funny look, but I didn't think anything of it at the time. I rewrapped the trident and stowed it in the cabin. He padlocked the door to the wheelhouse and walked me to my truck. He pumped my hand again as if he wanted to remind me of our deal. He headed in the direction of the Bradford, walking with the limp he had picked up when hot metal shredded his nerves and muscles in the rice paddy so many years ago. I climbed into my truck, thinking that the last thing I needed in my life was another complication. But if not for Joe, I wouldn't have that life to complicate.

Chapter Ten

A SURPRISE WAS WAITING for me when I got home from Provincetown. Kojak was asleep on the tattered old burlap welcome mat at the front doorstep. He was curled into himself, enjoying the warmth of the sun as cats like to do. When I left, he'd been inside the boathouse sleeping in his bed.

Kojak is a smart guy, but not clever enough to figure out how to turn the knob, open the door, and get outside on his own. I scooped him off the mat, carried him into the house, and poured him back into his bed without waking him up. Then I went out onto the deck and gazed at the area where I'd seen the white boat and the two fishermen who'd been so interested in my house. I called Flagg on his phone and told him what had happened with Kojak.

"You think someone let him outside?" Flagg said.

"He's an inside kitty. He'd be coyote or fox meat as soon as he stepped out of the house. He doesn't go outside unless I let him. I figure he could have slipped out while someone was nosing around in the house."

"Anyone special in mind?"

I told Flagg about the two guys in the boat. "They could have seen me leave. Front and back doors are unlocked. Anyone can walk in."

"Lucky you weren't home."

"Good point. If I hadn't gone to see my friend Joe in

Provincetown, I might have been at the boathouse when the fishermen came up to my dock. I would have gone down to see what they wanted. They'd say they were lost. Maybe they wouldn't even bother with the preliminaries before they muscled me into the house and out of sight of the world."

"You nailed it. Now that you've seen how fast this gang moves, let me ask again if you've given any more thought to my suggestion that you get out of town?"

"Sorry, Flagg. I've been too busy to think about it."

"Time you did. You can tell me what you want to do after I put out some feelers."

He said he'd get back to me, then he hung up and I went back into the house. The light was blinking on the phone message machine. I hit the reply button and got Jim, the rich guy who wanted to buy my boat. He said he was coming north next week.

I said, "I thought you were staying in Florida another month."

"I want to get this boat thing wrapped up. My boat broker will be with me when I come for my truck. He's a busy guy but I talked him into a meeting at the marina to discuss fleet expansion. I'd like to get together over lunch. Have you made up your mind?"

"Not really. It's a tough decision."

"Maybe the deal we come up with will help you decide to sell."

"Maybe it will," I said.

"Good. I don't mean to pressure you, but we've looked at some other boats. I'd love to get *Thalassa*. We'll have to move on the deal soon. I'd want the boat in the water and ready to fish as soon as the ink is dry on the agreement.

Hoping you can take the broker out so he can see how it does at sea."

I told him about the trouble I'd had getting *Thalassa* into its slip.

"Hold on," he said.

After a minute he came back on the line. "I gave the boat yard a call to see if I could light a fire under their butt. They're going to bring in a fork-lift from another yard."

"Thanks, Jim," I said. "And thank you for being so patient."

"No problem. I'll let you know about that lunch."

I hung up and stared into space.

I didn't like Jim treating me as if I was already a part of his boat fleet. Maybe I should get used to taking orders from a boss. I was clutching at straws thinking I could catch up with my loan payments even if I got my boat in the water and picked up a few charters. I was simply too far behind. If I entered deadbeat territory, the family schism would widen between my brother and sister. My mother is still a powerful figure, but I've seen her age since my father went into a nursing home. The last thing she needs is a family food fight at Parthenon Pizza. The last thing *I* needed was the smarmy grin I'd see on my brother's face if I screwed up the loan agreement.

Flagg could be right. Getting out of town made a lot of sense. I began to sketch out a plan. With help from Jim, *Thalassa* would go back in the water. Then I would bunk out on the boat while I was getting it ready to fish. That would buy time for Flagg to deal with his problem, and mine. Maybe I'd line up some charters.

I'd have to put off the job with Joe. The trident intrigued me, but it was still an *unknown*. My family, on the other hand, was very definitely a *known*. And as they say, blood is thicker than water. I'd have to tell Joe I couldn't get to the dive for a few days. With the complications in my life, I might not even keep that promise. Joe was in for a disappointment in any event.

I took a deep breath and picked up the phone to call Joe. I let it ring for a long time. He didn't answer. Probably hanging at the Bradford. I couldn't weasel out of the deal over the phone. It would be harder to tell Joe in person, but I had to do it. To soften the blow, I packed some clothes in a duffle. I'd leave the bag on the boat so Joe would figure I was coming back.

I told Kojak I'd be home in a while, gave him some extra treats, then got in the high lift truck and headed to Provincetown. I wasn't looking forward to the expression on Joe's face when I told him I was bailing. As things turned out, I needn't have worried about it.

Chapter Eleven

AN INVISIBLE HAND had woven the spidery wisps of fog drifting across Route 6 into a gauzy gray curtain that grew even more opaque the closer I got to Provincetown. The tiara of lights draped along the curve of the harbor was practically invisible when I got off the highway onto Beach Point. Minutes later, I came to a fork in the road and went left onto Commercial Street. As I drove through the thick fog at a crawl, the ragged sound of the truck's exhaust echoed off the corridor of closely built old houses. I stopped from time to time to avoid the few pedestrians who loomed in the headlights like the ghosts of dead sailors.

Near the center of the business district, the fog shifted in color from gunmetal gray to quickly alternating bursts of woolly blue and red in retina-burning mode. The disco effect was created by the roof lights of a police cruiser blocking vehicle access onto MacMillan Wharf. I left the truck in the town lot and walked out onto the wharf to see what was going on.

Yellow police tape stretched from one side of the wharf to the other. Beyond the tape barrier a second police cruiser and an ambulance were parked side-by-side. Muffled garbling crackled over police and fire radios like alien voices from another world. Some gawkers gathered on my side of the tape clicked away with their cameras and cells at the cops and emergency personnel milling near the top of the ramp.

The strobe flashes also washed over a slender woman and a thick-set man who stood apart from the others with their backs to me. They were looking down at the slips. The civilians turned to talk to a uniformed police officer who approached them, and I recognized Joe's sister Mary and her husband, Manny. As they talked, four EMTs carried a stretcher from the boat slips to the top of the ramp and stopped next to the couple. An EMT unzipped one end of the dark green plastic bag on the stretcher. Mary leaned over the bag, only to step back and bury her face in her hands.

The EMT rezipped the bag. The stretcher was carried to the ambulance and rolled inside. The EMTs closed the doors, and Mary and Manny headed in my direction. I lifted the tape so they could pass underneath. Mary mumbled a thank you and looked me directly in the eye. A stunned expression came to her tear-streaked face.

"Is that you, Soc?"

"Hi Mary," I said.

"What are you doing here?"

"I came to see Joe."

Mary's features dissolved into the kind of expression brought on by only the most desperate kind of grief.

"Joe's dead," she said in a leaden voice.

I had already figured out that the news would be bad. Body bags and grieving families are never a good mix.

Manny put his arm around Mary's shoulders and extended his free hand.

"I'm Manny, Mary's husband. We met a few years ago."

"Sure, Manny. I remember. The dune taxi." We shook hands and I turned back to his wife. "What happened,

Mary?"

She glanced at the morbid shutterbugs. They were edging closer, like feeding vultures, with cameras and phones raised to their eyes.

"I'll explain later." She grabbed my arm and urged me along the wharf. "Come with me."

Manny took up the rear. He's a big, wide-shouldered guy who would have intimidated anyone, but the pier paparazzi had drifted off to shoot pictures of the departing ambulance. We walked back to a Chevy Suburban SUV in the town parking lot. Painted on the door were scenes of dunes and beach scenes and the words M and M Dune Taxi. Mary got in back and I slid onto the passenger seat next to Manny.

"Where do you want to go, Mary?" Manny said.

"I don't care," she said. "Just drive."

Chapter Twelve

MANNY PUT THE SUV in gear and drove out of the parking lot onto Commercial Street, through the deserted West End, past the Provincetown Inn breakwater at the tip of the Cape. He followed the road that went by Herring Cove and through the Province Lands to Race Point beach. At the entrance to the beach parking lot, he turned onto a sand road that led into the dunes.

The road wound through rolling, grass-covered sand hills for a short distance, then ran along the shelf-like beach parallel to the surf line. After driving a few miles between the dunes and the surf he left the main track and followed a side road for a few minutes until a shape loomed black against the navy blue of the sky. The headlights swept the front of a two-story building hidden in a hollow.

Joe's dune shack had been in the family for generations. It was pretty much as I remembered from when Joe gave me a tour of the place a few years ago. Weathered clapboards sheathed the exterior except for the windows. It was square in shape, basically a large room, with a bed, stove and propane fridge and living spaces partitioned off by plywood walls. A metal spiral staircase ran from the first floor to the roof where Joe had built wooden rails to enclose an observation platform. It was the sort of architectural flourish you'd expect from Joe.

We got out of the parked SUV; Manny snagged a

flashlight from the glove box and led the way to the front door. Mary produced a key for the padlock, then pushed the door open and we stepped into the shack. After he lit some kerosene lamps, Manny started a fire in a wood-burning stove. I looked around the interior of the shack in the flickering yellow light. The fishing nets hanging from the oak-paneled walls were festooned with horseshoe crab shells, lobster buoys, conchs, and dried up starfish. A beachcomber's dream.

As the interior of the shack warmed up, Mary found a bottle of Jack Daniel's in a cupboard. She lined up three water glasses and poured out double shots straight. No water or ice to get in the way of a good buzz. We sat on keg stools at a wooden table that had a top made from a boat hatch.

Mary raised her drink. "To Joe."

"To Joe," we echoed, chugging from our glasses much faster than Tennessee sippin' whiskey was meant to go down.

I gazed at Mary over the rim of my glass. She had a few faint wrinkles around her mouth and eyes, but her olive complexion glowed with the health of a woman half her age. She was younger than Joe by around ten years. They had the same mother but different fathers which was why she had the good fortune to only resemble Joe a little.

She slugged half of her whiskey like a longshoreman coming off a shift, set the glass down, and stared at the highlights of the amber liquor dancing in the flickering light from the wood fire. She was ready to talk.

Mary said she had been tending the bar and running the show at Diva's, the nightclub she owns. Which explained why she was dressed in a slinky black dress with sequined flower blossom patterns that sparkled in the flicker of the lantern light.

"I got a call from my cousin, Ray Souza. He's a Provincetown cop. He said there'd been an accident and to get over to Joe's boat immediately. I could tell from his voice it was bad." She paused a few seconds to pull herself together, and in a voice as flat as day-old beer, said, "I told Joe he should have thrown that damned thing back into the ocean."

"I'll take a wild guess," I said, "You're talking about the trident that came up in Joe's net."

She shifted her gaze from the whiskey glass to my face. "You read the newspaper articles?"

"Nope. But Joe showed me the trident earlier today."

"I had no idea you'd been in town."

"It was a last-minute thing. Joe called and said he needed a diver. We met for beers at the Governor Bradford, then we went to the *Zora* where he had the trident. Joe didn't say anything to you?"

"He must have figured it was none of my business."

"I'm surprised to hear that. Joe and you were pretty close."

"*Were* is the operative word. Joe and I haven't talked in weeks."

"What's going on, Mary?"

"Money mostly. Or the lack of it. Joe has had a tough time with his fishing business. No one will work with him because of his temper. He's had to go it mostly alone. You've seen the *Zora*. It's falling apart. I've been pitching in with loans, but I had to tell Joe I couldn't keep supporting him and his boat forever. He would have to give up fishing."

"Joe's an old sea dog. Hard to imagine him doing

anything else."

"We suggested he work for Manny's dune taxi company," she said. "He couldn't see himself as a driver."

The comment brought a snort from Manny who'd been listening quietly to the conversation. "I've been doing all right since going out on my own after all those years I worked with Art's dune taxi. Joe thought driving tourists around the dunes was beneath him."

"Manny's right as far as it goes. We almost had Joe willing to give it a try. Then he found that pitchfork and it changed everything."

"Changed it in what way?"

"He turned down the driver's job," Mary said. "Said he was all done sponging off his sister. And he was going to pay back everything I'd loaned him, with interest."

"Where was that money going to come from?"

"He didn't say. All I know is that he started talking about payback. When you saw him today, did he say anything about his plans?"

"He figured the trident came from a statue that was on a shipwreck. He wanted my help to scope out the site for possible salvage."

"Did he tell you where he'd found the wreck?" Manny asked.

I shook my head. "I asked him that same question. Joe was cagey and said I'd see the location when we went out on the site."

"You were going to dive on the wreck?" Mary said.

"I told Joe the dive job was too big for me, but I'd run a remote search with an underwater drone. I just got back from Florida and had to deal with some boat business, so I couldn't give him a firm commitment. When I tried to reach him on the phone today to talk about it, there was no answer. I drove to P'town and saw what was going on with the police and EMTs on the wharf. What happened?

"What happened is that someone killed him," Mary said, almost spitting out the words.

I gaped like a codfish about to gulp down a baited hook. Joe had been beat up in the war and led a hard life that would have wiped out most men. I figured his lifestyle had put him in a body bag, not that he'd been murdered.

"I don't get it. Who would want to hurt Joe?"

"I don't know. Joe could be mean and ornery. But he was kind and generous too. People thought he was washed up. That wasn't true. He had so much more to give. He didn't deserve to die the way he did."

"You're right, Mary, it makes no sense."

"*Nothing* about this makes sense," Mary said. "Manny can fill you in. He's talked to Joe more than I have."

Manny had been watching with a pained expression in his eyes during Mary's lament.

"I don't have a taxi stand, so I pick passengers up at their location. I'd see Joe when I was running around town. Sometimes we'd chat. Like Mary said, he's been having a rough time lately. The boat is old and needs repairs. Trouble getting crew to work with him. He was going to see how things went this season."

"He seemed on edge when I talked to him earlier," I said. "Almost paranoid."

"Yeah, that's new. He's always been a little crazy since the war. Depression mostly, but he was doing better for a while after he found the trident. The Advocate sent a reporter over to interview Joe. Got his picture in the papers. You know how Joe likes to be the center of attention."

Mary smiled. "He enjoyed being a celebrity, especially when he got a story in the Boston papers." She pointed to a filing cabinet against a wall. "He even bought that thing to hold the stories about him."

"Did any of those stories hint at where he'd found the trident?"

"You've got to be kidding," Manny said. "Joe was famous around the wharf for keeping secrets. If you pushed him, he'd make believe he was telling you about his hot spot, but it would be phony information."

"I told him the trident looked like something you'd find in a museum."

"Bingo," Manny said. "A couple of experts said it could have been ancient Greek or Roman. But no one could figure out how something that old would have ended up in Cape Cod Bay."

"The locals joked that it was just Joe being a pirate," Mary said. "People said he'd picked up the trident in his travels and that he'd try to sell it. Everyone knows his business has been on the rocks. They got suspicious when he wouldn't say where he found it. Eventually people got tired of hearing Joe go on and on. The newspaper stories stopped after a while. It was a little sad about the mostly empty filing cabinet."

"What happened next?"

Mary swept the air with her arm. "Joe hung the trident on that wall with all the other crazy junk he's pulled out of the sea or off the beach."

"We thought that was the end of it," Manny said. "Then one day Joe let on that he was talking to someone he called 'the professor.' Said it had something to do with the trident. And that it was big. Really big."

Mary chimed in. "So big he got the thing out of here and stowed it on his boat. He told me that he was going to sell his boat and get out of fishing."

"All this would come from the trident?"

"It sounds crazy, doesn't it? He said the professor told him it might be the archaeological find of the century. That a lot of people would be interested in his discovery. He was acting like the king of the world. Then he read in the paper that the professor had died, and his whole attitude changed. He shut down. Wouldn't tell me or anyone what was going on. I laced into him. Said he had to snap out of whatever it was. He stopped talking to me."

"He clammed up with me too," Manny said.

"Joe told me it wasn't safe to talk," I said. "Any idea what he meant?"

"He was a big con man," Manny said. "My guess is he told people he couldn't talk because there was nothing to talk about."

"It's all my fault," Mary blurted. "The whole damned thing is on me. I nagged at him to quit fishing. He thought it was an attack on his manhood. He felt pressured into taking a risk."

"Don't blame yourself, Mary. Joe has always been a risk taker," I said. "He risked his life to save mine."

"I know you had some close calls in the war. You had that between you. You'd never stop believing in Joe. You'd never let him down."

I could have been honest and said I had come to Provincetown to do exactly that. I was going to let Joe down by telling him he'd have to wait for me to do the survey. I veered off on a conversational tangent instead.

"Did the police say where the investigation goes from

here?" I said.

"All I know is they've taken Joe's body to a state lab for an autopsy," Mary said. "He'll be released eventually to a funeral home."

"That's pretty standard procedure."

A surprised expression came to Mary's face, like someone had whispered a secret in her ear. "Oh right. I'd forgotten you used to be a detective."

"The cop habit is hard to kick. I've got my private detective license and take a case now and then."

A thoughtful expression came to her long-lashed eyes.

"Would you take a case for me? You can stay here in the dune shack while you're investigating. Please, Soc. I must know who killed my brother."

Joe had gone to his death thinking that his old war buddy was coming to his rescue to pay off a blood debt when it wasn't true at all. I still owed Joe, even if he was dead. *Especially* since he was dead.

There was only one answer I could give her.

Chapter Thirteen

THE AMBULANCE AND NOSY spectators were mostly gone from MacMillan Wharf, although the clinging fog had settled in for the night. We got out of the dune taxi at the town parking lot. Mary handed me the key to the shack. She gave me a quick hug, got back into the Suburban, then she and Manny drove off while I stood there in the damp mist trying to figure out where to start investigating the murder of an old friend.

The temperature had dropped into the chill zone. I got a windbreaker from my truck and walked out onto the wharf to survey the scene of the crime. A couple of Provincetown police cruisers were pulled up beside an unmarked car that had blue and white official license plates. The strobe units were shut down; floodlights on stands illuminated the scene. A dozen or so people in uniforms and suits were clustered near the boat slip ramp.

I bellied up to the tape to watch what was going on. Nobody noticed me at first. After a minute, someone wearing yellow foul weather gear stared at me for a few seconds, then broke from the knot of people and walked in my direction. I recognized the boyish face of assistant district attorney Francis X. Martin under the wide brim of the rain hat.

"Hello counselor," I said. "Nice to see you out and around this lovely night."

The ADA grinned. "Hi Soc. I thought that was you lurking in the shadows. You should have let me know you were here."

"You had me fooled, Frank. I thought you were the Morton salt girl."

"I was trying more for the old man and the sea. Kind of a dumb question, given your ghoulish history, but what are you doing here?"

"Nothing complicated. Joe Bones was a friend of mine. We go back to 'Nam."

"Sorry for your loss. I thought his name was Joe Bonega."

"Provincetown people use nicknames to avoid confusion. Lots of locals are related and have the same last names."

"That doesn't explain why you're here."

"I came by to pay my respects."

"Isn't that something usually done at the funeral?"

"I like to get an early start in case of traffic."

He chuckled. "Start on *what*, Mr. Socarides?"

"How about the cause of Joe's death?"

"Why do you want to know, if you don't mind me asking?"

"Not at all. The family of the deceased hired me to investigate the case."

"Wow! You work fast. I never figured you for an ambulance chaser."

"Looks like I'm a hearse chaser with this case. Joe's sister seemed particularly upset over the way he died."

"I don't blame her. This one is a *pissah*," he said, letting his Dorchester accent slip out. "The body was found in the wheelhouse under a net. There was blood on the deck, so he'd probably been moved inside after the murder. Vic had been stabbed three times in the chest."

Frank didn't notice me wince, but maybe he should have. Calling a murder victim the *vic* has always seemed a tad disrespectful, especially when the dead person was a full-blooded human being until the last breath.

"Multiple stab wounds are usually a crime of passion," I said, brushing off the TV cop talk.

"Maybe. But with only three wounds? I don't know."

"A *little* passion then?"

He narrowed his eyes. "It must have been a little passion by a methodical killer."

"What makes you say that?"

"The wound pattern. They were spaced apart equally from each other."

"Murder weapon?"

"Nothing on the boat. We've got people checking the beach on either side of the wharf. Divers are coming in tomorrow to search the water."

"How about witnesses? People are always wandering around the wharf even at night."

"You've got to be kidding! You could cut this fog with a knife. On top of the lousy visibility, the boat is off by itself where the light from the dock doesn't reach."

"The frontal attack suggests maybe Joe knew the killer and had his guard down."

"Highly possible. So, Sherlock, where do you suggest we start?"

"With the most likely murder weapon, based on your description of the attack. Joe had an ancient fish spear he dragged out of the sea on a fishing trip. It had three sharp prongs that could have made the wounds in his chest."

"How did you know about this thing?"

"Elementary my good fellow. I read the newspaper stories about Joe's find." It wasn't quite the truth, but it was close enough. "My guess is that the trident was a murder weapon of opportunity. Maybe the murderer needed something in a hurry and grabbed the nearest thing with a sharp point. Or three points in this case."

"Makes sense," Martin said. "The murder could have been unplanned, but the killer still made a half-hearted attempt to hide the body under the net and had the presence of mind to take the murder weapon with him."

"Or her."

"You really think the killer could have been a woman?"

"You never know. Think about Lizzie Borden."

"Who?"

"Never mind," I said. "Who found the body?"

"Pal of Bonega's who saw him earlier at the Bradford. He told his buddy he had to get to the boat but would be back to play cribbage. When he didn't show up for the game, his friend walked over to check on him. The deceased had been drinking and his pal figured he might have fallen asleep in his bunk. Found the body in the wheelhouse. Door was unlocked."

"Joe could take care of himself in a fight, but he had busted his arm, and it was in a cast."

"How'd that happen with his arm?"

"He fell off a ladder."

"He would have had a tough time defending himself."

"Joe would have tried, broken arm or not. The cribbage pal's story should give you a rough idea of the time of death."

"Won't know exact time until the autopsy." He

wrinkled his brow. "How'd you get hired by the family so soon after the murder?"

I didn't know what to say. Frank would ask questions if I told him I'd seen Joe and even held the probable murder weapon in my hands. Fortunately, I didn't have to come clean.

One of the suits gathered near the cars separated himself from the others and strode toward us like somebody on a mission. Even without the reflection of police lights on the shaved scalp I recognized the man as a state cop attached to the DA's office. His name was Corrigan and he'd had it in for me ever since I'd made his boss look bad in a murder case he'd bumbled.

Frank saw him charging in our direction. "Shit," he said. "I shouldn't be seen talking to you."

"I've got this," I said. As Corrigan approached, I said in a loud voice, "You don't scare me, Martin. I'm not afraid of you or your boss. Next time you see the DA, tell him I said to take a flying leap!"

Corrigan skidded to a cartoon stop. I got the chance to appreciate what a great job nature does of giving nasty people the face they deserve. He self-administered an extra dose of mean, then he kept on walking. Slower and more deliberate, like an Old West sheriff in a face-off with the hired gunfighter. Not the hot-headed buffoon he was.

He sidled up next to Frank, and with a growl like a bull mastiff, said, "Socarides here giving you a hard time?" He pronounced it *Socareyedes*. Probably trying to annoy me. It annoyed me.

Frank had caught on. Following my lead, he turned to face Corrigan. "No problem, lieutenant. I was just telling this fake cop to butt out if he knows what's good for him."

"Looks to me like he's interfering with an investigation," Corrigan snarled.

"Not as long as he stays on that side of the police tape."

"Too bad. I'd love the excuse to throw his sorry ass in the county jail."

I smiled. "Nice to see you, Lieutenant Corrigan."

"It's not nice to see you. What the hell are you doing here?"

"I wanted to ask if you were still molesting little girls."

It was a cheap shot and sucker punch combined into one. Corrigan hadn't *molested* anyone that I knew of, but he'd stood by while another cop used aggressive body search techniques on teenage girls. Corrigan said he had no idea what had been going on and would have arrested his pal on the spot if he'd known. He was politically connected, so his pal landed in jail, while Corrigan got a job in the DA's office.

He took a step toward me as if he were going to bust right through the tape. Corrigan is a big and burly guy and probably fights dirty. His belly drooped over his belt and red spiderwebs decorated his nose. I thought I could take him, but brawling with a state cop within sight of his pals probably wasn't a good idea.

Frank stepped in front of him.

"Don't let this jerk get under your skin, lieutenant. He isn't worth it."

Corrigan opened his mouth to say something, but one of the other uniforms called his name. He clamped his jaws shut, spun on his heel, and strode back to the group. I saw him point me out. He might have been saying what a fine fellow I am, but probably not.

Martin puffed his cheeks. "Thanks for the heads-up. I'd

be looking for a new job if the DA knew we were friends."

"A change of scenery for you might not be a bad thing."

"I know," he said with a shake of his head. "I can't wait to hand in my resignation and run against the DA in the next election. In the meantime, I've got to build up my resume and stay on the DA's good side."

"I didn't know he had a good side. By the way, calling me a fake cop was a little harsh."

He sighed. "Sorry. That was sort of cheesy."

"Pure Limburger."

"Guilty as charged. But where'd you come up with 'take a flying leap?'"

"Same Jimmy Cagney movie where you got 'if he knows what's good for him.' We'd better talk about our favorite tough guy cliches another time. Corrigan might have an attack of smartness and figure out we were playing him."

"Good idea. I'm still curious about how you got the gig with the family so damned fast."

"Joe wanted to hire me for a diving job. I came to Provincetown to talk to him about it and saw the ruckus on the wharf. I ran into his family, and they hired me to look into his death."

"That was a fortunate coincidence."

"Yeah," I said. "Some guys have all the luck. Nice talking to you."

I stuck my hand out and said it was great to see him. Before he could say another word, I wheeled around and headed to my truck. Frank was one of the good guys. I felt bad shutting down our conversation like that, but he was no dunce. He'd keep asking questions until he had all the answers.

I forced myself to amble as if I had all the time in the

world. I half-expected him to call me back to talk more but made it to my truck and slipped behind the wheel. When I glanced in the rear-view mirror, Frank was walking back to join the others. He was an experienced prosecutor, and I knew I'd be hearing from him again. I got out of town as fast as I could. I didn't breathe a sigh of relief until I turned onto the side road at Race Point and plunged into the sandy sanctuary of the Province Lands.

Chapter Fourteen

WHEN I GOT INTO the shack I poured a shot of whiskey, carried it up to the observation platform, plunked down in a beat-up old plastic stack chair, and stared off at the dunes that were bathed in the silvery light of the moon. The undulating sand hills were crowned with stunted trees, and gnarled, low-lying bushes that looked like flotsam on the rolling seas of a far-off planet. The air was cool with only a trace of the suffocating dampness of the fog-choked harbor.

The beauty of the other-worldly scene took my mind off murdered friends and corrupt cops for a few minutes, but my thoughts soon drifted back to Joe. From what I knew after talking with Mary and Manny, my old war buddy had been bumbling through life, trying to hold onto his business, probably destined to take a job driving tourists out to see the dunes. Everything changed when he found the trident.

If I wanted to find out why Joe was dead and who killed him, I'd have to go back to the time interval between the day he found the ancient relic and the night it was used to bring his life to an end. I polished off the whiskey like a riverboat gambler folding his cards and went back downstairs to look in the filing cabinet Joe bought to hold the stories about his discovery. In the top drawer I found some manila files and envelopes stuffed with news clips. I dumped the clips out onto the table and began to go through the articles one-by-one.

The stories reported Joe's account of how he'd caught the trident in his net. Some writers had talked to local fishermen about the crazy stuff they pull out of the sea. Even a live bomb in one case, but nothing like what Joe had hauled up. A few experts had chimed in, saying the trident was old, ancient maybe. But nobody could explain how it got to Cape Cod Bay. One scholar said flat out that unless there was evidence that ancient Greeks and Romans had visited Cape Cod, the trident would only qualify as a curiosity, not a relic.

Not every scholar pooh-poohed the find. The Boston Globe quoted an archaeologist named Dr. Emory Braddock, who took a slightly different tack. Braddock was a professor of Greco-Roman history attached to the Boston Museum of Fine Arts. He said the trident shown in the photo looked like it dated back to ancient times, but he couldn't tell for sure until he saw it first-hand. Braddock said the fact that it was found in an unlikely place shouldn't short-circuit the possibility that the thing was the real McCoy.

Fastened to the Globe article with a paper clip was a mailing envelope, addressed to Joe, that contained a single sheet of paper with the letterhead of the Boston Museum of Fine Arts. Printed in ballpoint on the paper was a short message: "Please call me," the initials EB, and a telephone number.

I folded the *Globe* article and letterhead, slid them into a pocket in my windbreaker and made a mental note to call Braddock. Then I stuffed the stories I hadn't read into a folder to be looked at later and put everything back in the filing cabinet. Digging a couple of musty woolen blankets out of an old steamer truck, I spread one out on the mattress and covered myself with the other. It was chilly in the shack, so I kept my clothes and jacket on. I lay on my back and stared at the ceiling. I tried to sleep but thoughts kept buzzing around in my mind.

I've only fished the Atlantic and Nantucket Sound. Cape Cod Bay is pretty much a mystery to me when it comes to dropping a hook. Playing a mind game to get my bearings, I pictured myself as a gull circling high above the Pilgrim monument, then flying over the harbor to hover above Wood End light. Like Joe, my imaginary gull could choose from several directions: south toward Billingsgate Shoal, west toward the canal, or north of the Cape to Stellwagen.

Joe had fished the bay for decades. He would have carried a chart around in his head, but he'd still have to rely on his Global Positioning System, or GPS, to put him on top of his favorite fishing hole. GPS also records where it's been, which means the instrument on Joe's boat might show his track on the day he found the trident.

The glowing face of the alarm clock on the table next to the bed told me it was nearly three o'clock in the morning. I tried to sleep but kept thinking about the GPS. I was already dressed. All I had to do was pull on my shoes, get in the truck and drive to town. Which is what I did.

Provincetown was deserted, as if someone had lifted one end of Commercial Street and emptied out every human being. With no police cars blocking the way, I drove onto the fog-shrouded wharf and parked across from the whale watch fleet. The yellow tape and the floodlights were gone, and so were the forensics people who must have finished with the crime scene. The only sounds were the mournful moan of the foghorn and gentle lap of waves against the pilings.

I got a crowbar and flashlight out of my toolbox and climbed onto Joe's boat. The *Zora* was almost lost in the mist-cloaked shadows. Picking my way around the fish tubs, nets, and coiled line, I went up to the wheelhouse and pried the latch off, padlock and all. It wasn't exactly a surgical procedure. The crowbar gouged a chunk of wood from the door jamb. I silently apologized to Joe for messing up his boat and stepped inside.

Joe operated with a portable GPS mounted on the dashboard to the right of the wheel. The screen section of the unit came easily out of the arms holding it to the instrument panel. I clutched the GPS in my left hand, slipped out of the house, and quietly closed the door behind me.

I was picking my way through the piles of fishing gear cluttering the deck when I heard a scuffing sound from behind me that could have been something accidentally kicked along the deck. I spun around as a shadow materialized in the gray fog from behind a stack of fish boxes. I brought up the crowbar defensively. Too late. The amorphous patch of darkness came in low under the crowbar and hit me hard in the mid-section.

The air whooshed out of my lungs. I went flying backwards and landed butt-first on the deck. The GPS slipped from my fingers and a blinding light flashed in my eyes. I flailed at it with the crowbar but swung in empty air. The light snapped off. When it went on again seconds later, the beam was pointed at the deck.

Motes of light swirled in the air, but I could make out the gloved hand that reached down and grabbed the GPS off the deck. The light went off again. Footsteps pounded along the pier. I got to my feet and rubbed my haunches.

Then I limped back to the truck and drove through the sleeping village and out to the dunes.

My aching ribs and posterior were telling me I had taken the Joe thing much too casually. I humored Joe when he warned me of danger. I blew him off because he had a talent for exaggeration. Even after he'd been killed, I wasted time baiting a rogue cop when I should have been nosing around the murder scene.

I would have kicked myself if my backside hadn't already been tender. I dragged the bottle of whiskey out of the cupboard and went to pour a shot. Instead, I put the cap back on, put the bottle back in the cupboard, and did the smartest thing I could think of. I went to bed.

Chapter Fifteen

MARY CAME BY THE shack early the next morning to drop off some groceries. I was having my coffee on the observation platform and saw the dune taxi winding its way along the sand road to the shack. Mary got out of the taxi holding a paper bag in her hands and called up to me.

"Good morning."

"Same to you," I said. "Where's Manny?"

"Working on a new taxi he bought. It was the one Joe was going to drive. How are you?"

"Doing fine," I lied.

My rear end and elbow were still smarting from the hard landing on the deck of Joe's boat. My ego was equally sore from letting the GPS go, and with it, any chance of finding Joe's phantom shipwreck.

"That's good. Brought you a few supplies." She reached into the taxi for a bag and headed for the door.

"I've got a coffee pot on the stove. Come on in."

I went downstairs and poured Mary a cup of coffee. We sat at the table and exchanged funny Joe stories. Talking about her brother seemed to lighten the load of sadness.

"You haven't told me how Joe dragged you into this mess," she said.

I told her about the phone call, the meeting at the Bradford, and the walk over to the boat where Joe had shown me the trident. As I rambled on, I recalled something from my talk with Joe.

"I just remembered. Joe mentioned that *we* found the trident. That sounds as if someone was with him on the boat."

"Probably Tink. Joe hired him as crew occasionally. He's about the only one in town who would work with my brother."

"Does Tink have a full name?"

"Tinkerbell."

Weird names are not uncommon in Provincetown, so I didn't pursue it. "How do I get in touch with Tink or Tinkerbell?"

"He's doing some handyman work for me at the club. You can catch him there."

"How will I know him?"

She smiled. "You'll know him. Say I sent you. That we're friends and it's okay to talk. I'll come by the club after I meet with the funeral director."

After Mary left, I cleaned up the kitchen, then got in my truck and drove back to town. Mary's club was a few minutes' walk from the town lot, off Commercial Street in the west end of town. I turned the corner into the alley and had what Yogi Berra would have called deja vu all over again.

The two-story building had been spruced up with paint and shingles, and the sign that said Diva's was different from the one I had remembered, but I'd stood in the same place years ago. I'd been investigating the death of a diver named Kip Scannell, who'd been diving on an old pirate ship. The path led to the club's door. My lead had been a female impersonator named Lady Brett who worked at the club and had an apartment upstairs.

The entrance to the club was unlocked. I stepped inside, walked past a vacant reception desk and down a hallway into a large room. Rows of chairs faced a curtained stage. I called out a hello. There was no answer. I went into a smaller, adjoining room where there was a bar. It was apparently unoccupied, so I went back into the stage room.

Fighting in an unnecessary war and working as a city cop had drained my capacity for astonishment. But I couldn't help doing a double eyebrow hike. Standing in my way was the biggest human being I had ever seen. I didn't even know they came in double extra-large size. He wore a denim jumper that had enough fabric to make a circus tent. A red bandana was wrapped around his head pirate style. The electric drill looked like a child's toy in his massive hand.

Baby blue eyes peered down at me from a roundish face. "Can I help you?" he said, drawing his lips into a deep frown.

"Maybe, if your name is Tink."

"That's me. Who are you?"

I gave him my business card. He glanced at the logo and said, "I'm not interested in fishing."

"Running a charter boat is my day job. I moonlight as a private investigator."

His expression didn't change. "I don't need a private investigator either."

"Maybe you don't but Mary does. She told me you fished with her brother Joe."

"I'll have to check with Mary before I talk about Joe."

"No problem." I looked around. "I knew someone who used to work here," I said. "Lady Brett."

Tink's lips drooped slightly less.

"You knew Lady Brett?"

"Not well. Our paths crossed. Brett was a key witness in a case I was investigating. He lived upstairs over the club."

"Mary's office and my apartment are there now. I've heard that Lady Brett was a legend in the business." He read the business card again. "You say Mary told you to talk to me?"

"She's coming in soon, so you can ask her yourself."

"No need to wait," he said. He swept the air with an arm that was like a log. "What can I do for you?"

"I need some information. Mary hired me to investigate Joe's death."

He shook his head. "Why hire you? If you don't mind me asking."

"I don't mind at all. I served with Joe in the Marines back in 'Nam."

He looked at the business card again and this time he must have read the name under the logo. "He talked about you! You're Soc. You were with him when he got busted up."

"I was the reason he got busted up. Joe took some shrapnel meant for me."

"I heard the story." We shook hands, which consisted mainly of my hand being clutched by fingers the size of bananas. "Great to meet you. How can I help?"

"I understand from Mary that you might have been fishing with Joe the day he found the trident."

"That's right. A few weeks ago. It was kind of dicey. Joe didn't want to lose the catch. He kept hauling the net in. The boat started to tip. We were afraid it was going to take on water and we'd get swamped."

"He told me he had his axe out ready to cut you free."

"Yeah, he had the axe, but you know how stubborn he can be. He couldn't afford to lose the net and the catch. I was afraid he wasn't going to cut the lines, but then the net came free. We saw the trident poking out of a mess of fish."

"Any idea where you fished up the trident?"

He wagged his head. "I'm basically a landlubber. I crewed with Joe because he was Mary's brother and he needed help. He hardly paid me, and I knew what money he did hand over came from his sister."

"Do you remember what you saw when the boat left the harbor?" Maybe I could piece together the route Joe followed the day he netted the trident. Where the boat was in relation to the Monument, the lighthouse, the cliffs and beaches, and whether it was headed due south, or around Race Point.

"It was dark except for lighthouses flashing," Tink said. "I had a nap on the way out. When the sun came up, we were already at the fishing hole. I was too busy to pay much attention to my surroundings. I remember it was after sunset when we headed home."

I tried another tack.

"Did you ever see the boat's position on the GPS?"

"Navigation's not my strong suit. Joe took care of that stuff."

"Too bad. The GPS would show where you'd been."

"I doubt if the GPS on the boat would tell you where we snagged the trident."

"Why wouldn't it?"

"It's not the same GPS we were using that day. He bought that new Garmin after we almost lost the net. Said he wanted something with all the bells and whistles. The new system wouldn't have the coordinates for the wreck."

"Do you know what he did with the original GPS?"

He shrugged. "Joe was pretty tight, so I can't imagine him throwing it away."

If what Tink told me was true, the person who'd knocked me to the deck of Joe's boat and stole the GPS would be in for a surprise. It was the new Garmin and wouldn't have any record of the trident trip. I smiled inwardly, but I was no closer to finding the wreck.

The club door opened, and Mary came in. "Glad to see you two have met," she said.

"Tink has been very helpful."

"Does that mean you've got a lead?" she said, an expectant expression on her face.

I didn't want to tell her we'd run out of options, which is why I said the first thing that popped into my mind.

"I read a news clip last night about Professor Braddock. He seemed very interested in the trident. I'll contact him if I can borrow a phone."

Mary said I could use the phone in her office. I thanked Tink again then followed Mary up a stairway to a landing. Posters for Manny's dune tours festooned the walls along with some for club acts. On top of a wooden desk was a laptop computer and next to it a telephone with an answering machine.

"This is my office," Mary said. "I've got to do some errands around down. You're welcome to work here. I do a lot of work on my cell phone, so I rarely use this space."

After she left, I called the neighbor who sometimes takes care of Kojak and asked her to keep him fed for a few days. Even better, she said he'd be her guest at her house. With my old pal taken care of, I dug into my pocket for the folded piece of paper with the professor's contact information and punched out the phone number. The woman who answered said, "Dr. Braddock's office. How may I help you?"

"I'd like to speak to Dr. Braddock," I said.

After a slight pause she answered, almost in a mumble. "I'm sorry. That's not possible."

A smart PI like me should have picked up on the change in tone, but I was busy scoping out my next move. I simply said, "Please have Dr. Braddock give me a call when it's convenient."

I gave her my name and the number of Mary's office but hung up before she had a chance to reply. I was in a hurry and maybe a little impatient. She never had the chance to explain that what I was asking of the professor was not only inconvenient. It was impossible.

Chapter Sixteen

EVERYTHING ABOUT JOE'S case seemed to come back to the trident. It was what got Joe murdered and maybe it was used to murder him. I recalled the thrill I'd imagined on his boat as I held the three-pronged spear above my head in throwing position. What was it about the ancient relic that was supposed to change Joe's life, but probably ended it?

After a few minutes of staring into space without getting answers to my questions from my brilliant detective brain, I picked up the phone again and called Assistant District Attorney Martin's number. He answered right away and said he was at the courthouse but would have a few minutes to talk. I asked if he'd heard the results of the autopsy. He said he'd seen a preliminary report. As he explained the night we talked at the crime scene, Joe had three wounds in his chest. None were deep, going in only few inches, but the middle prong had pierced his heart and killed him.

"Sorry about your pal," he said. "Not a good way to go. I'll get a copy of the full report for you as soon as it comes through. The divers we brought in checked out the water around the dock and didn't find a murder weapon. We're going to expand the search area in the water and on the land."

"Thanks," I said. "I'll keep you in the loop and let you know if I find anything."

Frank said he would appreciate whatever I could send

his way. I hung up and thought about Joe's theory that the trident came from a statue. I made another call, then walked back to my truck in the public lot and headed out of town onto Route 6. About an hour later I got off the Mid-Cape Highway at the Hyannis ramp and soon after that pulled into the parking lot of St. George Greek Orthodox Church.

Unlike the simple white-steeple churches you find all over New England, St. George's was designed in the architectural style called Byzantine. Back when the Greek population of Cape Cod was small enough to fit into an empty baklava pan, the church was in a former grange hall. As the Hellenic population grew and prospered, the parish built a new church on the outskirts of Hyannis.

`I walked under one of four arches set around a domed roof and through the main entrance. An elderly woman was on her way out of the church, and I asked if she knew where I could find Father Nicholas. She pointed to the sanctuary door.

"*Epharisto*" I said.

"*Parakalo*," she said with a golden smile.

I poked my head through the doorway into the main part of the church. The sweet smell of incense and the icons of haloed saints painted on the walls brought back long-forgotten memories of the church in the Greek section of the old factory city of Lowell, where my immigrant parents settled and built the Parthenon Pizza empire.

A man dressed in black stood at the front of the sanctuary with his back to me. He was bending over a table that had some religious objects on it and didn't hear me come up behind him until I said, "I thought you only worked on Sundays, Father Nick."

He turned, saw who it was and furrowed his brow. The

lips framed by the pepper-and-salt beard dipped into a ferocious frown.

"If you spent more time in this church, Aristotle, you'd know that a priest works twenty-four-seven."

"Just kidding, Father Nick. I know you're the hardest working priest since St. Basil fed the poor."

He clapped his hands lightly. His dark eyes twinkled with amusement and a toothy grin replaced the dour expression.

"Now *that's* the kind of respect a man of the cloth deserves." He set down the feather duster he'd been using and gave me a hug and a handshake. "I was surprised to get your call asking to see me. You're too early for the festival. Ah, I know. You are here to tell me you're rejoining the church community."

I scrunched my eyebrows. "Guess I had it all wrong. I thought all the fish I've given the church for the festival bought me a ticket to heaven."

"You wouldn't be the first sinner who tried to bribe his way into paradise," he said with a shrug of the shoulders. "I can't tell you if donating fish for the festival carries more weight than buying the church a stained-glass window, for instance, but the parish is truly grateful for your gifts."

The first time I met Father Nick he was busy trying to pull together the Grecian Festival, the weekend fund-raising bash the church holds every summer in July. I was commercial fishing on Sam's boat back then before I bought *Thalassa*. We'd had a good week fishing, so I called the church and asked if they would like some fish for the festival. Father Nick took me up on my offer and I donated a couple of boxes of cod, even offering to fillet them for *Psari Plaki*, baked fish with tomato and onion sauce. The tourists loved it. I've delivered fish every year since then.

"Glad to hear that," I said. "You can expect another load for the next festival."

"Thank you for carrying on the tradition of the Socarides family generosity."

Father Nicholas had recognized my last name the second I introduced myself at our first meeting. My parents have given piles of money to Orthodox charities. I'd explained that I was not involved with the family company. If he was curious why I wasn't part of the business or why I was hooking fish on Cape Cod instead of cranking out frozen pizzas and *spanakopita,* he didn't say so. That would come out later when we got to know each other better and we had some long conversations.

"I'll keep bringing in the fish as long as I catch them," I said, although most of what I bring in comes from fisherman pals who give me the wholesale rate.

"A deal. You've been well?"

"*Very* well. How's your family doing?"

"We couldn't be better. Thanks for asking. My wife is busy with church work and my children are excelling in school. What did you do this winter?"

"Worked on a charter boat in Florida. I just got back to the Cape a few days ago."

"Wonderful! Now tell me, how are your parents?"

"My mother is still company CEO," I said. "She leaves the day-to-day stuff up to my sister and brother while she deals with my father's care. He's in a nursing home with dementia."

"It must be very difficult for your family. Have you seen him?"

"Before I went to Florida. I was planning to make a visit

after I dealt with some boat business, then a friend died."

"Sorry to hear that. You certainly have your plate full. How can I help you?"

"I need to tap into your expertise on Greek mythology."

"I hardly qualify as an expert. Serious amateur would be more accurate."

"Good enough for me, if you have time."

"I always have time to talk about the religion of my ancestors. Have a seat."

We settled into the nearest pew. "You never told me how an Orthodox priest got to be so knowledgeable about pagan religion," I said.

"The Greeks have never had a problem merging the old beliefs with the new. When Christianity became ascendant, they transformed Dionysus, the God of wine, into St. Dionysus. They also built mountain top chapels for St. Elias just as they did for Helios, the sun god. Even Aphrodite merged into Christian iconography."

"What about Poseidon?"

"His Christian incarnation was St. Nicholas, patron saint of sailors and namesake of countless Greek males, later to become Santa Claus. Although Santa is a far cry from Poseidon, who was bad-tempered, moody, greedy, and vengeful."

"Not your jolly old elf?"

"There's nothing jolly about Poseidon. He joined with his brothers Zeus and Hades to depose their father Chronos and they split up their plunder. He became the god of the sea, his kingdom taking in the oceans and all bodies of water, along with earthquakes, storms, and horses."

"Where does the trident come into the Poseidon story?"

"It's originally a fish spear that became Poseidon's

weapon and main symbol. It was fashioned by the three Cyclops." He cocked his head. "What's your interest in Poseidon, if I may ask?"

I reached into my pocket, pulled out the *Boston Globe* article I'd borrowed from Joe's files and handed it to Father Nick.

"The fisherman holding the trident in the photo served with me in the war."

He read the story and handed the article back to me. "Fascinating. The trident certainly looks authentic."

I pointed to the picture. "You can see here that the end of the shaft is jagged, as if broke off from something, maybe a statue."

"That's certainly possible. Have you had a chance to see the trident up close?"

"Better still. I held it in my hand, and...."

Father Nick picked up on my hesitation. "And what, Aristotle?"

"I felt something. *Old.*"

"Aha. The ancient gods live after all."

"Not sure I follow you."

"I've experienced the same feeling back in Greece. I've visited an ancient place supposedly once frequented by mythological beings and sometimes felt a connection when I've touched things they left behind. There's nothing supernatural about it. Only a subconscious awareness that we human beings are relatively newcomers on the planet. The fact that there are ancient and mysterious forces we don't understand forms the basis for all modern religions." He tapped the photo. "I'd love to see this object."

"Might be hard to do. The trident has been stolen."

"A shame. And the fisherman in the picture?"

"Dead. He's been murdered."

His face turned as waxen as the candles in the sanctuary. "I don't understand."

"You knew that I was a Boston city detective before I became a fisherman."

"I was aware you had a background in police work. I thought that life was behind you."

"I'm officially a retired cop, but it was tough to let go of police work completely. I moonlight as a private detective. The fisherman's family hired me to find out why Joe is dead and who killed him."

Father Nick thought about what I had just told him, then said, "Let's take a walk."

We strolled out of the sanctuary down a hallway that led to his office. He sat in front of a computer and Googled Poseidon statues. Dozens of photos popped up showing the sea god in various poses. Some of the figures were standing upright, one leg in front of the other, arm up and holding the trident ready to throw. The tridents varied in style as well.

He ran through a batch of statues and enlarged the angular facial features of each one. The renditions of Poseidon were pretty much the same. Dark wavy hair down to his shoulders, and a beard big enough to hide an army. The sculptors had caught his bad-tempered personality. Almost every statue of Poseidon's face had similar sharp contours and piercing eyes.

"He looks like he's on the verge of violence but calm at the same time," I said. "Like a gunfighter who knows he's got the fastest draw in the West."

"Good comparison. Poseidon was like the unpredictable ocean he personified. He could be dangerous and serene as well. It comes with being a god, I suppose. He knows that with a single tap of his trident, he can trigger an earthquake, raise an island from the depths of the sea, or cause a spring to flow, even if its waters are salty. Aha. Here's what we're looking for."

He selected a picture on the screen that showed a trident like the one Joe found. It was part of a bronze statue made in Greece around 400 BC by an unknown artist. Father Nick held the news clipping next to the screen.

"Almost identical," I said.

"I agree. Let's assume that your trident is authentic and that it came from a statue of Poseidon. Any idea how an ancient Greek work of art thousands of years old wound up in Cape Cod Bay?"

"Not a clue. I don't even know where in the bay it was found."

"I have an idea. Let's use a simplified Socratic method of questioning and see where it gets us. I will be the inquisitor who asks questions, and you are the interlocutor who answers them. Let's start with the hypothesis that the spear came from a statue of Poseidon. And that statue may even be ancient Greek. How did it get to Cape Cod Bay from Greece?"

"That's easy. It was carried there from Greece in a ship."

"Why go through all that trouble?"

"Someone thought it was worth the time and money."

"What does that tell you about that someone?"

"Obviously wealthy."

"Do you think the statue came directly to Cape Cod from Greece?"

"No. It would probably have landed in New York."

"Why not Boston?"

"Possible, but New York is a bigger international commercial port than Boston."

"For the purposes of discussion, let's say it was transported from Greece to New York, where it stayed on board or was placed on another vessel that was on its way to Boston. What was it doing in Cape Cod Bay?"

"The Cape is between New York and Boston. The biggest harbor on the bay is Provincetown. It was going to stop there temporarily."

"Why do you say it was temporary?"

"Provincetown doesn't have a museum, which would be the logical destination for a piece like that."

"So there is no reason for it to be there?"

"It could have been going to a private collector, but there are more likely reasons for a stopover. "Repairs, refueling. Weather maybe. The Outer Cape is mostly unbroken coastline except for Provincetown, and the Atlantic Ocean can get cantankerous. Could be that the vessel was rounding the Cape, got into bad weather, put into the bay for protection and sank, maybe in a storm."

"Is there any way to prove that the main elements of your hypothesis are correct?"

"Sure. Find the ship. We might be able to trace its ownership."

"There we have it." Father Nick spread his hands. "An ancient Greek statue is being transported from Greece to Boston via New York by a wealthy individual, on a ship that was lost in a storm. That only took a few questions."

"You missed your calling, Father Sherlock."

"I'm not sure if the Greek Orthodox Church would consider a deerstalker cap as proper ecclesiastical garb."

"You never know," I rose from the pew. "Thanks for

your help, Father."

"Any time, Aristotle." He walked me to the front door, and we shook hands. "Before you go, I have a favor to ask."

"Sure, Father. Anything you'd like."

"I'll take you at your word. Don't be a stranger to your family."

I smiled. "Good advice, but I was thinking you wanted more fish."

"That *and* more fish. *Epharisto!*"

Chapter Seventeen

TALKING WITH FATHER NICK about the ancient gods who fascinate him must have whetted my appetite for things Greek because on the way out of Hyannis, I stopped off at the Royal II restaurant in Yarmouth Port and picked up a box of their amazing coconut baklava.

When I got back to Provincetown, I went directly to MacMillan Wharf. Joe's boat pulled at me like a magnet. Joe and I met for the last time on the *Zora*; it's where he had a fateful meeting with his killer and I'd been gut-slammed, maybe by the same person who'd murdered my pal.

I ambled along the wharf with my box of baklava, looking for a place to sit and sample the Greek delicacy. Gulls wheeled in lazy circles against the cloudless blue skies. Passengers waited for the high-speed ferry from Boston. The departing tourists were happy and tanned, blissfully ignorant of the fact that the sea-beaten fishing boat they were photographing for their vacation albums was a murder scene. Maybe an attempted murder too, if you count my encounter.

The famous Provincetown sunlight that had transformed the old fishing town into an artistic mecca slanted down through air that was clearer than fine crystal, but I was blindly groping my way through a mental fog. In desperation, I started playing around with a dangerous thought. Why waste time chasing shadows? If I could convince the killer I knew the whereabouts of the shipwreck, I mused, he might come to me. On the other hand, it's never a good thing to attract unhealthy interest from murderers. But if I wanted to catch Joe's killer, I needed more than a half-baked theory about some rich guy and a ship caught in a storm.

I came to the end of the wharf and turned around to look at the town. The skyline was dominated by the white steeple of the town library. New Englanders invented recycling. Use it up, make it do, wear it out, and do without. Like a lot of things in P'town, the library has an unconventional history. The building started life as a church, then became an arts museum and a cultural center. It's probably the only library in the country that has a half-scale replica of a fishing schooner in the children's section.

It was only a few minutes' walk from the wharf to the library. I went inside and asked the librarian at the desk where to find information on shipwrecks.

"That's a big subject," she said. "Can you be more specific?"

"How about a shipwreck in Cape Cod Bay? Does that help?"

"Not much. It narrows it down a little."

I recalled my Socratic back-and-forth with Father Nick.

"The ship might have been coming from New York and put into Provincetown to get away from bad weather."

"Wouldn't be the first boat to seek safe harbor in our town. Date?"

I shook my head. "Haven't a clue."

Puckering her lips in thought she said, "That could be a problem. I suggest you browse through the Provincetown Advocate. Scan the front pages for shipwreck news. You can aways check Google if you find a lead."

She sat me down in front of a screen and showed me how to call up the Advocate archives. It only took me a few minutes to discover that the newspaper had printed a lot of news since it started business in 1870 and that it might take me the same number of years to go through the paper's pages.

I got out the newspaper article I'd shown Father Nick and searched for nuggets of information I might have missed. Nothing popped up, so I typed the name Dr. Emory Braddock in the Google space and punched the enter key.

Dozens of posts about Braddock came onto the screen. Most were about his professional accomplishments, except for an article dated a couple of weeks earlier. The story had nothing to do with his life and everything to do with his death.

The Boston Herald headline read:

BOMB KILLS MFA PROF

I read the first paragraph of the news story:

"Leading Greco-Roman scholar Dr. Emory Braddock, 61, of Lexington, was killed yesterday by a device police say was a letter bomb delivered to his office at the Museum of Fine Arts."

The story said that the professor's secretary, who'd been working in an outer office, was unhurt. She told police the explosion sounded like a refrigerator door slamming.

A photo showed Dr. Braddock as a pleasant-faced man whose probing eyes were framed by horn-rimmed glasses. He had a nice smile and could have been sent by Central Casting to play the part of Dr. Gibbs in a production of Our Town. The rest of the piece talked about Braddock's work at the MFA. Another article dated a few days ago said the police were still exploring leads. There was a list of survivors and a notice that the funeral service would be private.

I laced my fingers around the back of my head and stared at the screen until the words started to swim. I was thinking it was funny in a peculiar way that the professor had died after he talked to Joe about the trident. Then Joe died, too.

I went up to the librarian's desk, thanked her, and asked if she liked baklava. When she said that she loved it, I handed her the box from Royal II and walked back to Mary's office. I used her phone to call the Boston Police Department, gave my name to the person who answered, and asked to be connected to Detective O'Leary on the bomb squad.

"As I live and breathe," said the gritty voice that came on the line. "Is it yourself, Detective Socarides?"

"It 'tis indeed, Detective O'Leary. And pleased am I that ye remember me name."

"Jeez. That's the worst godawful Irish accent I've ever heard."

"What did you expect, Pat O'Brien? Greece is a long way from County Cork."

"So it 'tis, my friend. You still running a fishing boat down there on old Cape Cod?"

"Yup. And you've got a standing invitation to cast a hook."

"Might take you up on your offer. But you didn't call today just to invite me to go fishing."

"I'm wearing my PI cap today. Chasing down info about the late Professor Braddock."

"Ouch. That was a nasty one. Why are you interested in

the professor?"

"I'm digging into the murder of a pal I served with in 'Nam. His family hired me to track down his killer. My friend and Braddock had been talking about an old fish spear that got dragged out of the sea in a fishnet. You may have seen something in the papers."

"I came across that story while I was doing background checks on the prof but didn't think much about it."

"Think about it. Both guys are dead within weeks of each other. Coincidence?"

"Depends. How was your pal killed?"

"Stabbed in the heart. Possibly with the fish spear, which is now missing."

"Whew! I thought my cases were weird. Can't see it being linked to Braddock though. MO is totally different."

"Tell me about the professor. The Herald story said he was killed by a letter bomb."

"Looks that way. Braddock gets a package in his mail. He slices it open with his letter opener and a battery activates a blasting cap, detonating a sheet of C-4. Bang. Just enough to blow his brains out. Didn't even mess up the papers on his desk."

"From what you're telling me, the hit was not an amateur job."

"Real pro, no doubt about it. Especially the C-4. Stuff comes in two varieties, military and commercial. This was the military variety."

"Will identifying it as military point to any leads?"

"Maybe, once we put that info together with the other evidence. There wasn't much blast debris to work with, but the forensic document examiners found fragments of postage. Greek stamps, as a matter of fact. What's going on with your countrymen that they don't like American professors?"

"First I heard of it. Working with Interpol?"

"Working with *every*one. You name it. State cops, FBI, ATF. Feds have been in contact with Greek law enforcement."

"Anyone come up with a motive?"

"Nope. The professor's friends and colleagues all said the same thing. Braddock didn't have an enemy in the world."

"He had at least one."

"Yeah. Seems that way. Sorry I don't have anything for you. Even sorrier I don't have anything for me! Lotta pressure on solving this because Braddock was so prominent."

"Thanks, O'Leary. I'll pass along anything I come across."

We exchanged cop gossip, mostly having to do with heart attacks and retirement. Then we hung up.

O'Leary didn't think the murders were connected because the MO was so different with each killing. Even if he was right, the Braddock murder was something to think hard about before I went off on some half-baked scheme to use myself as bait. If O'Leary's cop instincts were on the mark, I could have my hands full dealing with *two* killers instead of one.

And once I started the ball rolling there would be no stopping it.

Chapter Eighteen

WITH PROFESSOR BRADDOCK a dead end, I went back to Joe's murder. When you're investigating a homicide, the body is the center of the investigation. The cop homicide manual says the crime scene is where you have the best chance to find evidence or suspicious suspects to build your case on. I've never been a textbook kind of guy. If you really want to get to the bottom of a homicide, you start with the time *before* the victim got dead.

I was also at a distinct disadvantage on the crime scene because everything I knew about the murders of Joe and the professor so far had come to me second-hand. I only stumbled on the story of Braddock's murder because I was researching shipwrecks. After I left Mary's office I headed back to the library. Decades of Provincetown Advocate front pages awaited the attention of my gimlet eye.

As I walked past the Bradford bar, a yeasty fragrance drifted out the open door and tickled my nostrils. I stood on the corner, thinking that if I wanted to go back to the time before Joe became a corpse, there might be no better place than the bar stool he used as his office. Joe was always bragging about his exploits. Maybe one of his fellow barflies heard something important that Joe had said.

I was about to step through the door and into the bar when I heard the beep of a horn. Manny's dune taxi was coming down Commercial Street. He stopped in front of the

Bradford, waved me over and rolled down the window on the passenger side.

"Need a ride?"

"Thanks. I can walk back to Mary's club."

"I'll take you. Hop in."

Traffic was starting to pile up behind the truck. I opened the door and slid onto the seat.

"What's up, Cap?" Manny said. "Going in for a frosty?"

"Too early in the day, even for me. I was thinking about talking to Joe's drinking buddies. Maybe someone heard him say something that would help the investigation. You know this town better than I do. Good idea?"

"Bad idea unless you're really thirsty. Bradford's not the only place Joe hung out." He jerked his thumb at the Old Colony Tap, the vintage bar across the street. "You'd have to spend some time at the O.C. Tap. Or the upstairs bar at the Lobster Pot."

"Joe got around."

"He kinda had to. Joe pissed people off. He circulated from one place to another 'til the folks he upset cooled off."

"He called the Bradford his office."

"He spent the most time there, but they were *all* his offices. My advice? Go barhopping later. The regulars will be there 'til the place closes. Got a better idea anyway. Business is slow. You got some time; I'll take you out on a private tour of the Province Lands."

"Sure," I said. "Sounds a lot more appealing than being blasted in the face by boozy barflies."

Manny gave me the thumbs up. A short while later we turned onto the sand road near Race Point. He drove along the beach track, waving at the fishermen working the surf, then followed a winding, hilly sand road past Joe's shack and into the heart of dunes country.

As he drove through the Province Lands, Manny pointed out some shacks that went back to Provincetown's bohemian days, when they were used by writers who included Eugene O'Neill and John Dos Passos. We parked at the top of a hill and got out of the SUV. Manny took in the view of the rolling sand hills and the deep blue Atlantic.

"Straight shot east to Portugal from here. This is my most favorite spot in the whole world," he said, staring off at the horizon. "When I die, this is where I want it to be."

"Let's hope that's not too soon," I said.

He chuckled, and said, "So maybe I shouldn't ask, but you looked kind of lost hanging outside the Bradford. Investigation going okay?"

"Hard to say. An investigation is like a jigsaw puzzle. The pieces are people. You line up the edges of the pieces and work toward the center. After a while you start to see a picture. But pieces can be missing. Some pieces are on the move; some don't want you to find them."

"And some are getting toasted at the Bradford."

"There's that too. Sometimes the pieces are things, like the trident. You spend lots of time looking at pieces that seem like they should fit, but don't, so you've got to be patient."

"Good luck telling that to my wife." He pointed at his skull. "She's always been cray-zee when it comes to her brother."

"Mary knows I'm not going to let Joe down. Her brother is dead, and she wants the person who killed him brought to justice. I don't blame her."

"Yeah, she's tough, my wife."

"A lot like Joe."

"Tougher." He grinned. "Lot better looking, too."

His phone buzzed and he read the caller ID. "Speak of the devil." He clicked on and said, "Hello Angel. Just talking about you. Giving Soc a dunes tour. I'll be home soon. Sure."

He put the phone on speaker. Mary's voice said, "You're invited to dinner after you and Manny come off the dunes, Soc."

"Thanks, Mary. You sure it's no trouble?"

"Not at all. I've made enough kale soup to feed an army. I've got some meat pies from the Portuguese bakery. We can talk about Joe's case. I think of it constantly."

Manny pointed at his skull again and mouthed the word, cray-zee.

Chapter Nineteen

MANNY LOOKED AROUND at his most favorite spot in the whole world, then we got back in the taxi and headed to town. He parked at the end of the alley that runs past Diva's to the beach. We went up a set of exterior stairs onto a deck that had a view of the harbor and stepped into a big open space. Inset ceiling lights beamed down on the paintings hanging on the stark white walls.

Mary stood at a kitchen island stirring a big pot. She put the spoon down and came over to give me a hug and a double cheek kiss.

"Thanks for coming to dinner, Soc. You must be sick of our faces."

"Not a chance. You're stuck with me now that I know dunes tours, meals and art museums come with the job."

Manny slapped me on the back. "Hey, that's funny what you said about the museum. Mary and I call this place the Provincetown Guggenheim. The apartment's even got special air conditioning to keep it dry 'cause we're so close to the harbor."

"What do you think of our little collection?" Mary said.

"I should be wearing sunglasses. That's a lot of light coming off the walls."

"These are the best of the artists who lived and worked in Provincetown going back to its first days as an art colony. The sunlight drew them here."

"All originals, Cap." Manny stepped over to a rectangle of swirling lines and colors. "This is an early de Kooning. There's Karl Knaths, Hans Hoffman and some of the earlier P'town guys like Henry Hensche and Charles Hawthorne. Then there's the locals like Sal Del Deo and Ciro Cozzi. We got 'em all."

"You don't grow up in Provincetown without developing a love for the arts," Mary said. "Most of these paintings were owned by my parents, who ran the club before me. It was common for artists to pay for their drinks with their art. Or you could pick up paintings by young artists at bargain prices. My folks passed the art down to me."

Manny poured some Portuguese wine into three glasses. We sat on stools around the kitchen island and Mary spooned out servings of soup. She watched me devour a spoonful of steaming liquid, a combination of kale, linguica sausage, potatoes and white beans.

"Well? How is it?" she said.

"One more bite and I'll be speaking Portuguese," I said.

We practically inhaled our first servings and dug into seconds. When our bowls were empty, we finished off the meat pies she had heating in the oven. Dessert was a melt-in-your-mouth flan. She poured more wine and gazed out the picture window at the harbor.

"The harbor is the heart of everything I love about this town." she said. "The fishing boats. The whale watch fleet. The pirate museum. The hustle and bustle. I used to see Joe coming and going on his fishing trips. We'd wave at each other. Now it's all ruined for me. I can hardly bear to look at the damned thing." She pulled the drapes across the window. "I know there hasn't been much time, but do you have any idea yet why Joe died?"

"I'll tell you the same thing I told Manny. An investigation is like a jigsaw puzzle. This puzzle is like that painting," I said, pointing at the de Kooning. "All squiggly lines and color."

Mary nodded. "With abstract art, it's not only what you see, but what you feel in your gut."

I studied the painting on the wall. "Here's what my gut feeling tells me. Someone thinks what Joe found in the bay is worth killing for. There's more you should know."

I told them how someone jumped me on the boat and stole the GPS.

"Oh Soc, that's terrible," Mary said. "The attacker could have been the same one who killed Joe. Were you hurt?"

"Just my ego. But I feel like a jerk letting the GPS get away."

"I don't care about the GPS. I'm just glad you weren't seriously injured."

"Any idea who jumped you?" Manny asked.

"It happened too fast. But the joke's on the other guy."

"How's that?" Manny said.

"Tink told me Joe had installed a new GPS. The instrument that got ripped off wouldn't show the coordinates for the wreck site. Whoever swiped the GPS is in for a big surprise."

"I'll say. That means there's still a chance we can get to the wreck before anyone else."

"Sure. If we find the old GPS."

"That could work. Got any leads?"

"Nothing solid. There's been a complication. Joe had talked about the trident with a professor named Emory Braddock from the Boston Museum of Fine Arts. I thought the prof might know something and I called the museum. His secretary said he was unavailable. Seems he's been murdered. An old pal on the Boston bomb squad told me Braddock was killed with a letter bomb that came in his mail."

"Unbelievable," Mary said, "Do you think it had anything to do with Joe?"

"My friend on the bomb squad says he can't connect the two murders. Maybe I can if I dig deeper."

She shook her head. "I can't have you working on this case. It's too dangerous. You've got to pull out," Mary said.

"I don't think that's a great idea, Mary. I'm just getting started with the investigation."

"That's what I'm afraid of. The deeper you get into it, the riskier it will be. If you won't quit voluntarily, I'll have to fire you."

"You can't fire me. We don't have a contract."

She threw her hands up in exasperation. "Joe said you were stubborn."

"Goes with my Greek ancestry, but it's more than being mule-headed. Joe saved my life. I owe him, dead or alive."

She sighed. "I know you feel obligated, but Joe isn't going to know whether or not you paid him back."

"I'd know it, Mary. Tell you what, I can back off and see what the police investigation turns up. I'll keep in touch with my contact in the DA's office in the meantime. If anything develops, I'll let you know before I make a move. Deal?"

Her lips tightened in a firm line, then relaxed into a smile. "Deal. You can stay in the dune shack for as long as you like."

I thanked her, then excused myself and walked out onto

the deck. I punched out the number on the bootleg phone Flagg had given me. He answered as if he'd been waiting for my call.

"How are things in Provincetown?"

"How do you know I'm in P'town?"

"Easy. The phone in your hand has a locator."

"I knew there was a reason I don't like those things."

"What it doesn't tell me is why you're there."

"I've been working a job for a friend. It came up suddenly."

"Glad you followed my advice about getting out of your house."

"Looks like I'm coming back. I just got fired from my job."

"Not a good time, Soc. "The guys who went into your house could have found something that tells them where you are."

"Of course. That forwarding address I taped to the refrigerator would tell them exactly where I am," I joked.

"You have any messages you didn't clear off your phone message recorder?"

"Sure, my friend Joe called to ask a favor. They could trace me from that?"

"The phone number puts you in Provincetown."

"I knew there was a reason I don't like message recorders. Crap."

"Crap is right. You're up to your eyeballs in the stuff. These guys could have tracked you down even if you used a phone made of tin cans and string. Sorry I dragged you into this cesspool."

"How long do I have to get out of Dodge?"

"Next stagecoach out of town would be best. You've got

a couple of days. Maybe less than that."

"Where do I go then if I can't go home, and I can't stay here?"

"Up to you. We've got a safe house near Boston."

"Thanks, but no thanks. I know people find it hard to resist my outstanding personality, but why the interest in me from someone I don't even know?"

"They don't care about you. They'll use you to get to me. There were three brothers running the organization, or there were before they came to the Vineyard. One got away."

"The guy in the woods. You killed his brothers?"

"They got sloppy. I didn't. The third one wants revenge. Shows what happens when you leave loose ends."

"Any suggestions on how to tie up this particular loose end?"

"Where are you staying?"

"I'm hunkered down in a dune shack. Good place?"

"That could be good or bad, depending. Who knows about it?"

"A few people. Too many to keep it a secret."

"No such thing as a secret. Here's how it will work. A bunch of tough guys walking down Commercial Street or hanging out at a dive would attract attention. They'll send a lone scout in to check around. Friendly guy who smiles and talks a lot. Asks innocent-sounding questions. Could be a woman to throw you off. Might be a couple of people. Try to stay out of sight, especially in the daytime, keep your eyes open for talkative strangers and avoid bars."

"Bars? You're killing me, Flagg."

"No, I'm trying to keep you from being killed. I'll call you back within twenty-four hours."

Mary and Manny were cleaning up in the kitchen when I came back into their apartment.

"I just talked with someone who's working on my house," I said. "This is a good time to do the repairs. I'd like to take you up on your dune shack offer and stay a while longer. Maybe a few days."

Mary wagged her finger at me. "It's yours. Only if you promise not to work on Joe's case."

Flagg had already made it clear that my days in Provincetown were numbered, so it was easy for me to say, "Promise still in effect."

"No problem then. Since you're off the case, let's make a pact," Mary said. "For the rest of the night we talk about food and art, about Provincetown, about our own lives. We don't talk about Joe. Not one word. We'll fly off to that happy place where everything is peaceful and safe."

"Sounds good to me," I said. "How do we get to happy valley?"

Manny plunked a glass on the counter and poured it half full of wine.

"This is a start, Cap."

All went well for about an hour. The Provincetown stories tumbled out of Manny and Mary's memories like fruit flowing from an old cranberry scoop. They knew all the human flotsam and jetsam that had drifted ashore in Provincetown. Bootleggers. Pirates. Street performers. Drag queens. Writers. Artists. Sandal makers. Con men. The whole cast of talented oddballs who were drawn to Provincetown by its crystal-clear light and sea air, its live-and-let-live lifestyle and good-natured tolerance to nutcases.

Joe had been one of the Provincetown boys who dove from the wharf for coins tossed by tourists coming off the ferry. He would pick up a quarter and clench it between his teeth as if he'd scooped it off the bottom with his mouth. He'd make a big show of his fake feat, pounding his chest like Tarzan.

Mary said, "The tourists would throw more coins in the water. I thought Joe was the most amazing brother in the world." Her smile widened, but then her eyes welled with tears.

She put her glass down. "Sorry, but I don't think I can do this."

She got out of her chair and left us alone in the kitchen area.

"Damn," Manny said. He looked stricken. "Damn, damn."

I got up and said, "Thank Mary for dinner. I can find my way out."

And that's what I did.

Chapter Twenty

I SHOULD HAVE BEEN more up front with Mary and Manny. The story I spun about a murder investigation being like a puzzle was simply me doing a tap dance around the truth. The jigsaw puzzle comparison works if you're Inspector Poirot trying to pick the murderer out of a group of proper English ladies and gents on a luxury train or in an exotic hotel. But in a real-life investigation, you've got to find the pieces before you see if they fit.

As I drove the truck onto the access road at Race Point and plunged into the Province Lands, I thought that this investigation was more like a night-time ride in the dunes. The headlight beams that stabbed the darkness between the rolling sand hills showed only the twin tracks directly in front of me. The cones of yellow light caught fluttering moths or a suicidal rabbit dashing across the sand tracks, but only deepened the velvety blackness on either side. I almost drove into the dune shack before I saw it.

I parked in front of the shack, got out of the truck, and glanced up at the veil of stars draped against the blue-back sweep of the sky. The ocean breeze blew away the last of the wine fumes that had been filling my nostrils. I was staring toward the heavens when I heard an engine and seconds later a green-and-white SUV pulled up beside me.

The window on the driver's side rolled down to reveal the face of a woman wearing a park ranger hat. Blonde hair stuck out from under the broad brim.

"How's everything going?' she said.

"Going fine, thank you. Out on night patrol?"

"Sorta. The dunes are pretty after the sun goes down. You come across things you don't see in daytime."

"Yeah. I know. I had to watch out for bunny rabbits on the way in."

She smiled. "My name's Beth Williams if you need to get in touch."

"Mine's Socarides."

"You take care now, Mr. Socarides."

She put the SUV in gear and continued along the road until her taillights disappeared around a corner. Bunny rabbits. Real smooth, Soc.

I grabbed my duffle out of the truck and went inside the shack. When the sun drops into the sea, the shack becomes like the inside of a beer cooler. I lit some lanterns and got a couple of logs going in the stove. The crackling fire soon chased away the damp cold that had crept in through the uninsulated walls.

I made a cup of instant coffee, spiked it with whiskey and sat at the table thinking about the events of the last few days. Since driving over the canal bridge with Kojak, I'd reenacted the gunfight at the O.K. Corral with Flagg playing Wyatt Earp, one of my oldest friends had been murdered, I'd been mugged on Joe's boat, and I was hiding out in the dunes from some real bad guys.

In less than twenty-four hours, Flagg would call and urge me to relocate to a safe house before the nasties chasing him caught up with me. I dug into Joe's filing cabinet, hoping I'd find something I'd missed on the first round. Spreading the articles out on the table, I picked up a news clip to read, only to stop with my hand in mid-air. A movement outside a window had caught my eye. Hardly more than a shadow, it passed from one side of the window to the other and disappeared.

Maybe Flagg was wrong, and his friends had arrived early. Maybe it wasn't smart to sit there like a goldfish in a bowl. I reined in the impulse to dive under the table. With as steady a hand as I could muster, I put the news clipping down, took a sip of spiked coffee without really tasting it, then got up with my mug in my hand and walked over to the sink.

Putting the mug on the counter, I stepped over to the bottom of the spiral staircase. The lower stairs were mostly in shadows beyond the reach of the flickering lantern light. I gripped the railing, put my foot on the first step, and slowly began to climb.

At the top of the staircase, I unlatched the roof cover and opened it wide enough to slip through onto the platform. I lowered the cover back in place, using my fingers as cushions to keep it from slamming shut. Then I got into a half-crouch, took a few steps, and peered over the edge of the roof.

Seeing no one, I crossed to the opposite side of the roof. Paydirt. A hooded figure was looking in the window.

I took a deep breath and jumped off the roof, intending to land like a ton of bricks on the skulker. Too late. In the few seconds I hesitated, the prowler stepped back and turned away from the window. I dropped down behind instead of on the target. We both crashed forward with me on top. I got to my feet first. The intruder was slowly getting up. The face was hidden under the hood of a sweatshirt. I clutched the front of the sweatshirt under the chin with my left hand and cocked my right fist.

A voice came from under the hood. Hopping mad. And female.

"Let me go, you bastard!"

I lowered my fist. "Who are you?"

She pushed the hood back and spit out a mouthful of sand.

"Someone who's going to claw your eyes out if you don't let me go."

I released my hold on the sweatshirt. "Okay. Let's try again," I said. "What's your name?"

"My name is none of your damned business."

"Have it your way. You can tell the cops who you are when they arrest you for trespassing."

"Trespassing!" she blurted out. "You've got to be kidding. You jumped *me*."

"This is my shack. You were sneaking around and peeking in my windows. That makes you a trespasser."

"I wasn't trespassing, you jerk. I was looking for someone."

"Out here in the dunes this time of night?"

"That's right. Out here in the dunes. This time of night."

"Who's the lucky someone?"

"His name is Aristotle Socarides. He's a private detective."

"Weird name. Why do you want to see him?"

"None of your damned business."

Flagg had warned me that the killer gang might send a woman to throw me off. I figured it would be a pro who'd blend into the crowd. Not a sputtering, sand-covered amateur who got caught peeking in a window.

"Would it be my business if I said I'm the guy you're

looking for?"

"You're Aristotle Socarides?" Suspicious.

I nodded. "That's me. Who are you?"

"My name is Alyssa Braddock."

The last name jumped out at me. The connection to the professor seemed like a long shot, but I asked anyway.

"Any relation to Emory Braddock?"

"Yes, as a matter of fact. I'm his niece."

"Nice to meet you Ms. Braddock."

"I can't say the same for you."

"Sorry for the rough welcome. Are you okay?"

She brushed sand off her sweatshirt and jeans. "I'll live. But that wasn't very nice, diving bombing me."

"You're right. I shouldn't have jumped on you. My apologies."

"Accepted. Sorry I called you a jerk."

"You could have saved us both a lot of trouble if you'd knocked on the door."

"I was being cautious, I even parked behind a dune and walked up to the house. All I know about private investigators is what I see on TV. They seem a bit sketchy."

"Some are. Some aren't. Most try to do an honest job."

"Does that honest job include jumping on people?"

Alyssa wasn't going to let that one go. "Let me tell you something else about private eyes," I said. "They drink whiskey. Just like make-believe private eyes. Come inside, I'll pour a couple of shots, and we can talk about why you came to see me."

I went into the shack and left the door open.

Chapter Twenty-One

ALYSSA THOUGHT ABOUT it for a few seconds before she decided to come in. I tossed her a dish towel. She brushed the sand out of her face, giving me a chance to size her up. It only took a single glance to see that the Braddock family had a story to be told.

Alyssa had a wide face, with a flawless coffee and cream complexion, warm dark eyes, and cheekbones you could ski jump off. She was wearing oversized jade earrings in the shape of slithering serpents, and a silver ring in a nose that was slightly flat. The straight hair that hung down to her shoulders was the pinkish orange color you'd find on the inside of a conch shell.

I put two glasses on the table and poured out the booze. She was reading a news clipping I'd left out. Pointing to Braddock in the photo with Joe and the trident, she said, "This is why I'm here. My uncle came to Provincetown to see this man."

"That doesn't explain why you wanted to see me."

"My uncle's secretary told me you called the museum and asked to talk to him. I did some research and learned you were a private detective. I thought maybe you could help me find out why my uncle was murdered."

"How did you know I was out here on the dunes?"

"I tried the number you left with the secretary. The man who answered the phone told me how to find you. I had some work to do and couldn't get to Provincetown until late."

Nice of Tinkerbell to be so helpful to a stranger when a gang of murderers was trying to track me down.

"Let's go back to the beginning. Can I call you Alyssa?" I said.

"Of course."

"Good. You can call me Soc." I tapped the news clip. "Let me tell you why I wanted to talk to the professor. The other man in this photo was also murdered. His name is Joe Bonega and he was an old friend of mine. His family hired me to investigate his death. I saw Professor Braddock's name and picture in the news story. I wondered if the professor knew anything that could help my case."

"Dear God! Do you think the murders are connected?"

"Maybe. I talked to someone on the Boston bomb squad. They've turned up a few leads, but they're still investigating. Why not let the police handle the case? That's their job."

"I could ask you the same question."

"And I'd tell you I'm no longer investigating. The family has asked me to pull out of the case."

"Why would they do that?"

"They think it's too dangerous."

"Do you agree with them?"

"It doesn't matter what I think. I owe my friend a blood debt."

Her face hardened.

"Then you can understand why I'm fixated on finding the killer." She paused and took a deep breath. "Uncle Emory was a major influence in my life. My parents were both academics, specializing in Central American studies, which was fortunate for me. I was in an orphanage in Guatemala when they adopted me. I was still young when they were killed in a car accident while on a research trip. An oncoming truck went wide on a mountain road."

"Sorry to hear that. It must have been rough."

"It was very rough to become an orphan for a second time. I went to live with my Aunt Katherine and Uncle Emory. She was a like a mother to me and he fostered my interest in anthropology and archaeology. I went into Meso-American studies. I was on a dig in Honduras when I was notified about his death. I flew back as soon as I could."

"Any idea why someone might have wanted to kill your uncle?"

"Not specifically, but it could have been something related to his area of expertise. He specialized in ancient Greek and Roman studies."

"How would that be a motive for murder?"

"My uncle was a renowned expert on Alexander the Great."

"Impressive. But again, how would that get him killed?"

"You know where Alexander was born?"

"I studied the old philosophers in college before I went into the Marines. A little rubbed off. Alexander came from Macedonia, and he studied with Aristotle."

"You have a very Greek name, so you'd be aware of the dispute between Greece and its neighbor to the north about the name Macedonia."

"Sure. The Greeks say they have a historical right to the name. Their neighbors to the north say they do. The Balkan countries have been beating up on each other for centuries. Hard feelings tend to stick around for centuries in that part of the world."

She smiled for the first time since we'd met. "An understatement if I've ever heard one. The issues aren't simply ethnic or cultural. There are territorial claims that have international implications."

"So, your uncle was an expert on Alexander. I'm still not clear how that would get him killed."

"Neither am I. What I do know is that Uncle Emory wrote an article having do to with the ties of Alexander, a Macedonian, to Greek culture. He suggested that the northern country stop using provocative images like the Vergina Sun, the symbol on the tomb of Alexander's father, Phillip. And that they stop putting statues of Alexander in cities or naming stadiums and highways after him. He proposed that in return, Greece agree on a name that recognizes historical context and the cultural history of both countries. A short time after he wrote that article, he was dead."

"The article got your uncle killed?"

"I can't say for sure. But there are extreme nationalist groups who oppose any sort of compromise that goes against their claims to the name. They include people on both sides who are not above violence. One of these groups could have murdered my uncle."

I thought back to what my bomb squad buddy O'Leary said about the letter bomb's foreign-made parts and the Greek stamps on the envelope it came in. Maybe Alyssa had a point.

"You could be right about bomb-making crazies," I said. "But what about my friend Joe? He was a fisherman. Why kill him?"

"It's possible these extremists saw him as a threat to their interests."

"That seems pretty far-fetched."

"I agree. But if I'm right, the death of your friend might signal other killings to come."

"Why do you say that?"

"Apparently, knowing my uncle was dangerous."

"Okay, we'll use that premise. The professor was at the center of things and Joe was collateral damage. The question is where we go from here."

"I think we should talk to Avery Fowler. He's a wealthy antiquities collector and dealer. Fowler helped fund some projects my uncle worked on. He told me about the Alexander article and said it may have led to my uncle's death."

"Have you given Fowler's name to the police?"

"It would be a waste of time, in my opinion. The police seem more interested in physical evidence than theories involving ancient history and international politics. I didn't think they would ask the right questions."

"If you want me to, I can try to ask Fowler the right questions."

"You'd be willing to do that? I don't have much money, but I'd like to hire you to investigate my uncle's death."

I had hoped she'd go in that direction. Talking to Fowler would be a sneaky way of staying with Joe's case and keeping my promise to Mary at the same time.

"Here's the deal. My first hour of consultation is free. I'll work pro bono after that."

"In other words, you'll work for free."

I nodded. "Solving your uncle's murder may help me find my friend's killer."

"That's still very generous. Thank you."

"You're welcome. When and where can we see Fowler?"

"He's a waterfront real estate developer who lives south of Boston. I'll call tomorrow and see if I can arrange an interview. I can drive you up in the morning and drop you off at the Boston ferry after we talk to him."

"That works. Where are you staying in town tonight?"

"I don't know. This was a last-minute thing. I'll see if I can find a B&B or a motel."

"It's late. You can sleep on the couch. There's instant coffee and stale bagels for breakfast. Sorry it's not the Ritz."

"I'm an archaeologist so I'm used to primitive conditions."

"Then you should feel right at home. There's no electricity, and the plumbing is pre-Flintstones, but when you wake up, you'll have a spectacular view of the sun rising over the dunes."

"Hard to refuse an offer like that. I'll get my knapsack out in the car."

"See you in the morning. Sorry again for the airborne welcome."

She laughed over her shoulder as she headed for the door. "Next time I'll look up before I peek in someone's window."

I found some extra blankets and a pillow in a cupboard and tossed them onto the couch.

Alyssa Landry was smart and funny. She reminded me of my kid sister Chloe, which wasn't a bad thing. Jumping off the roof had been a good move after all. I'd picked up a lead and a now I had a smart young woman to assist in investigation. Even more important, I'd wormed my way back into Joe's case.

Chapter Twenty-Two

BACK AT THE BOATHOUSE, my day usually starts with a hungry cat walking on my head and a scratchy purr tickling my ears. But the next morning I woke up to the murmur of feminine voices and the scent of coffee someone else had made. I rolled out of bed, pulled on a fresh pair of jeans and T-shirt from my duffle bag and strolled into the kitchen area.

Alyssa and Mary sat at the table across from each other. They were chatting like a couple of old friends catching up on family news. The sad smiles on their faces suggested they were past the introductions and into the loss of loved ones.

Mary broke off their chat and gave me a bright smile. "Good morning, Soc. Alyssa and I are getting to know each other. It seems we have a lot in common."

"Good morning. Glad you had a chance to talk."

Mary pointed to the white paper bag on the table. "I came by with malassadas for breakfast and to see how you were doing. Imagine my surprise to find that you had company."

"It was a surprise to me too, Mary."

"Alyssa told me how you dropped from the sky. I didn't know flying was one of your talents."

Giving Mary my best evil grin, I said, "There's a lot you don't know about me. Thanks for the malassadas."

"They were delicious," Alyssa said. "It's been a pleasure meeting you, Mary. I'll let you two catch up while I make a phone call."

She shot a knowing glance my way, then picked up her cell phone and left me alone with Mary, who got some Portuguese donuts out of the stove where they'd been warming. I sat at the table, sank my teeth into a flattened blob of fried dough coated with sugar and cinnamon, and washed it down with coffee.

"Glad you guys got a chance to talk," I said.

"She's lovely," Mary said. "Intelligent, too."

"Did she tell you about her archaeological work?"

"She did. She also told me about her closeness to her uncle. And that she's hired you to investigate his death. It's a good thing you're no longer working for me."

"Yeah. Good thing." I savored another bite of dough. "Glad you're not thinking I took her case as a sneaky way to get around my promise to let the police handle Joe's investigation."

"Sneakiness never crossed my mind."

"I'd understand if you thought I was being devious."

"That would never occur to me," she said with a horrified expression.

"So here's how I look at it. If I find out that her uncle's death is linked to Joe's case, we can feed the information to the cops."

"I totally agree," Mary said. A cloud passed over her brow. "Alyssa told me that if something isn't done about the murders of Joe and her uncle, more deaths will follow."

"I can't say that's true, but it might be."

She waggled her finger at me like an old-fashioned schoolmarm giving the class clown a second chance. "Then you'll have to agree to one condition. You won't take any chances. Is that a promise?"

"Promise." I pointed with both hands at the rear of my skull. "Just like the Patti LaBelle song says. Eyes in the back of my head. Deal?"

She gave me a side look and a smile. "Okay. Deal."

I said I would let her know the second I turned up a lead. Mary gave me a peck on the cheek and was leaving the shack when Alyssa came back in. They exchanged hugs, and after Mary was gone, Alyssa gave me a thumbs-up. "Fowler will see us today."

We cleaned up after breakfast. I did a quick rinse in the outdoor shower and changed into chinos and an Aegean blue polo shirt. The logo for my charter business, the image of *Thalassa* over my name, was embroidered on the front.

We grabbed a couple of bottles of water for the road and set off in Alyssa's SUV. The drive to Scituate was over two hours, but time passed quickly. She talked about the archaeological dig she'd been doing in Central America. I told her how I made the move from Boston cop to fisherman, diver, and private eye.

Scituate is a toney South Shore enclave of seaside mega-mansions perched on the cliffs overlooking the waters of Massachusetts Bay. We stopped at an iron gate to check in over the intercom. The door swung open, and we drove up a long blacktop driveway to a pile of brownish-gray granite that must have taken the contents of an entire Quincy quarry to build.

After parking in a circular driveway as big as a racetrack, we climbed a broad set of stairs to the front door. I pushed the doorbell button. After a minute, the door was opened by a man in a wheelchair.

"Great to see you, Alyssa," he said before he turned his attention to me. "And you must be Mr. Socarides."

"Thanks for pronouncing my name right on the first try," I said.

He gave me a warm smile. "Ancient Greek antiquities have been a passion of the Fowler family going back several generations. Many of the pieces in this house were collected by my ancestors, and I've visited the country of your forefathers on numerous occasions. Come in."

Fowler was probably in his sixties. His lantern-jawed face had none of the fat that can come when you don't have the opportunity to burn off the calories, telling me he was disciplined in his lifestyle. Little details, like the perfect knot in his tie, the snug fit of his pale green linen sports jacket and the way his red pepper-and-salt hair was cut close to his scalp would have suggested a military background even if I hadn't noticed the West Point ring on his finger.

Fowler pressed a button on the arm of his wheelchair and backed up to let us in. The door closed by itself. The mosaic floor of the circular vestibule was laid out in inch squares that formed a picture with an ocean theme. Fishy creatures swam amid flowering seaweed. Scaled sea gods armored in shiny scales frolicked in the deep.

Fowler said, "The tilework came from a Roman temple to Neptune. What do you think?"

"I'm glad I don't get seasick." I pivoted slowly on my heel. "Nice collection of Olympians."

The curving walls of the vestibule were lined with statues of men and women standing on pedestals in half-nude poses that would have got them arrested if they weren't pagan gods carved in marble.

"Yes. All twelve of the Immortals. From Zeus on down.

I'm impressed. You know your gods."

"I know the ones that count. I took a gut course on mythology in college. Some of it stuck."

"A private detective versed in ancient religions is not someone you meet every day."

"Most PI clients are insurance companies checking on a bogus claim, or wives or husbands who want to know if their spouse is cheating on them. There's not a big call for detectives with mythological expertise."

"But it's precisely the kind of background that this situation demands. Let's go out on the porch and talk."

Fowler led the way. We hustled to keep up, walking past more statues in several rooms, and out onto the kind of porch you'd see on a resort hotel.

He motioned at some white wicker chairs set around a matching table. From the house, a vast lawn that looked as if it had been painted on the ground stretched off to the edge of a cliff and beyond that, as far as the eye could see, was blue water.

On the table were some glasses and a pitcher with lemons floating in it. Fowler poured our glasses full and said, "When Alyssa told me a private detective had called the MFA asking to talk to the professor, I urged her to get in touch with you."

Alyssa turned to me. "After my uncle's death I went straight to Avery thinking he'd know what to do."

Fowler nodded. "How did you get involved in this terrible business, Mr. Socarides?"

"My friend Joe Bonega was murdered a few days ago. His family hired me to investigate the case. I saw Professor Braddock's name in a newspaper article about an ancient trident Joe pulled from the sea. I called the museum, not knowing the professor was dead."

Fowler shook his head. "First Emory and then your friend. You don't think it's a coincidence, do you?"

"I don't know. The killings may be linked, based on circumstantial evidence."

"What evidence is that?"

"The trident ties everything together. Joe pulls it out of the sea and shows it to the professor. Next, Professor Braddock is killed after showing interest in the trident. Then the trident is used to kill Joe before it vanishes."

"You're thinking the same person murdered both men?"

"I might think that way if the murder weapons weren't so different. High-tech explosives versus an ancient spear."

"Are you saying there are two murderers?" he said.

"Anything is possible. Maybe after we talk, I'll have a better idea of what's been going on."

"I'd be glad to do what I can to help. Where would you like me to start?"

"Alyssa said you worked with the professor from time to time."

"Emory and I were on some of the same boards and foundations." Narrowing his flinty gray eyes, he said, "You don't have to be a detective to see that I'm an incurable collector. I've been very fortunate. I've benefited from commercial and residential real estate holdings my family has owned for generations. The business pretty much runs itself, and I've been able to indulge my real passion."

"Which is?"

"My love of ancient art. I'm not only a collector. I have a business that finds antiquities for other collectors. The trick is to locate relics that haven't been looted. Tracing lineage is no small task. Some of the people you deal with operate on the fringes of the law. Even the most prestigious museums are vulnerable."

"When did you first hear about the trident?"

"Emory called me several weeks ago with a fascinating story. A newspaper reporter had asked him for comment about an artifact dragged out of the sea by a Cape Cod fisherman. Emory was so intrigued he went to Provincetown to see for himself. In his opinion, the artifact was part of an ancient bronze statue."

"Poseidon?"

He stared at me. "That's right. How did you know?"

"I consulted an expert. He showed me photos of Poseidon statues throwing a three-pronged spear that was almost identical to the one Joe found."

"Your expert was correct, as far as it goes. This wasn't just any statue of Poseidon."

"What makes it so different?"

"You knew about the professor's specialty?"

"Alyssa told me he was an expert on Alexander the Great."

"He may have been the world's foremost authority on Alexander. He'd written far and wide on the subject."

"Alyssa also said the professor got death threats because of an article he'd written about Alexander."

"I hoped you'd be able to provide Mr. Socarides with details, Avery," Alyssa said.

"Of course." Fowler paused for a few seconds in thought, then said, "Let me take you back to 334 B.C. Alexander's army has swept down from Macedonia into Greece and he has his eye on the east. He pulls together more than a hundred boats to transport his army across the Hellespont from Europe. As his boat nears land, he leaps into the surf, wades to shore, and throws his spear into the beach to show he is taking possession of Asia."

"Alex was a showy guy," I observed.

"He was also a careful one. Alexander knew that the gods punished hubris. The sea god could be exceptionally cranky in that respect. He commissioned a statue of Poseidon to thank the sea god who allowed him and his army to get across four miles of open water."

"How did the professor know Joe's trident came from the statue Alexander commissioned?"

"Emory was the consummate scientist. He wouldn't declare something like that if he didn't have verifiable proof."

"Did the professor know how a more than two-thousand-year-old statue got from Greece to the bottom of Cape Cod Bay?"

"He was working on the provenance problem," Fowler said. "He'd make no official conclusion until he'd established the journey that brought the relic to its resting place at the bottom of the sea."

"Suppose the professor did nail the provenance all the way back to Alex. Who would care?"

"Pardon?"

"The main value of the statue would be scholarly."

"Yes. It would be a tremendously important scientific find. The rewards would be emotional rather than monetary. However, you can't put a value on the adulation that would be lavished on an amateur student of the past like me."

"The scientific lovefest only works if it's authentic."

"Yes, to that, too."

"Without that authentication it's just a hunk of bronze

and barnacles to most people."

He nodded.

"Let's go back to the theory that someone went to a lot of trouble to kill the professor in a spectacular way because of an article he wrote."

"It's difficult to write anything about the conflict over the name Macedonia that would not stir people up. The Greeks find the use of the name Macedonia by their northern neighbors to be offensive. They say Macedonia is inhabited by Slavs who came after Alexander's time, and that the newcomers have territorial ambitions. The present-day inhabitants of the old Macedonia think the Greeks are denying them their heritage."

"Let's agree that the article didn't make the professor any friends. The time to kill him would have been before the article was published. Why murder him after the fact? And why kill Joe?"

Fowler spread his hands. "Good questions, Mr. Socarides. You're the detective. Where do we go for answers?"

"To the bottom of Cape Cod Bay where Joe found the trident. He thought it was part of a statue from a sunken shipwreck and was planning to go back for a closer look."

"Any idea how far his plans had advanced?"

"He asked me to help him. I said it would be a complicated dive and we'd have to talk more about it. Obviously, we can't do that now."

"Have you given any thought to organizing a dive yourself?"

"Joe's boat has been impounded as evidence, so I'd have to bring in another vessel. That would take time and money, and I have neither."

"That's not a problem. I have both."

"You'd still have to know the location of the shipwreck."

"I was hoping you might have that information. It was one of the reasons I wanted to talk to you."

"Joe said he'd show me when we went out to do the dive."

Fowler cocked his head as if he were listening to something in the distance.

"You said you and Mr. Bonega were old friends?"

"That's right. We served in Vietnam together."

"Thank you for your service, but it just seems odd that an old friend wouldn't trust you enough to confide in."

"It had nothing to do with trust. Joe was looking out for me. Something was worrying him, and he didn't want to drag me into a dangerous situation. Given the way things turned out, seems he had good reason to worry."

Fowler gazed at me for a long time. It may have been a trick of the light, but there was a hardness in his face that didn't match the avuncular crinkle of his eyes. He opened his mouth to say something but paused to answer his chirping cell phone. After a brief conversation, he hung up and said, "Forget what I said about the business running itself. There's been a last-minute change on a meeting. Sorry, Alyssa."

"That's all right. We'll get together again when we have more to talk about."

"Absolutely." He extended his hand in a firm handshake. "Thank you for offering your keen insight as a trained investigator, Mr. Socarides. Plenty of food here for thought. Let's agree to keep in touch. If your investigation turns up the location of the statue, please let me know. I can have a salvage boat on site within twenty-four hours. Oh, hello, Wilma. Glad you're here."

Fowler was looking past our shoulders. I turned to see a tall, willowy woman who had quietly come from the house onto the porch.

"Sorry I'm late," she said.

Fowler said. "Your timing is fortunate, Wilma. I've been called away on business and had to cut our meeting short with Alyssa and Mr. Socarides."

She nodded familiarly at Alyssa. Extending her hand in my direction, she widened perfect lips in a smile and in a slight accent said, "Wilma Vladek. I'm in charge of acquisitions for Fowler Antiquities."

You wouldn't tag Wilma Vladek as someone whose job was to buy old things. With her matching black turtleneck, slender pants, polished leather boots and jet-black hair tied in a tight bun behind her head, she could have been a model in a fashion show with a Black Dahlia theme.

We shook hands and I said, "Nice to meet you, Ms. Vladek."

"And you as well, Mr. Socarides."

"Perhaps you could show our guests the family galleries on the way out, Wilma."

"I'd be happy to," she said.

Before heading back into the house, Fowler said, "Thanks again for coming to see me, Mr. Socarides. Dr. Braddock was a special person. It would honor his memory if we could carry out the work he started."

Wilma led us along a different route from the one Fowler had taken. The first gallery we passed through had a mix of marble and bronze statues, all women, frozen in various poses and sizes, ranging from a few feet tall to larger than life.

"This gallery has Greek and Roman female sculptures of goddesses and women, like Athena and Aspasia." We walked into another gallery, and she said, "As you can see, this room is all men, also a mix of gods like Hermes and mortals like Caesar and Pericles."

She stopped in the third room and swept her hand in the air.

"This one is a true rogues' gallery. A male and female mixture of immortal and mortal. That's Zeus and Hera, and Ares and Medusa. Then you have Caligula and Nero, Agrippina, and Messalina. Fascinating all."

"And all evil, too," I said.

"Evil and fascinating can be one in the same, you must admit."

"I've found that you don't have to be evil to be fascinating."

She arched a finely trimmed brow. "Avery said you were a private detective. Perhaps you're jaded by your exposure to evildoers."

"I don't think so. Most of the bad people I've come across would fall between rotten and nasty. Evil is in a class by itself."

"I suppose you're right," she said with a slight smile. "Even a cold marble rendition of a non-existent entity can do evil deeds."

"How is that possible?"

"That statue of Medusa was in an excavation in Greece Avery had financed. It toppled on Avery's legs when he was attempting to free it from the soil and destroyed his ability to walk."

I looked at the statue of the woman who had a nest of writhing serpents instead of hair. Her piercing gaze seemed fixed on me. "Medusa could turn people to stone. Are you saying that's what happened to Fowler? Figuratively speaking?"

"You have to admit it's an interesting concept."

"Sad story even if it is a reach," I said, although what I really should have admitted was my discomfort at the way Medusa had me in her sights. Glancing away to avoid her gaze, I said, "I'm surprised Mr. Fowler didn't destroy the statue, and gave it an exalted place in the house."

She smiled. "You obviously don't know Avery's capacity for acquisitiveness. He would never give up a classic sculpture, even one that maimed him for life."

She continued leading the way back to the mosaic vestibule, opened the front door and handed us a couple of business cards. "I'm available for any questions you might have about antiquities. Please call if I can ever be of help."

As we walked back to the SUV Alyssa said, "That was a spooky story about the Medusa statue."

"I think she was hinting that there's more than meets the eye when it comes to her boss."

"Maybe it was my imagination, but it seemed like he couldn't wait to get us out of the house when you started asking questions."

I shouldn't have been surprised that Alyssa picked up on the contradictory vibes Fowler projected. In her line of work, she would need a keen eye for details like a pottery shard or a button. One minute he was your favorite Uncle Dudley, all chuckles, and funny stories about faraway places. The next, he was acting like he'd caught me with my hand in the cookie jar.

I especially didn't like the way he insinuated that I was lying when I said Joe hadn't told me where he'd found the trident. One thing I was sure of with Fowler. He wanted the statue badly. I didn't want to worry Alyssa, so I brushed off her comment.

"Old Yankee families can be quirky. Maybe he isn't used to someone pinning him down. We shouldn't jump to conclusions, but until we know where this investigation is headed, let's keep anything we find to ourselves."

"I agree. What next?"

"I'll keep poking around in Provincetown. What about you?"

"My uncle kept an office at his house in Concord. I'm going to go through his files."

"What do you hope to find?"

With a hardness in her voice that surprised me, she said, "Something I can use to nail the monster who killed him."

Chapter Twenty-Three

THE HIGH-SPEED FERRY OUT of Boston made a quick dash across Massachusetts Bay and docked at MacMillan Wharf. While most of the gaggle of fun and sun seekers headed into town as soon as the ferry docked, I went over to the edge of the wharf and looked down at the *Zora*.

I stared at the boat for a couple of minutes, reconstructing my last conversation with Joe, going back to the first few minutes of our reunion at the Bradford. I had asked him about the cast on his arm. Joe said something about a woman being involved. The comment could have been nothing, but the fact he was so close-mouthed meant it was probably something.

I walked over to the Bradford bar, slid onto a corner stool, and ordered a beer. When the bartender set the mug down in front of me, I said, "Don't know if you remember me. I came in here a few days ago with Joe Bones."

"Sure, I remember. Joe called you the Mad Greek."

I nodded. "He gave me that nickname years ago."

"Nicknames are a Provincetown thing. They call me Beerman Bill."

"My other nickname is Soc. Short for Socarides."

"You'd fit right in with the locals. Tough about Joe. You served with him in 'Nam?"

"Same Marine unit. He saved my butt."

"Not surprised. Joe was a decent guy. I miss seeing him

on that stool."

"When I saw Joe that day, he had a cast on his arm. He said he'd been helping a lady friend and broke his arm falling off a ladder."

Bill chuckled. "Yeah, he told me the same story."

"I didn't know Joe had a girlfriend."

"Joe didn't talk much about his personal life, but he brought her in a couple of times. Her name's Diana. Real nice lady. She owns an art gallery on Bradford Street." He pointed at my chest. "Same name as on your shirt."

"*Thalassa*?"

"That's right. I'm sure of it."

"How do I get to the gallery?"

"Go out the door, take a right, then take another right. Gallery is up the hill on your left."

He went off to take care of another customer. I slapped some bills down on the bar top and stepped out into the fresh air. Then I followed Bill's directions to Bradford Street, walked up the hill, stopping at a sign that hung in front of a two-story Victorian-era house. Painted on the sign was an image of Cape Cod; the curled arm was wrapped around the word Thalassa printed in black letters over a wavy blue background.

A patch of blonde-colored shingles stood out from the silver-gray ones on the front of the house. I guessed that's where Joe's ladder was when he had his arm-breaking fall. An "Open" sign hung in the window. I walked up to the entrance and opened the door, triggering the bell. Stepping inside, I glanced around at the ocean-themed paintings and prints of every size that covered the white walls of the well-lit room.

I walked over for a closer look at a painting of dunes,

ocean and clouds that was made up of six separate frames. A hand pushed aside a curtain hiding a doorway and a woman stepped out into the gallery space. She came over and stood beside me.

"How do you like it?" she said.

"I like it a lot. I can feel the cool breeze off the water blowing in my face on a hot day."

"Thank you. That's exactly the effect I was striving for."

I squinted at the name scrawled in the lower right-hand corner of one panel. "You must be D. Oliver."

"The D stands for Diana." She regarded me for a few seconds with intelligent eyes that were the green-tinged blue of the summer sea. "And you must be Aristotle Socarides."

"How did you know my name?"

"Joe talked about you often." She pointed at the logo on the front of my shirt. "He told me your boat and my gallery had the same name."

"Thalassa, the mysterious sea."

"Exactly. I've been wondering when you would come by."

"I didn't know I was expected."

"From what Joe has told me about your friendship, I assumed a visit was inevitable."

"I would have been here sooner if I had known you existed. I saw Joe just before he-well, a few days ago. He had a cast on his arm. He said he'd been shingling a house for a lady friend and fell off a ladder."

"This is the house and I'm the lady friend. How did you find us?"

"The bartender at the Bradford told me where you lived."

"Well then, our rendezvous was meant to be. I'm so pleased to finally meet you. I have some tea brewing. Would you like to join me, Mr. Socarides?"

"Only if you call me Soc, like all my friends."

"And you will call me Diana." She shoved the curtain aside and we went into a combination kitchen and dining area off the gallery.

I would never have paired Joe with Diana Oliver. Where Joe was as gnarly as an oyster shell, Diana was refined and well-spoken. She had an artsy air and wore a smock over an ankle-length skirt and sandals. Long hair tied in a single brownish-gray braid went down to the small of her back. Her peach complexion was smooth and unblemished. Her expression alternated between a broad grin and a Mona Lisa smile.

Joe was a handsome man in his younger days, and charming, too. I'd lost count of the girlfriends and wives he'd had since I'd known him. However, even Joe's charm and good looks couldn't smooth the rough edgers of his personality. All his relationships eventually fell apart.

Diana invited me to sit down and filled two China cups from an antique teapot. Taking a chair at the table, she studied me like an artist sizing up a potential subject.

"I'm so glad we met. Joe thought the world of you."

"I owed Joe a lot. My life, in fact."

She raised her brows. "He only said that you served together in the war. And that you were there when he was wounded."

"I was the reason for his wounds. He was between me and a blast from a mortar round. He said it was dumb luck, but he insisted on taking the lead knowing he might draw fire."

"He never mentioned that important detail. I shouldn't be surprised, knowing Joe."

Talk of Joe brought on an awkward silence which lasted several seconds. I changed the subject before we got bogged down in memories. "How long have you owned the gallery?"

She smiled. "A long story."

"I have time."

"In that case pour yourself more tea while I put a closed sign in the door."

When she came back, she sat at the table and said, "I knew Joe going back to grade school. We both came from fishing families. After high school Joe fished with his father before joining the Marines. I married a fisherman. That's the way the town was back then. The women had children and cooked and the men fished. If you had a room, you rented it out to the summer folk."

Fishing is a tough life, and booze doesn't make it easier. Her husband had died early. No kids. She studied at Cape Cod Community College, became an art teacher at Provincetown High School, and worked summers for her sister, who'd started the art gallery. They sold large, abstract paintings to a New York clientele that wanted big art for loft walls. When her sister died, she left Diana the house and business. Diana changed the name of the gallery, got rid of the abstracts, and specialized in works that celebrated the sea.

She met Joe when he came in one day with a painting he'd done of his boat. She offered to sell the piece at commission and found a buyer. When he came in for his money, he asked her out for dinner to celebrate and they hit it off on their first date. Their personalities were as different as night and day, but they both loved art. They got along so well he soon moved in with her. As time passed, it got more difficult to make a living catching fish, especially as Joe and his boat got older. Joe's war wounds began to bother him, and he became even more cantankerous. It became harder to find crew to go out on the *Zora* with him.

"I've met Tink," I said.

"Oh yes, Tink. He has a good heart and Joe said he's a fast learner. But the business continued to decline. I was really worried about Joe. He was on the verge of depression. He spent less time here and more nights sleeping on his boat. I hardly saw him anymore. Then he dragged that thing out of the sea, and he changed completely."

"Changed in what way?"

"At first, he said finding it was no big deal, although I could tell he got a kick out of seeing his name and picture in the newspapers. He showed the spear around until people got tired of hearing about it. He seemed to be going back to his moody ways. Then he got a call from the professor in Boston."

"Dr. Braddock."

"That's right. The professor came over on the ferry. Joe brought him to the gallery to meet me. Joe said Professor Braddock got very excited when he saw the trident. I hadn't seen Joe that upbeat in a long time.'

"Any idea what was behind the mood change?"

"I asked Joe what was going on with the professor. He said the professor told him they were on the verge of one of the greatest archaeological discoveries of the century."

"Did he go into detail?"

She shook her head. "Joe and the professor talked several times by phone after the visit. You can understand how devastated he was when the professor was killed."

"Did you ever hear him talking to the professor?"

"He always took the phone outside. I finally brought it up. I told him that friends don't have secrets. He apologized and said he would explain soon; he was working on a deal that would get him out of fishing. After the professor was killed, he clammed up even tighter. Said it wasn't safe to talk. A few days ago, his attitude changed for the better again as if he had come to a decision."

"I think that's when Joe decided to call me. He was looking for a diver. I came to P'town and we went on his boat so he could show me the trident. He thought he had pulled it up from a statue on a sunken ship."

She sighed. "What is it about that old fish spear that gets people killed?"

"I wish I knew, Diana. The trident seems to be at the center of everything that's going on."

"It certainly was for Joe. He was fascinated with that thing. Let me show you."

We went back into the studio, and she picked a portfolio from a rack, placed it on a table and opened the folder. As she shuffled through some sketches of boats, she said, "You must have known Joe was a talented artist."

"I remember him sketching in a pad even in a war zone. I never saw any of his work."

"He destroyed all his war art. He said he only wanted to paint pretty things. He sketched mostly nudes of me at first. I was a convenient model and worked for free. I retired when I got old. Wrinkles and flab and all that."

Diana didn't have a wrinkle or an ounce of fat on her, but Joe knew boats and how to draw them. She showed me a dozen or so finely detailed pen-and-ink sketches of fishing boats, including some pictures of the *Zora*, then pulled out a drawing he'd done of the trident.

Joe's keen fisherman eye had caught every barnacle and flaw, and rendered them in fine detail, from the jagged end of the shaft to the flared barbs. One sketch showed what I had thought were scratches on a section of the shaft. Joe had seen the lines for what they were. Greek letters that spelled out a word or part of one.

SIPOS

I tapped the sketch with my fingertip. "What's this?"

"I have no idea, but Joe said the professor went crazy when he saw those letters. What do you think it means?"

"It could be a name or part of one. We'd have a better idea of what this is all about if we could see the statue the trident came from. Tink said Joe bought a new GPS. Do you know what he did with the old one?"

"The only place I can think of where it might be is his workshop he set up in the garage."

"Okay for me to take a look?"

"Of course. Follow me."

We went back into the kitchen and out the side door. At the end of the driveway was a quarter-size version of the main house with the same type of down-sweeping mansard roof. It was probably the old carriage house, judging from the doorway that was high enough to accommodate a horse and wagon. The doors were wide open. Joe's pickup was parked inside next to a Honda sedan I figured belonged to Diana.

She invited me to go in. I walked past the truck to the work bench at the back of the garage. Joe was not a tidy person. The bench was covered with tools, pieces of hose, sections of line, and old coffee cans filled with nails and screws.

A manufacturer's box for a GPS poked out from the stuff on the bench. I thought I had hit the jackpot, but the box was empty. I pawed through the pile of junk, then searched the cab of the truck. No GPS.

Joe wanted to keep the wreck site a secret. He wouldn't even divulge the location to an old pal like me and would not have left the GPS lying out in plain sight. I picked up the battered coffee pot sitting on a cold wood stove. Empty. I was putting the pot back on the stove when I noticed soot on the floor under the wide black pipe that took smoke outside.

I rapped the pipe with my knuckles; more soot fell from a joint. I got a grip on two adjoining sections and pulled them apart. A plastic bag with something inside fell onto the floor. I picked up the bag, removed the wire twistie around the neck, and pulled out a GPS.

I hit the "On" button and the display came to life telling me there was juice in the batteries. But when I searched the memory, I saw that the data had been scrubbed.

Diana was waiting outside the garage. I told her the GPS was worthless for the investigation and went to hand the instrument back. She told me to keep it.

I thanked her for the tea and conversation. She walked with me around to the front of the house and pointed to the new patch of shingles. "That's what Joe was doing when he fell," she said.

"He did a good job as far as he got," I said.

"It was the oddest thing, though. In the middle of shingling, he decided to touch up my sign. I don't know why. It had been painted only a few months ago. When he got back up on the ladder to shingle, he seemed preoccupied. Probably why he fell."

I thanked her again and she went back inside the gallery. I continued down the walk and stopped for a close look at the sign. I traced the shape of the Cape Cod peninsula with my fingertip and discovered why Joe had taken a break in shingling to touch up the sign.

Sandwiched between two of the parallel wavy lines were some newly painted letters and numbers. The latitude and longitude coordinates for a navigational position.

As I stared at the image of the Cape and the bay, I thought back to Joe's comment when I met with him in the bar. I'd told him what mother said about the sea. He'd smiled and said she was right. Thalassa holds the answer to everything.

Chapter Twenty-Four

PROVINCETOWN TURNS INTO a non-stop carnival when summer rolls around. Commercial Street is clogged with slow-moving traffic and crowds of people, and the restaurants and clubs are bursting at the seams. But the busy tourist season was still a few weeks off. Fewer than half of the tables in front of the stage at Diva's were occupied. The audience was the typical Provincetown variety pack of locals and a mix of couples in town to take advantage of the off-season lodging rates and uncrowded eateries.

Mary waved me over from behind the bar and went to pour a beer. I put my hand on the top of the mug.

"I'll pass for now, thanks. I need to keep my head clear." I gave Mary what I thought was a cat-who-swallowed-the-canary grin.

"Are you okay?"

"I'm fine. Why do you ask?"

"You don't look fine. You look like you've got a stomachache."

"My stomach is fine." I put my palms on the bar top, leaned forward, and lowered my voice. "I found Joe's wreck."

She clutched my arm in a lobster grip. "Damn, Soc. I knew you'd come through for me."

"Not quite there yet. I haven't found the actual site, but Joe left information telling me where it is."

"How-?"

"Tell you later. I need three favors from you. First, tell me if you want me to continue the investigation."

"Consider yourself rehired."

"Done. Second, I'll need to borrow Joe's boat."

"The *Zora* is yours. What's the third thing?"

"I'll need Tink to crew for me."

"Don't know if you've noticed, but Tink is a very big boy. He can make his own decisions. Ask him after the show." She glanced at her watch. "He's about to come on."

She pointed to an empty table directly in front of the stage. Seconds after I plunked down, the curtains parted and Tink came out onto the stage. He had exchanged his handyman jumpsuit for ruffled, skin-tight purple shorts, fish-net stockings, high heels, and a lacy white bustier. A curly black wig added six inches of height that he didn't need.

He pinned me with a fiendish gaze emphasized by heavy eyeliner, and I knew why the front table was empty.

"Aha! A new victim in the hot seat for Ms. Tinkerbell," he crooned. "What's your name, sailor?"

Flagg had warned me that bars were natural hunting grounds for the people trying to track me down. I figured no respecting hit man would search for me in a drag karaoke club, so I gave Tink my full name.

"That's certainly a mouthful," Tink said. "Is that Greek?"

"Any more Greek and it would open up a restaurant."

Tink pinched his chin between his finger and thumb. "If you're Greek, why aren't you wearing a toga?"

"Those are Romans. Greeks wear skirts."

He fluttered his out-sized eyelashes. "You really know

how to get a girl's attention. Can you say something in Greek?"

"Sure. *Kalispera*."

"Is that a proposal of marriage I hope?"

"I wished you a good evening."

"How disappointing. You have no idea how tough it is to find a *real* man in this town. I was hoping we could get to know each other better."

"Maybe we could go on a boat ride."

"I love that idea. Will you be the captain?"

"Yup."

"Even better. Well, captain, do you like karaoke?"

"Sure. There's nothing better."

"Then fill out the slip with the song you want to sing and put it in the hat."

Mary came out from behind the bar with a box of slips and stubby pencils that she passed around the room. On my slip I wrote, "See you on the *Zora* before dawn. S."

I put the slip in the bowler hat Mary used to collect requests from the audience. Tink picked my slip out of the batch, read it, nodded slightly, then chose another. I left while a woman in a black beret and the kind of haunted eyes I imagined Anna Christie might have had was doing a throaty rendition of Leonard Cohen's "Hallelujah."

I stopped at a convenience store and bought a loaf of bread and a package of boiled ham. Back at Joe's shack, I unpinned the Cape Cod marine chart from the wall and spread it out on the tabletop. The chart was frayed around the edges, but although Joe evidently used it a lot there wasn't a single position marked out. He didn't record coordinates. It would have been like leaving research notes from the Manhattan Project lying around for prying eyes to see. He would have kept the locations of his favorite fishing grounds locked in his memory and relied on his GPS to get him to the general area of a productive fishing hole.

Using the coordinates from the art gallery sign, I marked an X on the chart. I planned to sneak out of the harbor before the sun rose. This might be my only chance to get to the wreck site before the killer or killers figured things out.

Tink knew his way around Joe's boat and could man the wheel while I ran the ROV. Operating the vehicle at the end of its slender tether can be tricky if there are strong currents.

I made four ham-and-mustard sandwiches on white bread, thought about Tink's size, added a couple more, then set the alarm and crawled into bed. Tomorrow was going to be a long day.

Chapter Twenty-Five

JOE'S DUNE SHACK was as cold as a morgue when I rolled out of the warm bed at four o'clock in the morning. I hit the off switch on the buzzing alarm clock. Then I quickly pulled on a pair of jeans that were hanging near the stove. The fire had gone out hours before, so the jeans were as stiff as cardboard. By the time I buttoned up a work shirt under a wool sweater and zipped up a windbreaker, I had started to thaw out.

I packed the sandwiches in a cooler with some bottled water, got in the truck and drove through the pitch-black dunes to the marina. Tink was already aboard the *Zora*. Lights glowed in the wheelhouse and the diesel engine was rumbling as it warmed up. Tink welcome me aboard. He was wearing faded jeans, a Diva's sweatshirt, and a down vest. A navy knit cap was stretched to the seams on his head. Seeing him in normal clothes helped erase the picture of his karaoke outfit from my mind, but not enough.

"Mary gave me the keys to the *Zora* after I finished my act last night," he said. "I got here early to prep. Coffee will be ready in a few minutes. Got the ROV from down below."

"Thanks, Tink," I said. I knelt next to the ROV case and unsnapped the cover. Everything seemed in place.

"Ready to roll?" I said.

"Any time you are, Cap."

I manned the helm and Tink went out onto the deck to

untie the dock lines. I eased the boat slowly out of the slip. The growl of the engine echoed off the breakwater and wharf buildings. Once we were clear of the slip, I nudged the throttle and kept the boat at a crawl until we were out of the harbor. Then I throttled up to a cruising speed of fifteen knots. The hull sliced through low seas as we passed Long Point Lighthouse and emerged into Cape Cod Bay.

Tink poured coffee into a couple of mugs and handed one to me.

"Mind if I ask where we're going?" he said.

"According to Joe's coordinates, we need to head due south out of P'town, then steer west southwest on a course that will take us directly to the shipwreck."

I reattached the GPS I'd found in the stove pipe to its bracket.

His jaw dropped. "Where'd you find that?"

"Joe hid it. Unfortunately, the memory had been scrubbed."

"I don't get it. How do you know where to find the wreck?"

"I had some unexpected help from Joe."

I told him about my visit to Diana at the gallery and how I found Joe's notation on the Thalassa sign.

"That's real Treasure Island stuff," Tink said. "Joe was a surprising guy."

"No argument there. Now it's your turn to surprise me. I like Peter Pan as much as the next guy, and Tinkerbell was a real doll, but do you have a real name?"

His first name was Tony, and his last was that of an old Provincetown Portuguese family. "Tinkerbell is my stage name."

"Tell me how a P'town boy ended up working the stage

in a drag club."

"You can't be serious, Soc. Pretend you're an employment agency trying to match my size to a job in Provincetown."

"You'd make a kick-ass bouncer, Tink. No one's going to mess with you."

"Yeah, I'd scare off troublemakers, but I'd intimidate the regular customers as well. I have a degree in acting from Emerson. Going drag is just another role. Kinda like the guys who played women in Shakespeare's plays. Only larger and with more ooph."

"The *ooph* is the real deal, but the corset must get tight."

A pained expression came to his face. "Actors learn to suffer for their art. Besides, the money's not bad in the summer. If people are going to gawk at me because of my size, I might as well get paid for it. When you put on a good show, the tip jar stays full. Mary lets me use Lady Brett's old apartment, which means I don't pay rent. I used to pick up a few bucks with Joe, but he was erratic, especially after he found that old pitchfork." He gazed off through the windshield. "I miss Joe, and it's not just because of the money."

"I miss him too, Tink. That's why we're out here. Maybe we'll miss him less if we find out who killed him."

For the next half hour, we plowed through the semi-darkness, alone in our thoughts. I kept the boat at a steady fifteen knots, half-hypnotized by the rhythmic slap of the waves against the hull. Pinpoints of light from fishing boats blinked on like fireflies around the bay.

The sky to the east went from gray to pink, then shifted to orange as the sun rose over the outer arm of the Cape. A few sport fishing boats had ventured out of Rock Harbor to work Billingsgate Shoal for bass and blues. A trawler was coming out of Wellfleet Harbor.

With summer lurking in the wings, the dark blue of the warming bay waters was leavened with streaks of jade. The southwest breeze carried the smell of kelp and finny creatures and the promise of warmer temperatures.

Tink took the wheel and I spread the chart out on the instrument console. The coordinates from the Thalassa sign gave me a rough idea of the wreck's position. Pinpointing the exact site was going to take detective work. I checked the GPS screen and had Tink slow the boat to just above wake speed. The depth indicator showed about sixty feet of water under the hull.

"Hey Tink," I said. "Didn't you tell me Joe marked the spot with a buoy?"

"That's right. Tossed it over the side attached to a mushroom anchor. Marker's blue and white with *Zora* painted in big black letters on it."

"Cut the engine and we'll see what we can see."

Tink powered down and let the boat drift in the two-foot waves. Using Joe's binoculars, I scoured the area close to the boat, then far away. There was nothing out of the ordinary on the faceless blue-green sea.

The buoy could have come loose from its line and floated off, although that didn't seem likely. Joe was an experienced mariner. When he tied an anchor knot it came loose only when he wanted it to.

I lowered the binoculars, blinked my eyes to clear them, and tried again, checking the surface of the sea as I moved around the deck of the boat.

Nothing.

I lowered the binoculars. "Getting hungry, Tink?"

"Oh yeah. I skipped breakfast, and a monster body like mine needs lots of food to keep working," he said.

I got the ham sandwiches out of the cooler and passed one to Tink. It looked like a wafer in his big hand. I munched my sandwich and gazed out over the waves. I was thinking about how tough it had been for a survey boat loaded with instrumentation to find a big target like the *Titanic* even though the scientists knew the general area where it sank.

The encouraging news was that they found it. I waited ten seconds for Tink to devour his sandwich, then said, "We need a plan. Let's run the boat in parallel lines like a mower cutting a lawn. Standard search pattern. That way we can cover a lot of ground. Hundred-yard runs to begin with."

Tink asked if he could have another sandwich, then he headed back to the wheel. I finished my sandwich and made one more sweep with the binocs. This time I saw a silver glint in the waves that lasted a second before it vanished. I kept the binocs glued to the spot but there was no repeat of the sparkle and I began thinking I'd spotted a plastic bottle that had come off a boat.

A second later, the glint repeated, catching me in mid-doubt.

I yelled at Tink to start the engine. Then I raced to the bow where I stood, arm extended to point the way. We'd only moved a few yards before the reflection disappeared. I muttered a curse and signaled Tink with a wave of my arm to keep moving on the same line. We covered another hundred feet or so, and that's when I saw the glint off to starboard.

As we moved closer, I could see what had caused the lighthouse effect. Except for a fist-sized patch that was exposed to sunlight, the Styrofoam cylinder was almost completely covered with greenish-black seaweed. The buoy had to bob in the water at just the right angle and elevation for the sun's beams to reflect off the wet plastic surface.

I slashed the air with my hand. Tink killed the engine.

All was quiet except for the slosh of waves against the hull and the cry of gulls wheeling above in search of non-existent fish leavings.

"What next?" Tink said.

"We take a look under the water."

"Any idea what we're looking for?"

"Yeah. Whatever it was that got two men killed."

Chapter Twenty-Six

JOE'S BOAT WAS A true rust bucket. Practically every square inch of the *Zora* needed a coat of paint, the deck was like a marine junk yard, and the hull was in the advanced state of decrepitude that comes to boats and humans from too much time at sea. On the other hand, the *Zora* was heavy and wide, making it the perfect platform for undersea exploration.

It wasn't much of an edge, but I was glad to have it. I didn't have a clue what kind of wreck I was searching for. How big it might be. Or even if there *was* a wreck. All I had was Joe's story about how he pulled the trident up in his net. I didn't even have the trident. Only a vague notion that it had come off a statue.

We dropped the hook around fifty feet from the marker where the anchor's flukes would be less likely to snag on the bones of the wreck. I also needed elbow room to maneuver the robot. The joystick controls were built into the carrying case along with a video screen that would display what the main ROV camera was seeing. The camera could be switched from video to photo mode.

I gave Tink a quick show-and-tell, pointing out the vehicle's lights, camera, sensors, and propellors. Once the ROV started moving through the water, the lightweight fiberglass tether would unwind from a spool, carrying information and commands between the operator and the vehicle. Tink was way ahead of me. He had seen the ROV when Joe first acquired it and knew enough to bring along a laptop computer to download data from the robot.

I sat on an overturned fish box and set the monitor and controls on another box.

"Ready to launch," I said.

Tink picked the vehicle out of its case as if it were a rubber ducky then leaned over the rail and lowered it into the water. The ROV sank into the sea. I turned on the power and pointed the vehicle's nose downward. Tink watched until the yellow plastic housing was no longer visible, keeping an eye on the tether as it unreeled.

I shifted my attention to the screen and used the joystick control to point the ROV down at a sharper angle. When the vehicle reached a level where no surface light penetrated, I activated a switch; twin cones of yellowish green light came on and caught a few startled fish that darted out of the way.

I kept the vehicle on a dive trajectory, and at a depth of fifty feet, I leveled it off and aimed the ROV in the general direction of the anchor line. Visibility was about a dozen feet at that depth. The lights reflected off particles of marine growth that swirled in the beams like an undersea snowstorm. I increased speed to counter the buffeting effect of the bottom current.

"See anything yet?" Tink said.

"Fish and crud. Keep the tether moving so it doesn't kink up. Whoops!"

Tink leaned over my shoulder, blotting out the sunlight. "Whaddya see?"

"Anchor line for the buoy. ROV's on the right track."

I slowed the vehicle. The line running down to the mushroom anchor from the buoy was taut as a bow string and covered with furry brown marine growth. I backed the ROV away to avoid getting entangled in the line and sent the vehicle off at an angle.

Nothing showed up in the lights except for the sandy bottom, so I put the vehicle into a hover. I imagined I was straddling the protective casing like a cowboy on a horse. Once I had my bearings, I began to move the robot back and forth in a series of parallel lines, using the lawn-mowing search pattern.

More uncluttered bottom. More fish. More floating motes of marine growth. No shipwreck or statue. Maybe I was on the wrong side of the buoy. I decided to bring the ROV back on deck, move the boat and relaunch the vehicle on the other side of the buoy. I put the ROV into a tight turn in preparation to bring it back to the surface. As it followed the new track, its lights picked up some sand-covered objects on the bottom.

The cubes and cylinders were not the kind of shapes you'd normally find in nature. I followed the thickening trash trail like a hound hot on a scent until I came to the source of the undersea junk.

The vessel was broken in two amidships and lay at a slight angle. Drifting sand partially covered the deck and a section of smokestack that must have snapped off when the hull came apart. Standing on the bottom between the ghostly ship sections, as if it had hatched from an egg, was a pale green giant buried in sand up to the knees. The bare-chested figure was that of a man about seven or eight feet tall, and judging from the rippled ab muscles, he spent a lot of time in an undersea gym.

His right arm was raised above his shoulder and a shaft was clutched in his hand. The length behind his fist was a couple of feet long; the shorter front part had a jagged end. The left hand was extended for balance like that of a javelin thrower.

"Joe was right," I said.

"What do you see?" Tink said.

"Take a look. It's Poseidon, the god of the sea. And the front of his trident is missing."

He squinted at the screen. "Joe nailed it!"

I turned on the video camera and moved the ROV closer to the statue's head, but it was impossible to make out the features because the face was buried under a grassy layer of marine growth.

We stayed on the wreck until we had explored every square inch of the site. Before leaving, I went back and took some still photos of the statue from various angles, then backed the vehicle off and sent it over the stern section of the half-sunken hull. The currents had piled sand against the transom, hiding the name except for three letters: *AMP*

Chapter Twenty-Seven

THE SUN WAS ON ITS WAY down the western sky as the *Zora* came into Provincetown Harbor. Tink had made another pot of coffee and was raising his mug in toast.

"Here's to a successful mission!"

I tapped his coffee mug with mine. "Sorry to disappoint you, Tink, but there was no mission. We never left Provincetown. We never found a statue."

"Oh, I get it," he said, drawing out the words. "We never set foot on this boat. And the pictures and video I've downloaded into my laptop don't exist."

Tink was a quick study. Nodding, I said, "Mary knows we were out on the *Zora*. I think it's safer for everyone if we keep details of this trip to ourselves for now."

I removed the GPS and tucked it under a bunk pillow. We stopped off at the fuel dock to refill the tank, then headed for Joe's slip. As I brought the boat around the end of the pier, Tink said, "Uh-oh. What you said may be harder to do than we think."

Three men stood on the floating dock. The man in the navy-blue suit was Lieutenant Corrigan, and with him were two burly state police officers in uniform. Tink got off the boat and secured the dock lines. I killed the engine and stepped onto the dock.

"Good afternoon, Lieutenant. Nice to see you again," I said.

Corrigan's toothy alligator smile told me he wasn't buying my Eddy Haskell imitation. I figured we'd simply trade barbs and then we'd go our separate ways. I didn't expect him to whip out a pair of handcuffs from behind his back and dangle them under my nose. Nor did I expect him to say: "You won't think it's nice to see me after I slap these on your wrists and place you under arrest."

"Since when can you get arrested for saying 'good afternoon?'"

"You can't. But I can throw your sorry ass in the slammer for the unauthorized use of this vessel."

"Nice try, Corrigan. The owner gave me her okay to use the boat. Check with her if you want to."

"I don't have to check with anyone," he said. "The harbormaster has been keeping an eye on things for me. I know you've been gone for hours. Where have you been?"

"Nowhere," I said.

"Is that so? Well, I know just the place for you. I'm taking you in for tampering with evidence in an on-going homicide investigation."

Corrigan had a feral grin on his face that told me he'd love an excuse to have his minions light me up with tasers.

I turned to Tink who stood off to one side, listening to the back-and-forth with Corrigan.

"Tink, tell Mary I've been arrested," I said. I put my hands behind my back and turned around.

Corrigan clamped the cuffs extra-tight, then he shoved me toward the state cops. "Take this loser to the county jail, toss him in a cell, and throw the key away." Then to me, he said, "Enjoy your stay at the bad boy hotel. Maybe they'll let you out on a trash collection crew."

One officer shot a glance at Tink. "What should we do

with the big guy?" he asked Corrigan.

"Get his name and address. Tell him if he testifies against Socarides here we'll pin a medal on that big chest."

Corrigan handed the officer the key to the handcuffs and swaggered off as if he had just captured Billy the Kid. The officer watched him drive away, a stick-on bubble light blinking on the roof of the unmarked car. "What a jerk," the Statie said.

"Jeez, what did you do to piss him off like that?" the other trooper asked me.

"Nothing. I pissed his boss off."

"You talking about the DA?" the first officer said.

I nodded. "I made him look bad in a homicide investigation. It wasn't hard. The defendant's legal team hired me to investigate a murder case the DA's office screwed up."

"You're telling me you're a cop?"

"I used to be with the Boston PD. Now I run a fishing boat out of Hyannis and moonlight as a private detective."

"Crap! Corrigan never mentioned you'd been on the job."

"The other officer chimed in. "From what he told us, you were a combination of Whitey Bulger and Satan."

"Some people thought Whitey *was* Satan," I said.

They both laughed and the taller one said, "Careful how you talk about us Southie boys."

"I'll be careful. Wondered if you could do something about the cuffs. Corrigan clamped them on a lot tighter than necessary."

The taller officer dug out the key and loosened the cuffs. Turning to his partner, he said, "What are we going to do with public enemy number one?"

"Hell, I don't know. County jail's more than an hour from here. Even if we use the lights and siren to get there in a hurry, we'll have to deal with all that processing at the other end. My wife would kill me if I missed my kid's birthday party."

"I've got an easy way out of this. You could let me go," I said.

"Up to me it wouldn't be a problem, but Corrigan's got some clout with the DA. He can make trouble for us."

"Not if it's legit. Turn me over to the Provincetown cops. Say you got called in on an emergency."

"You sure you were a Boston cop?" the shorter officer said.

"I joined the BPD after I came home from Vietnam and mustered out of the Marines."

"Jeez. You were in 'Nam?" He turned to his partner. "We can't book this guy."

"County jail is out, but we still can't let you go." He unlocked the handcuffs. "We'll drive you to the station."

We went up onto the wharf where they'd left their car. A minute later we parked in front of a building on Shank Painter Road that used to be a funeral home before it was converted into the Provincetown Police Station. We went inside and the Staties explained to the dispatcher that they wanted to park me there for a while.

"Is this gentleman under arrest?" the dispatcher said.

"Not exactly," the taller cop said.

"It's kind of complicated," his partner said. "We've been instructed to arrest him, but we don't think there are sufficient charges."

"What *are* the charges if you don't mind me asking?"

She glanced from one trooper to the other. Then

everyone looked at me.

"I borrowed Joe Bones's boat," I said. "His sister Mary gave me permission to use it."

"You know Mary?" the dispatcher said.

I nodded. "I've known Joe longer, going back to the Marines. Mary hired me to investigate her brother's death. I'm a PI."

"I told you it was complicated," the tall Statie said.

The dispatcher shook her head and called someone on the intercom. A Provincetown police officer came out into the lobby. I recognized him from a past case I worked on. His name was Ray Souza. He looked at the two cops, then at me.

"Hi Soc. What's going on?"

"It's complicated," I said.

He let out a deep sigh. "Knowing you, I'll just bet it is. Give it a try anyway."

"Okay, here goes. A state police lieutenant named Corrigan wants these officers to put me in the county jail on a bogus charge of evidence tampering. They would rather not do it. I suggested they transport me to the P'town lockup instead. Here we are."

Ray smirked. "Nothing personal, Soc. We'd love to have you as a guest, but the Constitution frowns on locking folks up without a reason. I know Corrigan. Real hard ass. What does he say you did?"

"He claims I stole Joe Bones's boat."

Souza let out a short laugh. "The *Zora*? You gotta be kidding. Who in his right mind would steal that leaky old tub? Surprised it hasn't sunk at the mooring."

"The old gal is in rough shape, but I was desperate, and Mary gave me permission to use her. Corrigan says that doesn't matter because the boat is evidence in a homicide investigation."

"Is what he says true?" Ray said to the troopers.

They exchanged puzzled glances. Neither cop seemed eager to render an opinion, so I jumped in.

"Forensics went over every inch of the boat the night Joe was killed," I said. "The police tape barricade has been removed and there are no signs on or around the *Zora* warning people off."

A weary expression came to Ray's face. "I've got Mary's number. I'll give her a call," he said.

He got on his cellphone and said, "Hi, Mary. This is Ray Souza. I'm fine, thanks. Got a quick question. Did you give Aristotle Socarides permission to use Joe's boat? You did. Can you drop by the station and sign a statement to that effect? Okay. See you then. Bye."

"Sounds like I'm free to go," I said.

"Not exactly," he said. "Mary is at the undertaker's planning Joe's funeral. She won't be free for another hour at least."

"Guess that settles it," the shorter Statie said. "We don't have time to stick around. He's all yours. Nice meeting you, Socarides."

They started toward the door. Ray called after them. "Hey, you can't just waltz in here and start leaving people."

"Sorry. Not in our jurisdiction. We've got an emergency."

"What kind of emergency?"

"Socarides can explain."

They bolted out the front door as if they were trying to make last call at Dunkin Donuts. Ray turned to me. "What are they talking about with their emergency?"

"One of them has a kid's birthday party and his wife will divorce him if he doesn't show."

"Yeah, I guess that qualifies." He looked as if he were about to tell me my puppy had died. "Sorry, Soc. We can't have you hanging around the station."

"Sure, Ray. Don't want to give the place a bad name. Where do you suggest I go?"

"Take a walk. Or go have a beer. Have a couple! Then come back here. Maybe we'll have Mary's statement by then."

"What if you don't have it?"

He shrugged.

"First time I've been kicked out of jail," I said.

"I'll make sure it doesn't make it to your rap sheet."

I gave him a quick wave before he went back into his office, thanked the dispatcher for her trouble, and stepped out of the station onto Shank Painter Road. I headed back toward Commercial Street. A few minutes later I was climbing the stairs to the upstairs apartment and office at Diva's.

No one was around. A brown envelope with SOC written in Magic Marker on the outside lay on Mary's desk. I sat at the desk, opened the envelope, and pulled out a stack of eight by ten photos. Clipped to the pictures was a note from Tink:

Recorded ROV video on CD. Will show later. Busy with a handyman job. See you after the show.

I went through the photos. Even with my clumsy handling of the ROV controls, the photos of the broken ship and sea god statue were in sharp focus. I slipped the pictures back into the envelope and called Alyssa. She was driving from Boston with her uncle's files and would be in Provincetown in about a half hour.

We arranged to meet at a waterfront bistro named Bubala's by the Bay, a short distance from Diva's. I got there first and asked for a table off by itself. Alyssa arrived fifteen minutes later. I stood up to greet her and she put her briefcase down on the table and gave me a big hug. When the waiter came to the table, she ordered a fish sandwich and iced tea. I did the same.

She closed her eyes, filled her lungs, and let out a long breath. "Concord is lovely, but it's so good to breathe sea air."

"You're back in town sooner than I expected. That could mean your trip was either a success or a waste of time."

"Maybe you can tell me which it was after I bring you up to date. I went directly to Uncle Emory's house and spent several hours going through his files. The volume of material he has on paper and in his computer is simply overwhelming. He was extremely well-organized, luckily, so I quickly separated the wheat from the chaff."

"What did he have to say about the trident?"

"Quite a lot, as it turned out. But there was one thing that drew my interest." She opened her knapsack and pulled out a bound manila file. "He had a lot of material about a sculptor named Lyssipos."

She spelled out the name letter by letter.

"The last five letters of that same word were on a sketch Joe did of the trident shaft," I said. "The engraving couldn't be a coincidence."

Her eyes widened.

"That's wild!" She dug into the file. "Lyssipos was born

in 590 B.C. One of the greatest artists of classical times. The preferred sculptor of Alexander the Great. In fact, he was the only sculptor Alexander allowed to reproduce his likeness."

"Lucky guy to have a big shot like Alexander for his patron."

"He was more than lucky. He was extremely talented. He established two schools of sculpture and produced more than fifteen hundred bronze works. He developed a distinct style that used elongated body proportions. It came to be known as the Canon of Lyssipos. It's unmistakable. His figures were eight heads high instead of the one-to-seven ratio used by his contemporaries. The heads were smaller, but the bodies were slenderer and more naturalistic."

She removed a photo out of the file and handed it to me. The bronze showed a young nude man with his right arm raised to his head.

"Lyssipos?" I said.

"More than likely. The Getty bronze was pulled out of the Mediterranean and the artist is unknown. The youth is crowning himself with a laurel wreath. Look closely at the exaggerated facial features. They are consistent with what art scholars call the Lyssipian gaze. You see it in his representations of Alexander. Godlike, lips parted, and eyes lifted. Tousled hair, too."

I decided to tell Alyssa about the shipwreck and statue. I unclasped the envelope on my knees and slid the photos onto the table.

"These were taken today using a submersible camera. You can't see the face because of the seaweed, but the rest of it looks like the statues of Poseidon I've seen."

Alyssa picked up the photo and stared at it. After a few

seconds the puzzled pucker on her lips changed to a smile.

"I can't believe it, Soc. You found Joe's long-lost statue."

"Yup. Unless there's more than one bronze statue of Poseidon sitting at the bottom of Cape Cod Bay, arm raised as if he's ready to toss a trident. There's something wrong with the proportion ratio, though. This guy is built more like a line-backer than a fashion model."

"I see what you mean. He is chunky for a Lyssipos statue. Is that important?"

"I don't know. We'll decide after we see the video. I'm picking it up from Tink later. What else was in your uncle's files?"

Alyssa pulled a couple more folders from her briefcase. One had copies of the newspaper articles like the ones I'd found in Joe's filing cabinet.

I scanned the news clips and stopped to read a story from the international Herald-Tribune. "This is interesting. Seems Avery Fowler made the news. One of his antiquity suppliers got into trouble over stolen relics. There was a trial. Fowler testified on the defendant's behalf and the smuggler got off."

I handed her the clipping. She read the article and said, "Fowler told us he has to deal with sketchy people," she said.

"Same thing goes for private investigators, so I'll give him a pass on this." I asked to borrow the clipping and said, "What else do you have?"

She went into another folder and handed me what looked like copies of book pages. Some of the passages were underlined with ballpoint pen and notated with exclamation marks.

"Your uncle must have thought this was important," I

said.

"*Some*one did. These are excerpts from the Alexander romances, versions of his adventures that sprang up in Medieval times long after his death. The stories describe Alexander crossing the Hellespont to invade Persia and going down in a glass diving bell so he can conquer the sea."

"I came across the dive legend when I studied Aristotle," I said. "He was Alexander's tutor and taught him to have curiosity about the world. In the story, Alex gets snatched up by a giant fish. He survives, but he's learned the folly of his arrogance."

"That's quite the fish tale," she said. "I wonder why my uncle thought these legends were significant."

I handed the pages back. "We'll figure it out sooner or later. Anything more from Uncle Emory?"

She gave me a sheet of paper enclosed in transparent plastic. "I'm not sure what to make of this note. The writer was Arthur Kellogg."

"The cereal guy?"

"Not even close, Mr. Private Detective. Kellogg was a curator at the Museum of Fine Arts long before my uncle joined the staff."

The letter on Arthur Kellogg's MFA letterhead was dated April 11, 1897. There was no indication who the letter was going to, and it had only a brief message:

"Mr. and Mrs. Neptune are expected to arrive in Boston in two days. Can hardly wait!" It was signed with the initials AK.

"Any idea what this is about?" I asked Alyssa.

"I know that Neptune is another name for Poseidon. I didn't know he was married."

"The name of his wife was Amphitrite. She was the

goddess of the sea. Hello!"

"What's wrong?"

"Not a thing," I said. I shuffled through the ROV photos and found what I was looking for. "This is a shot of the boat from the rear. The stern is mostly buried under sand, but you can make out part of the name."

She studied the photo and spelled out the letters. "A…M…P."

"Amphitrite. Also known as Mrs. Neptune."

"I know that must be important, but I'm not sure where it fits into the whole picture," she said.

"Then let's sketch out what we have so far. Lyssipos created a statue at the request of Alexander the Great. Thousands of years later and a long way from Greece, the statue ends up on a boat that sinks in Cape Cod Bay."

"That's all plausible, but it's still conjecture. As a scientist, I need facts."

"Here are a couple for you. Joe finds part of the statue and tells the professor, who says it's an important discovery. Both men are murdered."

She shook her head. "As much as I want to, there's no way to deny the fact of the murders. But why would the discovery of the statue get them killed?"

"I can't answer that, but maybe Tink's video will show us why the statue is so lethal and who killed Joe and the professor."

"And if we do find that person, what are you going to do?"

I wanted to find Joe's killer because that's what you do when someone kills the person who saved your life. I hadn't thought what I'd do, so I pitched her an easy answer.

"I'd tell the cops and hope the law throws the book at

the killer."

"And if the law falls short. What will you do? Would you shoot the murderer?"

"I don't own a gun."

"But you could get one."

"Yes, I could. But that would make me a murderer, too. I was thinking more along the lines of making the guilty person wish he'd never been born. Details to come."

The smile returned. "I think I like that."

"And you, Alyssa? What will you do when we find the person who killed your uncle?"

"Life behind bars would be a good start."

"We're on the same wavelength. Revenge is sweet, but it's distracting, and if we're not paying attention, we might not be aware of something that could spoil our plans."

"What sort of something?"

"Something that would let the killer, or the killers, get to us before we get to them."

Chapter Twenty-Eight

ALYSSA WAS SO UPBEAT I couldn't bring myself to tell her we had a long way to go before we figured out who murdered her uncle and my friend Joe. We had an ancient statue of Poseidon at the bottom of the sea. And we might even know the name of the sculptor who made it, but he was just as dead as my case.

I was trying to figure out how to let her down gently when the waiter swooped in with our order. As we munched fish sandwiches and fries, I asked Alyssa to tell me about the future of her central American research. Her face lit up. It was a nice change from murder talk.

"That's pretty much it for me," she said. "Now it's your turn, Mr. Detective. What comes next?"

"I'm too stuffed for dessert," I said. "Maybe an ice cream cone later?'

"Sounds good. But I'm not talking about dessert. I'm talking about our case."

"We can't do this alone. I'd like you to talk to a friend who might be able to help. His name is Father Nick."

"A priest?"

"A very good one, in fact. He's also an expert on ancient Greek and Roman art and mythology."

"I've got nothing planned today except for an ice cream cone. I'd love to talk to him."

I dug Father Nick's number out of my wallet and

borrowed Alyssa's cell phone. When he answered my call, I asked the priest if he could look at a photo that had to do with the subject of our last meeting.

"Of course," he said. "Always a pleasure to see you."

"It won't be me. I'm sending a friend in my place. Her name is Alyssa, and she's an archaeologist."

"Fascinating! I'd love to talk to her. I'll be at the church all afternoon."

I gave Alyssa the photograph of the statue, taken from the front, and asked her to show it to Father Nick.

"Should I take some of the other pictures as well?" she asked.

"I may need them. Father Nick can make a judgment based on that one photo."

After lunch, I walked with Alyssa as far as Mary's club. She asked me to hold her uncle's files for safekeeping, and said she'd meet me later at the dune shack. We parted ways, and I followed the alleyway past Diva's entrance to the beach. Plunking down on the sand with my back to a fence, I gazed out at the harbor. I wanted to think.

Alyssa's meeting with Father Nick might turn into something we could use in the investigation. Mainly, it was an attempt on my part to buy time and put distance between us. Even if Father Nick confirmed the statue was Poseidon, that still wouldn't lead me to the murderer or murderers. But maybe my discovery of the statue and shipwreck would make the killer or killers come to me. And if I became a target, I didn't want Alyssa in the line of fire.

Hanging myself out as bait wasn't something I looked forward to, but I seemed to be good at it. I'd lured Flagg's bad guys into his trap without even trying. Just think what

I could accomplish if I put my mind to it. The work was easy. All I had to do was walk around with a target on my back.

Joe had warned me to keep my mouth shut. Given what happened to him after he started talking about the trident and the shipwreck, keeping a low profile seemed like good advice. Putting myself out there would be risky, but if I wanted to solve Joe's murder, I couldn't sneak around like a thief. I'd have to be Mr. Big Mouth. Luckily, talking out of turn was something that has never been hard for me.

My life wasn't the only one that would be complicated if I went public with the story. I called Flagg on his donated cell phone to ask his advice.

"I think I have a way to move my murder investigation along," I said.

"That's good."

"What's not good is that it's going to attract your bad guys. We might get into a game of bad guy tanglefoot."

"That's not good. I'm listening."

"You remember me telling you about an old war pal named Joe Bones?"

"Sure. He saved your ass back in 'Nam.

"Joe was the one who was murdered."

I told him about the call from Joe, the trident, and how I'd found the statue and the shipwreck.

"Congratulations. Seems like your investigation is on track."

"I've hit the wall, Flagg. I don't know where to go from here. I figure if I go public about finding the statue, Joe's killer will make a move that will kickstart the case."

"Huh," he said. Which could have meant anything. "That kick might knock the legs out from under you."

"I know it will be risky, but Joe did something dangerous when he saved my life. You think it's a bad plan?"

"It's crazy as hell, but it would do what you said. Going public will bring in your bad guy or guys. That's your problem. But it's going to attract my gang like flies on molasses."

"That's what's got me worried."

"This wouldn't be the first time I had a bunch of killers running around with my picture in their wallets. Goes with my job description. You're a paid snoop. You don't get into the hard-ass stuff unless it's by accident. You go public, the guys who want me dead will find you."

"I'll have to take that chance. I owe it to Joe."

The phone went silent. After a few seconds Flagg said, "And I dragged you into my mess. I'll meet you tomorrow and we can talk about it."

He named a time and place. I said the location surprised me.

"Looking at the big picture might give us some perspective. You could probably use the exercise," he added before he hung up.

In his own peculiar way, Flagg had given my crazy and dangerous scheme his blessing. Now it was time for me to put it in motion.

Chapter Twenty-Nine

LEAVING THE PEACE and quiet of the beach behind me, I climbed the stairs to Mary's second floor office and spread Joe's newspaper clips out on the desk. It only took a few seconds to find the article from *The Boston Globe* that quoted the professor saying the trident could be a very important discovery.

The name in the byline with the title of special writer was Jerry McGuire. The name was circled with a ballpoint pen and a line drawn to a phone number in the margin of the story. I called the number and left a message on the recording machine.

"My name is Socarides. I read the stories you wrote about the trident that came into Provincetown. I have new information I'd like to share with you. Please call me back."

My phone rang a few seconds after I hung up.

"This is Jerry McGuire," the voice said. "Sorry not to pick up. I like to screen my calls. Your message said you've got something new on the trident?"

"That's right. I saw your byline and thought I'd give you a jingle."

"Jingle away. What have you got?"

"Confirmation that the trident came from an ancient Greek statue."

"Sorry Mr. Socarides, but the Greek statue angle was in the original piece I wrote."

"That was supposition, as I recall. No hard evidence."

"Correct. It was a theory, based on expert opinion."

"Here's what you don't have. I've located the statue the trident came from."

"Wow! Now you're talking. Where'd did you find it?"

"On a shipwreck in Cape Cod Bay. Can't say where. The wreck will be swarming with poachers if the exact location gets out. I've got photos of both the statue and the ship that will prove I found them. How do I get the pictures to you? I'm calling from Provincetown."

"That works for me. I'm in P'town doing a story on the whale watch fleet."

"See you at the Bradford. I'll be the guy holding a brown envelope."

A few minutes later I walked into the bar and glanced around. Someone waved from a table. When I held up the envelope he pointed at his chest. I went over to the table and shook hands with a man wearing shorts and a New England Patriots T-shirt. A Red Sox ball cap was pulled down on pure white hair worn over the ears. Sports fans in Massachusetts aren't shy about advertising their loyalties.

Jerry asked for my beer order and went to the bar. He came back with a couple of foaming glasses and set one on the table in front of me. "Down payment on the story."

We clinked beers. "Thanks. Lucky for you I work cheap."

"I really appreciate you getting in touch. In my excitement I forgot to ask how you got pulled into this story."

"Joe and I were in Vietnam together. In fact, he was wounded when he blocked some shrapnel headed my way. I'm a diver, so I was the first one he thought of to survey the site where he netted the trident. We were going to use a remote-operated vehicle he'd picked up from the pirate museum. After he died, I figured I still owed him for that business back in 'Nam. I went out in his boat and used the ROV. I found the statue where he said it was."

"He told you?"

"Let's say he left a posthumous message."

Jerry frowned. "This whole thing with Joe's murder is crazy. He was a little crusty maybe, but a nice guy. Who would want to kill him over an old relic, or a statue?"

"Dunno. You have any ideas?"

"Maybe." He took a slug of beer and set the glass down harder than necessary. "I think there's a connection between your friend's death and the professor's."

"Tell me more."

He pointed his finger at me. "That's exactly what my editors should have said. I worked for years at the *Globe*. Retired now and living in a condo. Stringing is a way to keep my hand in the game and stay out of my wife's hair. Instead of assigning someone who knew Joe and the back story, the paper sent one of their staff people to cover the murder. Kid reporter who buried the dead professor link."

"How would you have handled it differently?"

"I would have put both the murders in the lede and used the trident to connect them."

"Sounds like you've got a solid take on a link between the two homicides."

He tapped his nose. "I may be an over-the-hill stringer, but I can still sniff out a story. All you've got to do is lay out what happened. Joe shows the trident to Professor Braddock. Within a short period of time, he and the prof are dead. Murdered. Trident disappears. What's that tell you?"

"The trident was a link."

"Kinda jumps out at you, doesn't it? The story the *Globe* carried barely mentioned the missing trident. I guess they figured that old pitchfork sprouted legs and walked out the door."

"That's exactly what happened, only in this case the legs belonged to Joe's murderer."

An alert expression came to his eyes. "You said you were a diver?"

"Part-time. My main business is running a charter fishing boat. Before that, I was a cop in Boston. When I moved to the Cape to fish and dive, I got my private detective's license and take a case now and then. Mostly minor stuff. But like you said, it's a way of keeping my hand in the game."

"You're a PI? This story just gets wilder and wilder."

"Yes, it does. And it's all yours if you want it. You can have the exclusive."

"Thanks! That's very generous of you."

"It's not entirely generosity. There's a quid pro quo."

"Quid pro all you want."

"In return for the info, I'd like you to write a story about me finding the wreck for tomorrow's edition of the *Globe*."

"The pub date is up to the editors, but I can write the story and file it tonight. The fact it's coming from a private investigator who was a Boston cop may give it some weight."

"Here's even more weight."

I unclasped the envelope, used a wad of napkins to wipe the beer circles off the table, and slid out the photos. "I shot these with Joe's ROV camera."

McGuire went through the pile and gave a long, low

whistle.

"These are simply amazing! My editor is going to go gah-gah when he sees them."

"He can gah as much as he wants to if he publishes tomorrow and spells my name right. Where do we start?"

He reached into the pocket of the knapsack hanging from his chair and pulled out a miniature recorder and a steno pad with a pen clipped to the cover. He asked if he could record our conversation for accuracy and I said that would be no problem.

Before the interview began, I laid out some ground rules. I wanted the interview to concentrate on the discovery of the statue and the shipwreck. He could make the connections between Joe and the professor, but that wouldn't come from me.

"I agree to all those conditions," he said.

"Ask away then."

"Okay. First question. How did you get into this deal?"

I glanced at the corner stools where I'd met Joe on the last day of his life.

"Like a lot of things, it began here at the Bradford over a couple of beers."

Chapter Thirty

THE REPORTER JUMPED into the interview like a puppy with a bone. I answered every question he fired my way, except when he asked me how I knew where to find the ship. I didn't want Diana to be part of the story. I said Joe had left a marked chart, which was partly true.

The bar started to fill up. The happy hour patrons at the Bradford wasted no time in the pursuit of happiness. The noise level reached a dull roar, and it was getting impossible to talk.

McGuire closed the cover on his notebook. "That should do it."

He said he would head directly home to write the article. Short and sweet. The photos would sell the story to his editors. Tink had made duplicate photos, so I let McGuire borrow the pictures to fax to Boston. He asked about a follow-up story. I said I'd call him after the article was published.

We stepped out of the noisy bar, and he shot a photo of me for the article. Then we shook hands. I wished him good luck. McGuire hustled off to his car. As I watched him head to the town parking lot I wondered if it had been smart to go public. Too late now, Socarides. I gave a mental shrug and joined the stream of strollers heading toward the West End.

I walked down the alley at Diva's and climbed the stairs.

I figured Tink would be getting dressed for his act but there was no one in his apartment. I went back down to the club. A few tables were occupied. Mary was mixing and pouring.

She smiled when I came up to the bar.

"Sorry I couldn't get to the police station when you called," she said.

"That's okay. I heard you were at the funeral parlor. How did it go?"

"Not very well. Hard to plan a funeral when you don't have the guest of honor. Still waiting for the medical examiner to release Joe's body."

"I know someone in the DA's office. I'll ask around."

Mary brightened. "That would be great. I went by the police station later, looking for you, but Ray said they kicked you out."

"I was giving the cop house a bad name and he threatened to arrest me for loitering. Did anyone ask you for a statement saying I had permission to use the *Zora*?"

"Ray said to drop a note off some time. No rush. Case of CYA, he said. "What was it all about?'

"A state cop named Corrigan wanted to throw me in jail for using the *Zora*."

"I might throw you in the nuthouse for going out in that old tub, but not jail."

"Ray said kind of the same thing. Turns out it wasn't so crazy after all. Tink and I found Joe's statue and the shipwreck."

She sloshed the margarita she was pouring.

"You've got to be kidding. I can't believe it."

"Believe it," I said. "Joe made an amazing discovery."

She refilled the margarita glass to the rim, then leaned across the bar, wrapped her fingers around the back of my neck and gave me a big wet kiss on the lips.

"Manny didn't think it was a good idea to hire you. I told him you'd come through for us. I don't know how I can thank you."

"Thank Tink, too, when you see him. He's got a video that shows the statue and the ship. He wasn't in the apartment. Any idea where he is?"

"He never showed up. He usually checks in with me before he goes upstairs to get into his outfit. We may have to call off karaoke. I thought he might be with you."

"I haven't seen him since I got hauled off to jail."

I'm getting worried. I've asked Manny to look out for him. Tink usually keeps his van parked outside the club but it's not there."

"He left me a note in your office saying he had a handyman job and would see me after the show."

"If he had an outside job, he might have stopped by his tool shed."

"I didn't know he had one."

"There's no room in the apartment and he doesn't like to leave tools in the van, so he rents a shed off Beach Point. I didn't think to send Manny there because I didn't know about Tink's job. I'll call him."

"I'll check it out in the meantime."

Beach Point is a wide causeway that runs between Pilgrim Lake and the harbor. The locals built the land bridge in the nineteenth century to stop sand drifting in from what was called East Harbor. Before Route 6 was built, the two-lane road used to be the main route to Provincetown. Through the years, cottage colonies, motels and houses sprang up along the road along with a few businesses. Every artist with a paintbrush or photographer with a camera has been inspired by the cottages named after flowers that line the beach side of the road.

Mary's directions led me to a two-story house that looked as if it hadn't been lived in for a while. Shingles had fallen off the roof and sides. The sandy driveway was hemmed in on both sides by tall compass grass.

I pulled into the driveway next to the house, grabbed a flashlight from my glove box, and got out of the truck. I stood in the darkness listening to the stiff fingers of wind strum the utility lines like guitar strings, then I walked around behind the house. Tink's van was parked between the house and a beat-up old shed about half the size of an ordinary garage that looked like it could have been around before the Pilgrims blew into town on the *Mayflower*.

I called Tink's name, shouting to be heard over the wind coming off the bay. After a couple of tries with no reply, I went over to the shed. The padlock hung from the latch and the door was open a couple of inches. I called Tink's name again. No answer. I opened the door and flashed the beam of the light around the inside.

The interior was neater than I expected. Tink had used the same care he brought to applying lipstick and mascara in arranging the cans of paint lined up neatly on the shelves. Brushes and tools hung from hooks. The workbench was as uncluttered as a surgical instrument table. The only thing out of place was a pile of black plastic tarps that had been tossed carelessly in a heap on the plank floor.

I glanced around and was about to step out of the shed, only to stop at the sound of a muffled groan.

I said, "Tink? Is that you?"

The groan repeated. It seemed to be coming from under the tarps. I pulled off the sheets of plastic one by one. Tink lay face down on the wooden floor. The back of his head was matted with blood that had dripped down his neck and was starting to dry.

Tink must have weighed close to four hundred pounds. I'd need a fork-lift to roll him over. Kneeling, I put my ear close to his mouth. His breathing was heavy and labored.

I put my hand on his shoulder and called his name.

A wet gargle that sounded like a broken garbage disposal unit came from deep in his throat. He was still alive, but he might not be if he didn't get medical help in a hurry. I went out to my truck and found the phone Flagg had given me. He said to use it only to call him, but this was an emergency. I tapped out 911, told the dispatcher where I was, and said that I needed an ambulance.

The dispatcher asked my name. "Please hurry," I said. Then I hung up.

After the kerfuffle with the state and local cops earlier that day, I didn't feel like dancing around the question of how I came to be at the scene of an assault and battery.

I searched the interior of Tink's van. There was no sign of the video CD or the second set of photographs. The laptop computer was gone as well. I wondered why whoever beat Tink up didn't come after me instead of someone the size and shape of a refrigerator. Well of course, I had been safely tucked in the tender arms of the State Police, and after my visit to the Provincetown jailhouse I was being interviewed at the Bradford.

I took a wild guess. The assault on Tink had something to do with our undersea discovery. But that raised the question of how anyone knew Tink and I had found the statue and wreck. Before talking to the *Globe* reporter, I told Alyssa, but hadn't even mentioned it to Mary until I'd popped into the club looking for Tink.

Tink didn't know the exact location of the statue. The people who mugged him seemed to know a lot, so they might look for me at the dune shack. And if they did, they'd find Alyssa alone and defenseless. I couldn't let that happen.

Chapter Thirty-One

I WAS DRIVING WAY over the speed limit when the ambulance passed me going in the other direction. Minutes later, I drove the truck onto the dune road at Race Point. The trick to sand driving is to stay loose and let the wheels follow the tracks. The sand is like mashed potatoes. Play lead foot with the accelerator pedal and you'll fish-tail out of control. But it's hard to stay calm when bad thoughts are buzzing around inside your skull like angry bees.

And even harder when someone is on your tail.

The vehicle must have been sitting on a side road with its lights off. The sudden reflection of headlights in the rear-view mirror almost blinded me. I adjusted the mirror to dim the reflection and gave the engine more gas. The lights stayed with me. I kicked up my speed and tightened my grip on the steering wheel.

The beat-up old truck I'd been ashamed to drive morphed from a knock-kneed old nag on the way to the glue factory into a Kentucky Derby winner. The big tires gripped the sand as if they had spurs on them. Once I got on the straightaway that ran along the shoreline my pursuer fell behind.

My lead would only last for a mile or so, until the beach road ended, and I was back on the winding, hilly sand track hemmed in by dunes on both sides, where I'd have to slow down to stay in control.

Except for the beach route, the road system through the Province Lands is laid out like a web woven by a drunken spider. I kept my eyes peeled for a side road where I might be able to lose my pursuer.

Rounding a curve, I saw an opening into the dunes. The bend in the road would hide me for a few seconds. I whipped the steering wheel over and nailed the accelerator.

The muscular pickup did fine on the straight stretches, but it had trouble making the turn. The wheels went wide and dug into the side of a dune. I slammed the gear shift into reverse. But in my haste, I gave the engine too much gas and the wheels spun without gaining traction.

Alternating the transmission lever between low and reverse, I rocked the truck back and forth until the wheels were in the track once more. I'd lost time and the chaser had narrowed the gap. I drove deeper into the Province Lands without a clue where I was or where I was going. The dunes were getting higher and the grass taller, restricting my field of vision to the track I could see in my headlights. I guessed that I was traveling toward the ocean. The chase would end when I ran out of land.

A glance into the rear-view mirror told me it might be sooner than that. The headlights were about to catch up with me, but then, suddenly, a second set flicked on directly ahead. I mashed the brakes and the truck plowed to a stop. Wild thoughts raced through my mind. There were two chasers and somehow, one of them had cut me off.

Then a funny thing happened.

The headlights behind me shrank. The chaser was backing up. Then the vehicle made a U-turn and disappeared around a bend. The other vehicle still blocked the road. The only way I might escape was to drive up onto the dunes. My hand reached for the gear shift lever.

That's when another funny thing happened.

The headlights that had lit up my bug-speckled windshield went dark. The vehicle's door opened, and the interior light went on. Someone got out of the cab. The parking lights cast enough illumination for me to see the dark green uniform of a national park ranger who came up to the driver's side of the high lift. I rolled the window down. The face under the wide-brimmed hat was that of Beth Williams, the ranger who had stopped by the dunes shack on night patrol.

"Did you see what that guy did?" she said. "He drove out of the track onto the dunes. Big no-no. Breaks down the grass and destroys the roots that hold the dunes in place. We've got enough natural erosion around here without someone promoting it with bad behavior."

"He was right on my tail. Guess I wasn't going fast enough for him," I said.

She shook her head in disgust. "You headed to the beach for some night fishing?"

"I'm on my way to Joe Bonega's shack."

She glanced left and right. "You're nowhere near it."

"Yeah, I know. Hard to see where I was going with the high beams in my eyes. Maybe the guy behind me was lost, too."

"Maybe," she said, sounding unconvinced. "I'll show you how to get to the shack."

"Thanks. It's lucky for me you were here," I said.

"I was out for a night ride and saw a couple of vehicles moving fast. Might be kids with a case of beer looking for a place to party. Like I said the other night, you'd be surprised what happens out here when the sun goes down."

"Not anymore," I said.

Ranger Williams backed up to a wide place in the road where she could turn around without destroying the beach grass. I followed her through the maze of trails to Joe's shack. She blinked her headlights and disappeared into the night probably to look for kids with beers.

I pulled up beside Alyssa's SUV and went to the front door. Not wanting to startle her, I knocked lightly and called her name before I went inside. She was kneeling on the floor in the light from a couple of kerosene lanterns, picking up sheets of paper and stacking them in a neat pile. Joe's filing cabinet lay on its side. Drawers had been pulled out of the dressers and the clothes emptied out on the floor.

Alyssa looked up at me, a sad expression on her face. I went over and knelt beside her. "Helluva mess," I said.

"I got here around half an hour ago and this is what I found. What on earth did they want? There's nothing in the dressers but old clothes."

"They emptied out the drawers because they didn't find what they were looking for in the filing cabinet."

"Omigod! This must have something to do with your discovery of the statue and shipwreck."

"I'll take that theory one step further. The people who broke in are probably the same ones who beat up Tink and stole photos and video of our underwater survey."

A horrified expression came to her face. "What are you saying?"

I told her how I had found Tink in his workshop.

"I'm so sorry. Will he be all right?"

"He's young and strong," I said, without answering her question. "I'll check the ER in a while."

"How would they have known so quickly that you had

found the shipwreck?"

"Can't say. What I can tell you is that the whole world is going to know tomorrow."

I told her about the interview with the Globe reporter.

She frowned. "Is it wise to attract attention?"

"I won't know the answer to that question until the whole thing plays out, but it will switch attention to me, which is where I want it. Tink got beat up today. Tomorrow it could be you or anyone else who's been too close to this thing."

"I know, but...."

I raised a finger. "We can talk later. Someone followed me into the dunes. Leave this mess for now and we can clean it up in the daylight. The ones who did this might still be in the neighborhood."

She glanced around, alarm in her eyes.

"You're right. We'd better go."

We killed the oil lamps, shut the door without locking it, and got into our trucks. I led the way out of the dunes. I'd kept calm for Alyssa's sake, but my case of the jitters didn't end until we got back to Provincetown.

With Tink in the hospital, I could use his apartment, but Alyssa needed a place to flop. I drove to the Thalassa art gallery. Alyssa pulled in behind me. I asked her to stay put, then went to the front door and rang the bell. The outside light flicked on, and Diana came to the door wearing a pink terry cloth bathrobe. I apologized for waking her up. She said she had been watching television and told me not to worry.

"Is there anything wrong?" she asked apprehensively.

"I need a favor. There's a young woman named Alyssa Braddock parked out front. Her uncle was Joe's friend, the professor. She needs a place to stay tonight. I wondered if you had a room to spare."

"My goodness. I have plenty of space in this big old house. My sister used to rent rooms when she had the gallery. I'd love to have Alyssa for as long as she needs. I'd be glad to have the company. Please tell her to come in."

I thanked her and told Alyssa she had a place to stay that night. I'd see her the next day. As we walked up to the front door she said, "In all the excitement I forgot to tell you about my meeting with Father Nick."

"Did he ID the photo?"

"He said the statue is definitely Poseidon, even though he couldn't see the face because of the marine vegetation."

"Anything else?'

"Yes, as a matter of fact." She paused and said, "He crossed himself and said for you to be careful."

Chapter Thirty-Two

PILGRIM MONUMENT IS where middle-aged men who think they're in good shape learn the hard way that the sweet bird of youth has flown south. Every step I took to get to the top of the two-hundred-fifty-foot-tall granite tower was a painful reminder of all the empty vows I'd made to follow a pure and wholesome lifestyle.

I'd walked over to the monument after a fitful sleep in Tink's apartment. By the time I set foot on the observation platform after taking the last of the hundred-and-sixteen steps, I was huffing and puffing like the Little Engine that Couldn't. But the view from the top of the tower built on a hill overlooking Provincetown was worth the climb. I walked around the platform, taking in the long curving sweep of Cape Cod, the rolling hills of the Province Lands and the narrow streets of what used to be called Helltown.

Rounding a corner, I almost bumped into Flagg. He's a big man, but he can be as stealthy as a cat stalking a mouse. When he's not setting deadly ambushes, his normal working outfit is a navy suit, blue shirt, and conservative tie. Today must have been office casual. He wore a black-and-white running suit and high-end track shoes. Pulled down over the black hair that was cut slightly long was a Washington Nationals baseball cap. A knapsack hung over his left shoulder.

His eyes were hidden behind reflective aviator

sunglasses that rested on a broad, hawkish nose. I was still breathing hard from my climb, and my mouth opened and closed like a hungry guppy. His thin lips were set in a tight smile, and he showed no sign of exertion.

"Fancy meeting you here," he said.

"I never figured you as a fan of the Pilgrims."

"But I am a big fan of irony, and this hunk of rock is as ironic as it can get," He gazed out at the bay through the safety screen enclosing the platform. "Pilgrims steal Indian corn, cheat us out of our land, and they get a national holiday and nice Italian style monument."

Flagg had a tough childhood growing up on Martha's Vineyard. He was a popular student and a good athlete, but he spent too much time in fistfights with boys who called him Chief. The year he was voted in as class president the principal nixed the deal, saying it wasn't his time.

"Maybe we can dig into the roots of Native American and European conflict another time. I've got a few things on my mind. Like trying not to be killed by your pals."

"Sorry for dragging you into this mess. I never thought you'd show up at my place in the middle of an operation."

"You said you broke your leg. I came by to help because that's what friends do."

He sighed heavily. "You're right. That's what they do. Look, I let this thing get personal. Big mistake. But I've been cleaning up after these scumbags for years."

"Who are they?"

"Names aren't important. Everyone knows them as the Three Brothers. They've left a trail of death around the globe. Men, women, and children. Doesn't matter. Real equal opportunity outfit. When I saw a chance to sink them and their organization, I took it."

"The guys who showed up at your house were brothers?"

"Hard to believe one family had a monopoly on cruelty. I don't know how many more people are going to die because I got sloppy and one of them got away."

"That bad?"

"That bad. Fact you're not dead yet is a good sign," he said.

"I'm not sure I like the *yet* part."

"Slip of the tongue. What I meant is that killing off two brothers slowed things down, but with one alive, their organization is still intact and bound to cause trouble. How's your investigation going?"

I told Flagg about Tink getting mugged, the chase through the dunes, and the mess at Joe's shack.

"Sounds like you've had your hands full. Your bad guys are way ahead of mine."

"Tink and I went out on the boat early yesterday morning, found the statue and the wreck, and came back with the proof. Within hours, Tink gets mugged and robbed, I go on a merry chase through the Province Lands, and Joe's shack gets tossed. What does that look like to you?"

"Someone knew you'd found something."

"But how? The only ones I told were Mary and Alyssa."

"Could be you let the secret out to the bad guys."

I shook my head. "How would I have done that if I didn't even know who the bad guys are?"

"What if someone bugged the boat? They would have heard everything you did and been ready for action when you came back in."

"I'm an idiot," I said.

"Naw. Technically challenged, maybe. Easy enough to do a sweep of the boat."

"Good idea." I'd been gazing out at the harbor while I talked with Flagg. "Wish I'd brought my binoculars."

"No problem." He reached into his knapsack and handed me a pair of compact binoculars.

I raised the lenses to my eyes. "There's a boat anchored near the breakwater that appears to be outfitted for marine salvage. It's got an A-frame crane on the stern."

I handed him the binoculars and he put them to his eyes.

"Huh," he said. "Definitely a work boat."

"It must have just arrived. I would have seen it when Tink and I came in with the *Zora*."

"What are you thinking?"

"Alyssa arranged a conversation a few days ago with a guy named Fowler. He's a Boston real estate developer and antiquities collector and dealer who was a friend of the professor. We talked about Joe's theory that the trident came from a statue. He said he had access to a salvage vessel. Maybe this is it."

"Salvage boat could have made the crossing from Boston in a few hours."

"That's what I'm thinking. I'd like to take a closer look."

"Do it soon. Things might get complicated with the *Globe* story in circulation," Flagg said.

"How long before we have to worry?"

"Can't say for sure, but this is what we're dealing with. The three brothers brought their technical savvy to stuff like drug and human trafficking. They cut through layers of security to find me on the Vineyard. All it took was one small info breach. Once you're in their system, programs run constant search checks. Your name or mine pops up on the internet and it rings an alarm bell. The *Globe* story will tell them you're in Provincetown. They'll look into your bio. They'll know all your habits. You like to drink?"

"I've been known to partake."

"They'll send people to check every bar in town."

"Not a bad strategy. The bartender at the Bradford knows a lot about Joe and me."

"Lots of opportunities. They'll say they're pals of yours. They'll contact the reporter. Maybe pose as experts who want to talk to you, or lawyers specializing in marine salvage."

"What should I do?"

"Stay out of sight for starters and keep an eye peeled."

"We should check out that bug now. It might take a while to find it."

He removed a small black plastic box with buttons and lights on it from his pack.

"Probably not," he said.

We made a quick descent from the top of the monument and got into Flagg's black Crown Victoria. A couple of minutes later, we were in the *Zora*'s wheelhouse. Flagg got down on one knee and pointed the black box at the underside of the instrument console. He put his finger to his lips, then stood and waved at me to step out onto the deck.

"The bug is still active and broadcasting," he said.

"That means they would have heard everything Tink and I said."

"And maybe a lot more. No telling how long it's been there. Could have been worse. In addition to the bug, they could have put in a locator beacon and tracked you out to the wreck site."

"Lucky for us they didn't. I showed Tink the position on the chart, but we never talked about the coordinates. Can we rip the bug out?"

"You might not want to do that until you find out who put it there. Could be useful later if you want to push some disinformation."

"Good point. Then it stays."

"For now. In the meantime, I've got a team coming down to provide back-up."

"Thanks for the help, but I don't want your people to get in the way."

"You won't even know they're around."

"Don't be too sure. I'll bet a streetwise private eye like me can make your guys in a second."

"Easy money. You didn't ID the agent I sent out to watch the dunes shack. You got fooled by a pretty woman in a Smokey hat."

"The park ranger was one of yours?'

"Works out of our Boston office. The National Park Service is a government agency. Just like mine. All it takes is a phone call to borrow a uniform and NPS vehicle."

"You win. When will your team be here?"

"Can't say. We had to round up people from various departments. Might be a few hours. Can you stay out of trouble?"

"I can't get into much trouble going to the hospital to see how Tink is doing."

"I'm not too sure of that. If someone shows unhealthy interest when you get back to town, the team will move in and roll them up in a hurry. Don't take any chances. There's no room for error. Remember that stuff you've told me about fate being on the knees of the gods."

Over the years, I'd worn Flagg down with my talk about our fate being out of our hands. I only half-believed what he called the knees of the gods stuff. At the same time, it was never wise to ignore the lessons of mythology. As Father Nick reminded me, when Poseidon gets his temper up, people get hurt.

Chapter Thirty-Three

THE VOLUNTEER AT THE front desk of Cape Cod Hospital looked up Tink's room number and confirmed that he was allowed visitors. On the way to his room, I stopped in the lobby to pick up a copy of the *Globe*. The story was on the first page of the regional section under the headline:

Cape Cod Mystery: Ancient Statue Found in the Bay

McGuire had done a good job hitting all the important points. He mentioned the strange coincidence of two deaths, leaving it up to the reader to link them. The paper ran a picture from the original article that showed Joe, the professor, and the trident. The head shot McGuire took of me outside the Bradford bar wasn't too bad. All that was missing was a bull's-eye between my eyes.

Tink's room was on the third floor. I peeked in through the open door. Tink looked like an Oriental potentate. Two beds had been pushed together to accommodate his massive body. Bandages enveloped his head like a turban. He saw me peering around the corner and gave me a big smile.

Relieved that he wasn't in a coma, I stepped into the room and went over to shake hands. His grip wasn't the knuckle-cruncher of our first meeting, but it was still strong.

"Thanks for coming. How do you like this rig?" he said.

"Clever. How are you feeling?"

"Okay. Being a big guy has its advantages. The regular

rooms were too small for my fabulous bod, so they gave me the deluxe. Hospital johnnies were a problem. They hooked two johnnies together with safety pins."

"You look better than the last time I saw you."

"I guess I clean up good. Most of the blood was from a head wound. Not as bad as it looked. The EMTs said someone called them."

"That would be me."

"How did you know where I was?"

"Mary said you went to the tool shed sometimes when you had a job."

"Thanks for following up."

"Any time. Sorry I got you into this, Tink. A cracked skull wasn't part of the job description."

He gingerly touched his turban. "I'm used to headaches from listening to croaky old winos sing about lost love."

I pulled a chair up to his bed. "Do you feel like talking about what happened?"

"No problem. What I can remember, anyway." He adjusted his body on the beds. "We'd come off the boat and the cops were hauling you away. Hey, how come you're not in jail?"

"We worked out an arrangement. What happened while I was headed to the slammer?"

He wrinkled his brow in thought. "I took my laptop to the club and ran the photos off on the printer. Two sets. One for you and one for me."

"They're sharp and clear."

"The video was spectacular. Like being down there on Joe's wreck. I got a call on my cell phone while I was finishing up with the photos. It was a woman who called, saying she had a rush job. Wanted to know where we could meet that was private."

"Why the need for privacy?"

"She said her husband thinks of himself as a handyman. He'd go off on her if he knew she was hiring a professional."

"So, you met at your toolshed."

"Yeah. The house has been tied up for years in an estate. The family lets me use the shed to store my stuff. When I got there, no one was around. I keep the door locked because of the tools, but the latch was pried from the wood. I had just stepped inside when I felt something hard shoved into my back. They must have been waiting behind the shed."

"They?"

"Yeah. The guy at my back spoke to someone else."

"What did he say?"

"He talked in some kind of language I'd never heard before. The other guy said something back in a similar language."

"What happened next?"

"They didn't waste time with preliminaries. A house fell on my head and the lights went out."

"You say there were two of them?"

"Three actually, if you count the woman."

"You didn't say anything about a woman."

"Sorry. I heard a female voice just before I passed out. She sounded like the woman who called for the job."

"Anything distinctive about the voice?"

"Maybe a slight accent when we talked on the phone. She only said one word in the shed. Sounded like she said *duster*."

"Like feather duster?"

"Yes, only without the feather. I know it doesn't make

sense. Any idea why they picked on me?"

"Probably because they couldn't find me. I went out to Joe's dune shack after I called in help. The place had been broken into. Someone followed me, but they turned back after a park ranger showed up."

"That was lucky." A thought seemed to come to him. "My laptop with the video was in the van!"

"I searched the van before the rescue squad arrived. Nothing."

"Crap. What about the duplicate photos?"

"Alyssa showed one photo to an expert who says the statue is Poseidon. The other pix went to the *Globe*. Read all about it."

I handed him the newspaper and walked over to the window while he read the article. From the window I could see the Hyannis marina. *Thalassa* had been moved from its boat rack and was in its regular slip, ready to fish or be sold. I wondered what was going on with my family. I should be getting back to Chloe and George.

Tink's voice broke into my thoughts.

"*Jeez!*" he said. "This is a big deal, isn't it?

I turned away from the window and went back to Tink's bedside. "We'll see how it plays out. Even with the photos and video, the people who bopped you still don't know the exact location of the wreck. They'll come after me."

"Be careful, Soc! You don't want to get busted up like this."

I tapped the newspaper. "I'm hoping this story is my insurance. After beating you up, tossing Joe's shack and chasing me around the dunes, they've got nothing but a bunch of pretty pictures like the ones with the story. Maybe they'll figure the strongarm stuff doesn't work and they'll try to make a deal."

"You really think that's possible?"

"No. But it's worth a try. They'll have to come out of the shadows and into the sunlight where we can see them."

"I should be helping you instead of taking up two beds."

"You can help me by healing fast. Your karaoke fans demand it."

"Ah yes, the fans." He rolled his eyes, then closed them, and drifted off to sleep. I quietly left the room.

Chapter Thirty-Four

ABOUT AN HOUR AFTER leaving the hospital, with a stop at the office to check for phone messages, I walked into the Bradford bar and saw McGuire sitting at a table, his eyes glued to the screen of his laptop. I pulled up a chair and said, "Got your call. Great story! Congratulations."

He glanced up from his computer. "Glad you liked it."

"Reads like a murder mystery. I liked the way you connected the trident to the two murders without exactly saying so."

"I had to sneak that part in, or the editors would have cut the balls off what I filed." He handed me the envelope with the photos. "The underwater shots of the wreck and the statue really caught their attention. My words were window dressing. And an even bigger thanks for the background material on how you got pulled into this crazy story."

"No problem. Any response yet?"

He nodded. "Lots of people responded to the story. I'm logging in the calls from ones who want to get in touch with you."

"Anything stand out?"

"Most were what you might expect. Divers who want to explore the wreck. Academics who want to show you how smart they are by pooh-poohing the discovery. Someone from the state archaeological board got in touch to tell you not to try a salvage job without their okay. Lawyer who specializes in salvage law. Even the Greek consul in Boston, who wondered if the statue had been stolen from his country."

"It wouldn't be the first work of art to leave Greece by dead of night. Anyone else?"

"One of the callers left her number, but she didn't say who she was. I told everyone that I'd see you got their messages."

He turned his computer around and slid it across the table. I went down the list on the screen, then borrowed his cellphone and called the number next to Unknown Woman. After a couple of rings, a female voice answered the phone and said, "Yes?"

"This is Aristotle Socarides," I said.

"Hello, Mr. Socarides. Wilma Vladik speaking. We met at Mr. Fowler's."

The Black Dahlia, Fowler's assistant in charge of acquisitions. "Sure, I remember you well, Ms. Vladik. How can I help you?"

"Mr. Fowler read the article in the *Globe* and asked me to get in touch with you. He's very interested in your find. Congratulations."

"Thanks. I got lucky."

"You're being modest. He'd like to learn more about your discovery."

"The *Globe* story was pretty comprehensive," I said.

"Yes, it was, but I was wondering if we could talk further."

"I'm busy with a case right now. I wouldn't be able to come to Scituate."

"That's all right. I can fly to Provincetown this

afternoon. Can you meet me at the airport in two hours?"

I said, "I'll see you there."

I handed the phone back to McGuire. "Thanks. Can I buy you a beer?"

"Sure, but even better, you can tell me what's going on with all this cloak and dagger stuff."

"That will have to wait. Sorry."

He shrugged. "Then I'll take that beer now."

I went to the bar. Bill the Beerman came over. After taking my order, he said, "Your friends ever get in touch with you?"

"What friends are those?"

"Couple of guys came in earlier today. They ordered top drawer whiskey straight up and asked if you ever dropped by the Bradford. Said I saw you from time to time. They said they were pals of yours from the old days and asked me not to tell you they'd been in. Wanted to surprise you."

"Did they leave their names?"

"Mike and Rick. No last names, but they left a big tip."

"What did these big tippers look like?"

"Tourists. You know the rig. Hawaiian shirts, shorts, sneakers with white socks, and straw hats. Oh yeah. These guys were buff. Lotsa muscle. Sound like anyone you know?"

"Maybe. Thanks for the heads-up. If they come in again, please don't mention we talked. I'd like to surprise them."

I carried the beer to the table and told McGuire I'd be in touch with him. I probably should have called Flagg to let him know that his friends were nosing around town. I didn't want him sending in the cavalry just yet, so I put it off while I dealt with Joe's case.

A few minutes later I walked into the Thalassa gallery.

Diana was busy with a potential customer. She pointed toward a door. I went through the doorway onto a brick patio bordered by flowerbeds. In the center of the patio was a round wooden table. Alyssa was sitting under an umbrella, a stack of file folders on the table in front of her.

"Hi Soc," she said, giving me a smile. "Just thinking about you. I've come across something in my uncle's files."

"The last will and testament of Alexander the Great?"

"That would be the *what*. This may be the *why*." Lowering her voice she said, "*Cherchez la femme*."

"Look for the woman?"

She nodded and opened a file folder. "My uncle's notes mentioned a Ruth W. a couple of times. One notation had the full name. Ruth Wonderly."

I gave her a look. "Did your uncle like detective stories?"

"He read mysteries of all kinds. How did you know?"

"I used to read hard-boiled detective novels. It's probably why I got into cop work. Ruth Wonderly is the alias Brigid O'Shaughnessy uses when she comes into Sam Spade's office in *The Maltese Falcon*. What was the context?"

She scanned her uncle's notes. "Ruth W. wants to meet with Joe."

"Interesting."

"I can run through the other files while you're here and see if she pops up again. Anything new since the last time I saw you?"

"The newspaper story stirred up some interest, including a call from Wilma Vladik, the woman we met at Fowler's place."

"Wow! Did she say what she wanted?"

"Only that Fowler read the *Globe* story and wants to talk to me about the statue."

"That ties in. His specialty is antiquities from the time of Alexander. Are you going to see her?"

"She's flying to Provincetown in a little while. There's something else. Fowler said he could bring in a marine salvage boat on short notice. Before Wilma arrives, I want to look at a boat fitted out for salvage that arrived in P'town harbor earlier today. I can do it alone, but a nosy guy in a boat might attract attention where a couple would look like they're just out for a cruise."

"If you're asking me to go with you the answer is 'yes'."

"Thanks, Alyssa." I set a leather case down on the table. "We're going to get as close to the boat as we can, so we'll need a disguise. I borrowed Tink's makeup kit. Maybe there's something here we can use."

"Oh goodie," she said, clapping her hands. "Dress up."

She dug inside the case, pulling out a curly blonde wig that she yanked down on her head. She gave me a coy look from under the wild fringe of platinum blonde hair that hung over her forehead.

"What do you think?"

"You've unleashed your hidden Dolly Parton. We're trying to be inconspicuous. Maybe if you wear a hat."

"Let's see what I can find for you." She reached into Tink's case again and came out with a dark brown wig that she draped over a fist. "You'd make a wonderful Cher," she said.

"Like I said, inconspicuous. Any scissors in that case?"

She poked around and came out with a pair of shears that were small but sharp. She winced when I used them to trim a strip off the bottom of the wig.

"Tink's not going to like that," she said.

"He won't need it in the hospital." I held up the trimmed

wig. "Voila," I said.

"It looks like a furry snake."

"Watch the master of disguise work his magic." I wrapped the strip of fake hair around my neck and tucked it in under my chin. "Captain Ahab?"

She wrinkled her nose. "You'll be fine if you wear a hat."

"I'm already wearing one."

"It was so inconspicuous I hadn't noticed."

I was beginning to like Alyssa. "Let's go for a boat ride," I said.

Alyssa pulled her ball cap down over her wig. We put on sunglasses and went back through the gallery. Diana was still with her customer. She raised an eyebrow as we went by, but otherwise didn't seem surprised at our change. Maybe she thought Provincetown's weirdness is catching.

I drove onto the wharf and a few minutes later we climbed into Joe's inflatable boat which was tied to the dock behind the *Zora*. I still had Joe's boat key ring from the boat trip. I started the outboard motor and Alyssa uncleated the dock line. She pushed us from the dock, and I pointed the blunt rubberized prow out into the harbor.

The salvage boat was anchored off by itself. If we headed directly toward it, someone on board might see us and wonder what we were up to. Instead, I wove in and around the other moored boats while Alyssa shot photos of our target at a distance with her cell phone camera.

After a while, I veered off at an angle that brought us closer to the yacht. The vessel was around seventy-five-feet-long. It had a white hull and a profile that would have been sleek except for the sturdy boom mounted on the stern where the crane could be used to lower and lift heavy loads.

As I began a turn that would take us parallel to the boat, a man emerged from the main cabin and walked casually along the deck. He stopped around midships and raised a pair of binoculars to his eyes. I didn't worry until two more men came out onto the deck. The first one pointed his finger in our direction and handed the binoculars to one of the newcomers. He checked us out and gave the glasses to the third man.

"Don't look now, Dolly," I said. "Guys on the boat are giving us the eye. I'm going to ease off and head back to the wharf."

Alyssa stopped taking pictures of the salvage boat and aimed her phone camera in the direction of Pilgrim Monument as if she were taking photos of the town.

I swung the inflatable around, allowing me a quick glance at the yacht. Two men were walking toward the stern where an inflatable twice the size of ours was tied up. If they launched the boat and came close, our amateur disguises wouldn't hold up for a second.

The man with the binoculars must have said something because his pals turned back from the stern, and they all went into the cabin. I meandered the inflatable slowly across the harbor and didn't return to the *Zora* until I was sure no one was following. We tied up the inflatable. The fake beard was hot and scratchy, and I was glad to take it off.

"That was scary," Alyssa said as she removed her wig. "I thought they were going to come after us."

"It was worth the risk for what we learned."

"The only thing I learned was that we stink at disguise," she said.

"Maybe not. Something changed their minds about

checking us out. Anyway, we now know that the yacht has enough mechanical muscle to raise a substantial load off the ocean bottom. The crane appears to be a retrofit. Also, we know that the crew is touchy about strangers nosing around. Too bad we had to leave before we could do a close inspection."

"I got some shots of the equipment on deck if that helps," Alyssa said. She handed me her cell phone.

I scrolled through the photos on the display screen. Some were blurred and off-kilter, but they confirmed my assessment that the yacht had been modified for salvage. One photo caught my attention.

"How do I make this bigger?" I said.

"Put your thumb and forefinger on the screen and spread them apart."

I did as she suggested and read the words on the stern of the yacht. "This is crazy."

"Is there something wrong with the pictures?"

"Depends on how you look at it." I handed the phone back.

She read the yacht's name. "Amphitrite II," she said. "Similar to the partial name on the sunken boat."

"Alias Mrs. Neptune."

"That's a wild coincidence. It *is* a "coincidence, isn't it?"

"Could be, but it doesn't seem likely. All this time I've been thinking the statue was the key to the secret of who killed Joe and your uncle. But it was the boat carrying the statue that ties it all together."

"I think you're saying that it would be helpful to know who owned the boat when it sunk."

"I think that's what I mean but I don't know for sure. I'll check with the library later. Maybe they can help ID the yacht's ownership."

I glanced at my watch. It was time to meet Wilma.

Chapter Thirty-Five

A FEW MINUTES LATER, I was walking into the lobby of the Provincetown airport. It was in between Boston flights. The place was deserted except for the ticket sellers at the Cape Air counter, a couple of bored-looking TSA agents, and me. I stood in the waiting area where I had a view of the runway. Not long after I arrived, a twin-engine plane swooped out of a cloudless sky, touched down on the landing strip, and taxied up to the terminal.

Wilma stepped from the plane, and as she walked across the tarmac, the ocean breeze played with her hair. She wore a shark gray pantsuit that fit her body like a glove, but my guess is she would have looked good wearing a burlap bag. She entered the terminal, saw me waiting, and came over to shake hands.

"Thank you for meeting me," she said. She removed her sunglasses and brushed the hair out of her jade-colored eyes. "Hope it was no trouble getting together on such short notice."

"Happy to be of service." I glanced out the window at the plane. "Your pilot must have had the propellers spinning when I called."

"Something like that," she said with a quick smile. "Opportunity can be fleeting in the antiquities acquisition business. We have a contract with a company that has pilots on call 24/7, ready to fly us anywhere we want to go. The pilot will wait until I'm done here and fly me back to Boston."

"We'd better get going in that case. I've got a ride outside. We can go somewhere less public to talk."

"This is your neighborhood. I'll leave that decision in your hands."

We walked through the lobby and out into the warm sun to the high lift truck parked outside the terminal.

"Are we going on a peace mission?" she said. "This looks like it belongs to the UN."

"The truck was a gift from a friend. It was painted camouflage and I thought blue might work better with a charter fishing business."

"I like it," she said.

She stepped onto the high running board and launched her lithe body easily into the passenger seat. I got behind the steering wheel and drove a few miles from the airport to Herring Cove beach. We found a picnic table at the edge of the beach away from some people who'd spread blankets and were soaking up the sun's rays.

I offered her a bottle of water I had picked up at a convenience store on the drive to the airport.

"Thank you. That's very kind," she said. "I had something on the flight." She unsnapped her purse and extracted a copy of the *Boston Globe* story laminated in plastic. "Congratulations again on finding the statue and the shipwreck."

I unscrewed the bottle cap and took a swig. "It's easy when you have the coordinates for the site."

She cocked her head. "I thought that information died with Mr. Bonega."

"Like I said, I got lucky."

Wilma placed the *Globe* article down and tapped it with a long, tapered fingernail. "The story quotes you as saying you intend to keep the location a secret."

"For now. If I went public, poachers would clean the wreck out within twenty-four hours. I'm thinking of turning the coordinates over to a university or non-profit that would salvage the site the way it should be done. I'll be talking to the state, since Massachusetts salvage law may be involved."

"All responsible courses of action." She paused for a second or two, then said, "As you know from talking to him, Mr. Fowler is intensely interested in your find. He has a non-profit foundation in place that has the means to recover the statue and salvage the wreck. He'd like you to consider a joint venture."

"That's very tempting, but...."

"But what, Mr. Socarides?"

I pulled out my wallet and extracted the Herald-Tribune piece I'd found in Joe's files; the story said Fowler had testified on behalf of a smuggler who'd been charged with selling stolen antiquities. Making a show of it, I flattened the article out on top of the Globe story.

"Since you're the one who brought up Fowler's name, maybe you can explain what this is all about."

Wilma picked up the clipping and glanced at the headline. She must have seen the article before, because without reading it she said, "You're very thorough."

"I like to know who I might be doing business with."

"There's an explanation for this," she said, placing the article back on the table.

"I'm sure there is, but is it one I'd buy?"

"That's entirely up to you. You know the commodities

Mr. Fowler's company deals in."

"Greek and Roman antiquities, with an emphasis on the time of Alexander the Great."

"Correct. There is a small but highly profitable market for those artifacts. You might be surprised at the number of oligarchs who like to think they are marching in the footsteps of Alexander. They try to emulate his attributes."

I gave her a Socarides smirk. "What attributes would those be? His ruthlessness? Disregard for life? His vanity? His egomania?"

"All of those and more. The collectors see themselves as his metaphysical heirs."

"That seems sad."

"Thinking that owning something from Alexander's time will make them great? Yes, it probably is, but it means they will pay anything for objects that link to Alexander."

"What does an unhealthy preoccupation with a questionable historical figure have to do with Fowler's brush with the law?"

"Anyone who trades in antiquities risks legal exposure. The origins of relics are often murky. Say you're offered a marble bust of Alexander. Those who dug up the relic are long dead. The chain of ownership is often impossible to establish. Most police departments give art theft low priority. You often deal with unreliable people. Sometimes the line between the legal and illegal is blurred. Fowler testified on behalf of one of his suppliers."

"So, Fowler got dragged into a mess by being a nice guy."

"I didn't say he was nice. Only that he was tarnished by his ties to shady characters and by his fixation with acquiring objects from the ancient world."

"Fowler's obsession affected his judgement, and he screwed up. How does that apply to Joe?"

"When Fowler heard about the statue, he sent me to make Joe an offer. He'd finance the salvage of the statue and your friend would get the credit for making that possible."

"What did Joe say?"

"He was interested at first. It would be a way of showing doubters that what he'd found was important. Then the professor intervened, and Joe began having second thoughts about Fowler's offer."

"Fowler's reaction?"

"Disappointment of course."

"Anger, too?"

She raised an eyebrow. "Are you asking me if Mr. Fowler had anything to do with your friend's death?"

"I might be."

She laughed. "I can't believe you're serious. An old man in a wheelchair?"

"Fowler could have hired someone to take care of Joe."

"Yes, he could have. But he didn't. Why kill the only one who knew where to find the statue?"

"Only the killer can answer that question. I've got one of my own. Joe finds the trident, and after he talks to the professor, he starts acting as if he's going to be filthy rich. What was that all about?"

"In trying to woo Mr. Bonega back, Mr. Fowler became more forthcoming. He told your friend that the statue could be extremely valuable, and that he would share in this bounty."

"Valuable in what way?"

"There's a legend of a treasure associated with the statue."

"So, Joe is leaning toward Fowler, then the professor comes in and tells him about the treasure. Fowler sweetens the deal, but Joe no longer trusts your boss."

"Apparently the professor was very persuasive."

"Apparently. The next thing we know, the professor is dead. But Joe doesn't go back to Fowler, he comes to me. Then he's dead. Now you show up and start talking a deal, just like you did with Joe. You can see why I'm a little jittery. It's not only Fowler. I checked on you. There is no Wilma Vladek on record with your credentials."

It was a big bluff on my part. She gazed at me for a few seconds, then said, "I underestimated you."

"You wouldn't be the first one. Who are you, really, Ms. Vladek?"

Without missing a beat, she said, "I'm someone who is warning that you are getting in over your head. These are dangerous waters. You don't know the whole story."

"Tell me what I'm missing, then. I love fairy tales."

She clamped her lips in a tight line and looked out at the water.

"Here's my problem," I said. "I'm being asked to turn over something of potentially great value to a man who hides his past and a woman who doesn't have a past."

Turning to face me, she said in a soft voice, "This is not how it appears. No matter how this seems to you, I am not a part of it."

"What *are* you a part of?"

"I can't tell you now. You don't understand that the forces at play go back thousands of years."

"And you don't understand that when a friend asks for your help you give it to him whether he is dead or alive."

"I appreciate your desire to avenge Mr. Bonega, but it

will be dangerous if you don't accept Mr. Fowler's offer."

"Sounds like a threat, Wilma."

"That's because it is a threat. But not from me. Fowler will stop at nothing to get the statue. He considers it his property."

"He told me ancient Greece has been a passion of his family for generations."

"The strength of that family passion is obvious to anyone who has seen his collection. And it's why I feel so strongly that if you give him enough rope, he will hang himself."

"Suppose I go along with your suggestion. What would I have to do to keep my side of the deal?"

"Simple. Tell Fowler where to find the statue."

Wilma was beautiful and persuasive, and she seemed to want to distance herself from Fowler. On the other hand, she hung out with the wrong crowd. Maybe Fowler didn't kill Joe, but my gut instinct was telling me that he was up to his eyeballs in Joe's death. If I could get closer to him maybe I might find the real murderer.

"What would Fowler do if I gave him the location?"

"He'd probably launch a salvage operation immediately."

"And when he brings up the statue, then what? He returns it to Greece where it belongs?"

"Eventually. Maybe."

"Like Lord Elgin?"

Elgin was the British nobleman who stole the frieze sculptures from the Parthenon in 1801 and gave them to the British Museum, which has kept a lock grip on them since then.

"I can't tell you that. Only that refusing his offer would

be an unwise decision on your part."

"Maybe, but I'm keeping the location a secret for now. Before I do anything, I want to talk face-to-face with him. Maybe he'll change my mind. Maybe I'll get a better offer."

"I can't guarantee he'll agree to your terms."

"He will unless he wants Alexander sitting at the bottom of the sea forever."

"I'll tell him what you said. I wish you had agreed to his proposal without conditions but thank you for your time. Perhaps we should head back to the airport."

We got in the truck for the short drive through the Province Lands. Wilma made a few observations about the beauty of the scenery, but that was about it until we got to the airport. I walked her to the lobby. She thanked me again. Minutes later, the plane rolled down the runway and angled up and into the air.

I watched the plane shrink in size until it vanished, thinking about what I'd learned from my strange conversation with Wilma.

Fowler was dangerously obsessed with the statue and not to be trusted, but she urged me to give him the information he wanted. She said I was dealing with matters that went back thousands of years. And that no matter how it looked, she was not a part of what was going on.

This is not what it seems, she said.

I might not know what was going on, but there was one thing I was sure of. From the day Joe called me, *nothing* about the case was as it seemed.

Chapter Thirty-Six

THE LIBRARIAN AT THE Provincetown Library desk greeted me with a full-face smile. "I read the fascinating article in the Globe this morning," she said. "I didn't realize you were quite the celebrity."

"Andy Warhol said everyone gets fifteen minutes of fame."

"Well-deserved in this case. Congratulations. How on earth did an ancient Greek statue wind up where Joe found it?"

"That's the big question. There's a good chance that it was carried there by a boat named the *Amphitrite*."

"I don't remember seeing that name in the newspaper story."

"I kept that detail out because I wasn't sure of it. If I were wrong, it would cast doubt on the whole story. The hull was partially buried under sand. I only saw part of the name, but the boat had sleek lines, so I assume it was a yacht. I'd like to track down the ownership."

"Hmmm. Hold on." She clicked her computer mouse a few times. "There are some classic yacht organizations online that might be of help. This is a down time. Let me see what I can find out."

I left her with the information I had and said I'd be back in an hour. I wanted to tell Alyssa about my talk with Wilma. From the library, I drove straight to the gallery.

Alyssa was sitting at a low table in the showroom looking through a sketchbook.

"Diana has been showing me Joe's work," she said. "He was a fabulous artist."

"I've seen some of his paintings at Mary and Manny's," I said, settling into a chair. "He used to sketch back in 'Nam but kept the drawings to himself. I had no idea he was so good. There was a sketchbook on his boat, so I guess he was still at it."

"You can see his progression as an artist in this sketch pad. The sketches are even more interesting than his finished product," Alyssa said. "His first images are powerful but on the rough side. His technique became polished after he took a few art classes, although he still retained his power."

She handed me the sketchbook. In the first few pages Joe's sketches were almost primitive. The pencil strokes were thick and drawn rapidly, as if Joe were afraid the subject would vanish before he could capture it. In later work, the lines were finer and more detailed, and Joe showed he had a talent for drawing.

Most of the sketches were of boats, except for a diagram on one of the last pages in the book. It was a simple drawing, dated a few weeks earlier, that showed two more or less parallel lines connected by a dotted line. There was an X at the midpoint of the dotted line, and two more Xs where it connected to the parallel strokes.

I showed the sketch to Alyssa. "What do you make of this?"

She studied the drawing. "Could it be a map of one of Joe's fishing holes?"

I let my mind's eye follow the shoreline of Cape Cod Bay

from Provincetown around the curving peninsula to the canal.

"I can think of a couple of rivers and harbors where water is bordered on two sides by land, but Joe fished mainly in the bay. And if this was a favorite fishing spot, why would it be in a sketch pad?"

She sighed. "I wish I had known Joe. He's far more complicated than the common stereotype of a simple fisherman."

"Simple is not a word I'd use in the same sentence with Joe's name. I just came from the library. The librarian is seeing if she can track down a yacht named *Amphitrite*. I told her that I could only see part of the name in the ROV pictures."

I opened the envelope I'd retrieved from the *Globe* reporter and slid out the packet of photos. Alyssa idly browsed through the pile and stopped to study one drawing of the statue. "If only old Poseidon here could talk."

I asked to see the photo. "Maybe he can."

"What do you mean?"

"As a detective, I look for inconsistencies. There's a big one. Literally. What did you tell me about the guy who probably sculpted the statue? Something to do with body proportions."

"My uncle's notes say that the figures Lysippos sculpted were noted for their symmetry and grace. He made their heads smaller in proportion to their bodies so they would appear taller and slenderer. The common ratio for sculpture was seven to one. In the Canon of Lyssipos he used a scale of one to eight for the head and total height of the body."

"We talked about the chunky proportions on this guy

when I first showed you the photos." I pointed to the figure in the photo she'd passed me. "Does that look like one-to-eight to you?"

Alyssa used her thumb to measure. "This is more like a one to seven ratio. Maybe one to six."

"That's right. Old Poseidon looks as if he's survived on fish and chips all the time he's been down there."

"What do you mean?"

"He's sturdy, but almost porky. Alexander had the final say on the statues Lyssipos made. Why would he allow the god of the sea to be portrayed in a way that was less than flattering?"

"I don't know. Why?"

"Maybe he didn't want a simple statue."

"What do you mean?"

"Suppose the statue had multiple functions. Alexander could thank his patron god Poseidon for allowing him to move his army across the Hellespont. And it could serve as a container of some kind."

"That last would seem far-fetched."

"I agree, except for Joe's drawing. What if it was a map showing where Alexander dropped the statue? Put yourself in Alexander's place. He wants to move fast. He doesn't want his pack animals or soldiers to be burdened with plunder. What would he do?"

"He would want to leave it somewhere safe."

"What would be safer than the bottom of the sea?"

"Which suggests that he was planning to come back to retrieve it."

"It also suggests that the story of Alexander going down in the diving bell was based on something that really happened."

"You really think that's possible?"

"Alexander's army carried some sophisticated war gear. Catapults and other siege machines. Equipment that could have been adapted for marine engineering. Look at the belt on the statue. See anything odd about it?"

"The metal loops at the hips?"

"That's right. You could hook lines to those and pull the statue out of the water. I think Alexander had something valuable he didn't want to take with him."

"Yes, but what?"

"He could have been safeguarding loot from the last campaign he conducted before crossing the Hellespont."

"You think Alexander commissioned the overweight statue to hide a stash while he conquered Persia and put the treasure in a place he could come back to?"

It seemed like a long shot, but then I thought about the young red-haired man who leaped off a boat into the surf, brimming with audacity, throwing his spear into the beach to claim an entire continent.

"Kinda looks that way," I said.

Chapter Thirty-Seven

ALYSSA SAID SHE WOULD dig into her uncle's files to see if she had missed anything that might relate to my weird theory. We'd get together for dinner at the Lobster Pot to talk over our findings. On the walk back to the library, I encountered tendrils of fog that were snaking off the harbor and into town. But I was starting to feel my way through the mists that had clouded my mind since I'd driven into Provincetown on the murky night Joe died.

The librarian was pecking away at the keyboard of her computer when I came back. She waved at me to come over. The librarian's name was Cindy. She was so eager to help she made me feel like a researcher for National Geographic instead of a cut-rate gumshoe trying to build a homicide investigation out of suppositions, hunches, and wild guesses.

I pulled up a chair and studied the photo on the screen. "What have we got?"

"I dug into the archives of several classic yacht associations and managed to patch together a history of *Amphitrite*. This picture was from a newspaper article."

The seaworthy boat in the picture was a far cry from the cracked-open wreck lying at the bottom of Cape Cod Bay.

"Handsome vessel," I said. "What do we know about her?"

"She was built in 1895 and owned by Seven Seas

Shipping. The owner of Seven Seas Shipping was a New Englander named Lysander Fowler. He lived on the South Shore of Massachusetts."

"Scituate?" I said.

"That's right. How did you know?"

"I made a wild guess. Did those records say anything about her sinking?"

"No. It was supposedly sold to the Venezuelan navy in 1897. The trail ends there."

"That would make it tough to trace," I said.

"It's not a warship, so it would have been acquired as a pleasure craft, probably by someone high up in government," Cindy said. "People with that sort of influence might not want the public to learn that yachts for politicians or high-ranking navy people are being purchased at taxpayer expense. You never know."

"That's right. You never do know. On the other hand, the owners of the yacht may have said they sold it to the Venezuelans so they wouldn't have to explain why it disappeared."

"The sale story is a fraud?"

"Possibly."

Cindy arched an eyebrow. "Maybe it would help if you told me what this research is for."

"I'm a private investigator. My client's family had ties to the yacht. There may have been valuable cargo on board the *Amphitrite*. They're wondering what became of it."

"How exciting! The only private detectives I know are the fictional ones. I run the mystery book club for the library. We've read *The Maltese Falcon*. I saw the movie, too," she said with a wink. "You're not at all like the hard-boiled private eye in the book or Humprey Bogart in the film."

"I prefer my eggs soft-boiled," I said with a wink back. "Detectives have different styles, but some things never change. Like greed and friendship."

"In the story Sam Spade wants to avenge the murder of his friend and partner, Miles Archer."

"That's right. And the bird?"

She smiled. "The statue was made of lead, not gold and jewels."

"In other words, not everything is as it seems," I said.

"The stuff dreams are made of," she said, quoting Sam Spade.

I smiled and said, "Thank you for your help, Cindy."

We shook hands. I was headed for the door when she called after me, "There was one more thing, Mr. Socarides."

I stopped in my tracks, wondering what other bombshell Cindy had for me.

"What's that, Cindy?" I said.

"Thank you for the baklava."

I had told Manny that a homicide investigation is like a jigsaw puzzle. Find the pieces and fit them together. Some pieces are people. Some are things. Like a busted-up old yacht at the bottom of the sea. If you have enough of the right pieces, a picture will come together.

What was coming into view was more like a photo montage. Lysander spiriting the Poseidon statue out of Greece. Shipping it to America. Putting it on a yacht bound from New York to Boston. And finally, the yacht sinking in Cape Cod Bay, where it languished until Joe's net snagged the trident and broke it off.

Avery was likely a descendant of Lysander. He would have known about his ancestor's misadventure. And he would have considered the statue valuable family property, which is why he tried to talk Joe into giving up the location of the yacht and the statue.

Wilma said it would be senseless for Avery to kill Joe, the only person who knew where to find the statue. But it made very good sense for Fowler to knock off the professor who was talking Joe out of taking his offer.

If Fowler didn't kill Joe, then who did?

Once you round up a list of likely suspects, you build a case based on motive, method, and opportunity. The motive was easy. With the professor out of the way, Joe might be more amenable to Fowler's offer. The means was more complicated.

My bomb squad pal O'Leary said the letter bomb parts that killed Professor Braddock had originated in foreign countries. Fowler had testified on behalf of a smuggler. Maybe I was wrong about Fowler, that he was a kind-hearted and generous guy who gives his all in the service of mankind. But from what I knew, he didn't seem like someone who'd stick his neck out in a courtroom for an antiquities smuggler without demanding a quid pro quo.

Smugglers know a lot of sketchy people, Wilma said. The smuggler Fowler helped could have known someone who dabbled in the type of material needed to assemble a letter bomb.

The pay-back to Fowler might have gone beyond bomb parts. The smuggler could have sweetened the deal with the loan of a gang of thugs who would give the house-bound old man all the muscle he would need.

Opportunities to do in the professor abounded. Braddock would never suspect that his good old friend and benefactor might consider him an obstacle to be removed. Fowler had a perfect red herring in the article the professor wrote about the Greeks and the Macedonians. What better way to deflect suspicion than to say the professor got caught in the middle of an age-old feud?

A lot about the case was still a mystery, but one thing was very clear. Alyssa should be informed that her uncle's friend was not the kindly old man he pretended to be. I drove from the library to the Thalassa gallery but didn't see Alyssa's SUV parked outside. I went into the gallery and found Diana puttering around in the showroom.

I said hello and asked where Alyssa was.

"She went out a while ago," Diana said.

"Did she say where she was going?"

"Oh yes. She was stopping by Joe's boat on the way to the restaurant. You had mentioned seeing another sketchbook on the *Zora* and she wanted to look at it."

I tossed Diana a quick good night and hurried out the door to the truck. A few minutes later I pulled the high lift next to Alyssa's SUV at the end of MacMillan Wharf. I got a flashlight out of the glove box, climbed onto the boat, and made my way to the wheelhouse.

The door was wide open. I stepped inside and flashed the light around. The beam picked out a cell phone lying on the top of the steering console. I knew right away from its pink casing that the phone was Alyssa's. The phone lay on top of a sketchbook. Most of the pages had been ripped out except for one. Written in ballpoint on the page was a telephone number and two words: Call me.

I grabbed up the phone and sketchbook and stepped onto the dock. Fowler's yacht was gone. I hustled back to the high lift and drove the short distance to the nightclub office. The light was blinking on the answering machine. I pressed the button. Alyssa's voice came on. She sounded excited.

"Hi Soc. It's me. I'll be a little late meeting you at the restaurant. I'm at Joe's boat looking at another sketch pad. Interesting stuff. Ties right in with your theory about the Alexander statue. I think you're right about this turning into a good old-fashioned treasure hunt. I'll bring the sketch pad with me."

It didn't take a genius to figure out what had happened. Alyssa would have called me from the *Zora*. Since I don't have a cell phone, she would have used the number I'd given her for the office at Diva's. The listening device on the boat had picked up her words about a treasure hunt and transmitted them to whoever was monitoring the bug. The thugs jumped into the inflatable, traveled the short distance across the harbor, and snatched her off the boat. All in a matter of minutes.

I slid Flagg's phone from my pocket and punched the call button. When he answered, I said, "I need your help, John."

He would know that the call was serious because I'd used his first name.

"Tell me about it."

When I was through explaining what had happened with Alyssa, he said, "Now give me a quick run-down of the salvage site."

"It's southwesterly of Provincetown. Joe dropped a lobster buoy in the water to mark the wreck. The water's around ten fathoms deep. That's about it."

"We're going to need a boat. That old tub your friend owned still available?"

"The *Zora*? Sure. I never gave back the keys."

"Make sure it's ready to go."

"We gassed up on the way in."

"Good. You told me the wreck is marked with a lobster buoy?"

"That's right. White and black with the *Zora*'s name on it"

"Any more buoys on the boat?"

"Sure. He had a pile left over from his lobstering days."

"Make sure they're still there," he said. "Now this is what I want you to do. Call the number in the sketchpad and tell whoever answers you'll give them the coordinates for the wreck site."

"Is that a good idea? I'll lose my only bargaining chip. Once they have the info, they can do what they want with Alyssa."

"That's why you have to control the situation by laying out your terms."

"What *are* my terms?"

"Still thinking about that. Wait."

He hung up and I sweated it out until he called back a couple of minutes later.

"I had to check on something. You can make your play. The important thing is to buy time. Say you will call them at dawn from the wreck site. You'll give them the coordinates. They can meet you at the buoy at first light and transfer Alyssa at the same time. No arguments."

"They can still pull some funny stuff. Joe's boat isn't exactly a battleship."

"You might be surprised. Call me back and tell me what they say."

"And if they don't go for it?"

"From what you told me, Fowler is calling the shots. He kills Alyssa, he'll never see his statue. You think that's going to happen?"

I hoped Flagg was right. I hung up and called the number on the sketchpad.

Fowler's razor-edged voice came on the line.

"Nice of you to call, Mr. Socarides. How can I help you?

"Don't play games with me, Fowler. Where's Alyssa?"

"She's safe. For now. How much longer she remains in that condition depends entirely on you."

"It depends on you too, Mr. Fowler. Any harm comes to Alyssa, and you'll never get the statue."

"Are you really prepared to gamble with the young lady's life?"

"What I know about your great-grandfather makes it less of a gamble."

He chuckled softly. "Oh, what is that?"

"Your family has been waiting more than a hundred years for the Alexander statue, ever since Lysander pulled it out of the sea. You're not going to let it go now that it's almost in your grasp."

There was a pause of a few seconds, then Fowler said, "You've done your homework, Mr. Socarides. You must know that one more life is not going to stand in the way of my goal."

"You'd kill an innocent woman?"

"As you said, I won't let anything stand between me and the statue."

I let out an exaggerated sigh. "You win. I'll give you the navigational co-ordinates for the site, but this has to be done my way."

He chuckled softly. "You're in no position to bargain but go ahead. I might find it amusing."

"I can guarantee that you'll laugh your head off when I

tell you how I want it to go. I'll call you at dawn and we'll meet int the general vicinity of the site. You transfer Alyssa. I'll pinpoint the wreck. That's the only way I'll do it. Alyssa comes on board. You go your way and I go mine."

"A rendezvous at dawn? How dramatic. I've waited this long; I can wait a few hours longer. I'll expect your call."

The line went dead as soon as I gave him the wreck's position. I called Flagg and told him about the conversation.

"The fact that he caved in so easy tells us he's planning a double cross," Flagg said.

"That's what I figured. So what do we do?"

"Ever hear of a triple cross?"

"Didn't know there was such a thing?"

"Meet me at Race Point beach in an hour and I'll show you how it works."

"What if it doesn't work?"

"Easy. We go to quadruple cross."

Chapter Thirty-Eight

A FEW MINUTES LATER, I was back on the *Zora*. I gathered the lobster buoys that Flagg wanted and piled them on the deck.

I went below and made sure the old GPS was under the pillow where I left it, and that's when I came across a bottle of cheap whiskey. I poured the contents into the harbor as an offering to Poseidon, thinking that if ever we needed the sea god's favor, this was the time.

Then, with the *Zora* ready to go, I headed to Race Point. The parking lot was mostly empty except for a few cars and trucks parked close to the beach where their owners were probably surf fishing. Flagg's Crown Victoria was off by itself near the old Coast Guard station. No one was in it.

I parked next to the car and got out of the truck. About a hundred feet away a light went rapidly on and off several times. I walked over to where Flagg was standing, a flashlight held in his hand.

"What's going on?" I said.

"The package I'm expecting is about to arrive. You might want to stand back."

I went to ask Flagg what he was talking about, but he stepped away. He pointed his light toward the sky and waggled the beam. I looked up and saw a blinking cluster of lights moving across the dark gray sky. About then, my ears picked up the distant thump-thump of helicopter rotors.

Taking Flagg's advice, I walked toward the Coast Guard station. I stopped and turned to look back just as a flare blossomed hot red and white from where Flagg had been standing, flew in a blazing arc, and landed on the tarmac in a shower of sparks.

Seconds later, a helicopter hovered above the parking lot and its thrashing rotors kicked up a cloud of sand that stung my face. I turned away and put my hands over my ears in a futile attempt to block out the racket. The helicopter set down and cut its engine. When I turned and opened my clamped-down eyes, I saw Flagg moving in under the slowly spinning blades. The door of the cockpit opened, and an arm handed Flagg an object.

He trotted over and said, "Let's get out of here before the cops hear all the ruckus and start asking questions. Joe's boat ready to go?"

I put an optimistic spin on my reply. "*Zora*'s raring to go."

We hurried back to our vehicles. Flagg opened the rear door of the Crown Vic and put a hard-plastic black suitcase on the floor. As I got in the truck, the chopper's engine ramped up. On our way out of the parking lot we passed a police cruiser going the other way. By then the helicopter was rising above the tarmac. It circled over the Coast Guard station, then flew out over the ocean.

Minutes later, we were aboard the *Zora*. While I got the engine going and set up the GPS, Flagg disconnected the listening device, then carried four of the lobster buoys I'd rounded up below along with his suitcase. He said he'd be busy on the trip out to the site. I cast off the lines, eased the boat away from the dock and pointed the bow toward the channel. Ignoring the speed limit, I goosed the throttle. *Zora* kicked up a wake that rocked the other boats anchored in the harbor. Before long, we were running past the breakwater on a course that would take us into Cape Cod Bay.

I didn't have a lot of confidence in the old rust bucket's engine, but I pushed it as far as I dared. Following the GPS track from my trip with Tink, we got to the wreck site area about forty-five minutes after leaving Provincetown. I reduced speed to a crawl and ran the boat in parallel lines until the bow spotlight picked out the reflection of Joe's buoy bobbing in the waves.

"On target," I yelled down to Flagg.

He passed the buoys up and climbed back on deck, where he laid out the markers in a row. Duct tape had been wrapped around each of the buoys. He picked up one of the buoys and pointed to a bulge under the tape.

"I've attached a cube of C-4 to each marker." He took a remote-control unit out of his bag and held it in his big palm. "Pop in a couple of batteries, turn this baby on, and I can light them up with the push of a button."

C-4 is a plastic explosive powerful enough to destroy a tank. "That's what the chopper brought in," I said.

"Had to call in a few IOUs to get this stuff so fast. We're probably outnumbered and outgunned, and they've got Alyssa. I figured we needed some bang for the buck."

Flagg attached anchors to each buoy line, then he had me run the boat in a circle. He dropped the improvised floats into the water with the wreck buoy at the center.

I checked my watch. Dawn was still a few hours off.

"Now what?" I said.

"We try to get some shut eye. I'll take first watch."

I went below and crawled into a bunk. Sleep wouldn't come, and I tried to clear my mind. The slosh of waves against the hull and the rocking of the boat had a hypnotic effect and eventually I dozed off. The smell of brewing coffee woke me up. Flagg was in the captain's chair sipping from a mug.

"I was supposed to take a shift," I said.

"You were sleeping like a baby. I wanted to go over some things, so we'll be ready when the time comes."

I poured a mugful of coffee and listened as Flagg ran through the fine points of his plan.

"That's it. What do you think?" he said.

While I pondered an answer, I looked out the window. Against the gray backdrop of sea and sky, a boat's running lights could be seen coming in our direction. I gulped the rest of my coffee and set the mug down.

"I think that the time has come," I said.

Chapter Thirty-Nine

THE SUN POKED UP OVER the horizon like an orange eyebrow. The first faint rays of dawn fell on the silhouette of a boat that materialized about a quarter mile away. Alyssa's phone chirped. I glanced at Flagg, who nodded. I went out on the deck and answered the call.

Fowler's voice came on the line. "Good morning, Mr. Socarides. Up bright and early I see."

"I wanted to be ready for our face-to-face meeting."

"That's not going to happen. As you know, I'm limited in my mobility and must forgo the pleasure of meeting in the flesh. The *Amphitrite* is outfitted with cameras from stem to stern. Although I'm not on the boat, I can clearly see you standing on the deck."

The yacht had slowed to a walk around a hundred yards away.

"Then you'll know I'm ready to make the exchange."

"First things first," Fowler said. "I want you to point out the location of my great-grandfather's boat."

"About fifty feet to the right of your position, you'll see a lobster buoy. The wreck is almost directly below the marker in sixty feet of water. I've carried out my part of the bargain. Now you can send Alyssa over in the launch."

"How do I know you're telling the truth? You could have tossed the buoy in the water at a random site."

"I could have, but I didn't. You probably have side scan

sonar that will give you a picture of what's on the bottom or you can put an ROV down to see for yourself. Before you do that, I want Alyssa back on my boat."

"You'll have to wait until I first do a subsurface survey to verify you've kept your side of the bargain."

"That's not going to work, Mr. Fowler."

"Then it appears we have a stalemate."

"Maybe not. See those four markers around the wreck buoy? They're loaded with plastic explosives, and I've got the remote. Here's what happens if I press the button. There will be four loud, wet bangs. The downward water pressure will bust your statue open like a ripe watermelon, and you'll be picking pieces of Poseidon and whatever's inside the statue off the ocean floor."

"You're bluffing," Fowler said. "I know everything about you. You would never have access to material like that nor the expertise to put it to use. You're nothing but a cut-rate private detective who thinks he's going to make a score."

I had to admit that Fowler was half-right. I worked for peanuts, and most of the time I didn't even get paid for my services, but the only score I wanted was to get Alyssa safely back on the *Zora*.

"I can light up one of these poppers to show you I'm telling the truth," I said. "The explosion might set off the other floaters. Can't say for sure. As you said, I'm no expert with this stuff."

After a brief silence Fowler said, "I'll order my crew to send the woman over. In return, you will give them the remote."

"How dumb do you think I am? I'd be giving you my best bargaining chip."

"Think again, Socarides. You get the girl in exchange for the remote, then you can be on your way while I start salvage operations. The statue means nothing to you. You've got thirty seconds to decide."

To drive the point home, a couple of guys came out of the cabin onto the deck holding Alyssa between them. One man pointed a pistol at her head.

"Fifteen seconds."

"Okay, Fowler, the remote's yours. Send her over."

The men muscled Alyssa into the launch, got in the inflatable with her, then started the outboard and slowly closed the short distance between the two boats.

As they came up alongside the *Zora*, the man in the bow tossed me a line. I pulled the inflatable against the hull. He and his friend both wore headphones. I guessed Fowler was directing their every move.

Alyssa stood up unsteadily in the inflatable, which was rising and falling in the waves, and reached for my free hand to steady herself. As I went to help her, the bow man pulled a pistol from under his shirt. He would have used it on me if Flagg hadn't stepped out of the captain's house with a gun in his hand.

"Toss it," he snapped.

Fowler's man hesitated as if he were going to try something, but he must have figured out that making a move would end badly. He dropped his weapon over the side.

While Flagg kept watch on the men in the inflatable, I grabbed Alyssa's hand and pulled her up onto the *Zora*. Once she was safely on the deck, I tossed the remote into the launch along with the loose end of the line.

"Get lost," I said.

The tiller man goosed the throttle. The inflatable sped back toward the yacht at least three times as fast as the trip over.

I asked Alyssa if she was all right.

"I'll be fine once I stop trembling."

She gave me a rib-breaking hug that was interrupted by the chirping cellphone. I answered the call and heard Fowler say, "You never said you had someone else on board."

"You never told me you were going to pull a double-cross," I said. "We're getting out of here. Have fun with your statue."

"I don't think you and your friends will be going anywhere." Fowler said in voice colder than ice.

The inflatable was coming alongside the yacht. The third crewman stood at the rail, holding a long cylindrical object against his shoulder.

"Rocket-launcher!" Flagg shouted. "Get moving."

Springing into the wheelhouse, I got the engine going and started the motor for the anchor line winch. While I reeled in the anchor, I pushed the throttle ahead. The boat began to move. Flagg raised his pistol in both hands, aimed at the yacht and emptied the magazine. Most of the bullets went wild. The man at the rail wasn't taking any chances and threw himself belly-down on the deck.

The fusillade bought a few seconds of time. Unless Flagg had an anti-missile in his bag, Joe's boat was about to become splinters. The anchor was still on its way up. With the line dragging in the water, I put the old tub into a tight turn.

Flagg had reloaded and was pointing his pistol at the yacht. I expected another round of shots, but he held off, even though the man he'd shot at was back on his feet. The rocket launcher dangled by his side. He and another crewman had their heads together.

I gunned the throttle. The cranky old engine poured enough power into the propellor to gain another knot or two. About then, I became aware of a pulsating racket. A Coast Guard helicopter hovered above the yacht. A Coast Guard cutter was making its way toward the yacht at high speed.

"I put the Coasties on standby last night and said there might be an incident," Flagg said.

I looked across the water at the yacht. "Guess this qualifies," I said.

Chapter Forty

MAYBE FOWLER DIDN'T want his pretty yacht caught in the middle of a fire fight, because his crew surrendered peacefully. As soon as a boarding party secured the yacht, Flagg got on the phone with someone at Coast Guard headquarters who told him that the yacht and its crew would be escorted to Boston for questioning.

We hung around until they gave us permission to leave the scene, then Flagg collected the lobster buoys and deactivated the C-4 charges while I pointed the *Zora* back to Provincetown. On the return trip, Alyssa told us how she wound up on the yacht. Minutes after she called me from Joe's boat, she'd stepped out onto the dock and three men had surrounded her. One had pressed something hard and cold against her neck. She heard a hissing sound and seconds later fell unconscious.

She woke up in a boat cabin. The chemicals injected into her bloodstream caused her intense thirst. A kidnapper came in with water. She took a few gulps, then fell asleep and didn't wake up until they hauled her out onto the deck, and she saw me on Joe's boat.

"I knew then that everything was going to be okay," she said before she went below to sleep off the hangover from the knock-out cocktail.

Flagg had maintained telephone contact with the Coast Guard. He hung up and said, "Coast Guard will hold the crew on weapons charges until they can pull together a kidnapping case. After we get in, I'll head to Boston to return the unused C-4. How do you want to handle the charges against their boss? Fowler's going to be tricky. He wasn't even on the yacht."

"Maybe he's not as smart as he thinks."

"What makes you say that?"

I reached into my jacket pocket and pulled out a remote control that was identical to the one I'd tossed to the man in the inflatable. "Fowler told me he didn't think I was bright enough to come up with the floating explosives."

"And he never figured I'd give you a second remote. Shows he's the dumb one for underestimating you."

"That's what I was thinking."

"Would you have set off the buoys and messed up his ol' statue?"

"If I thought it could neutralize the rocket-launcher. Sure."

Flagg stretched his lips in a wide grin. "It would have given Fowler quite the hotfoot."

After we got to port and pulled the *Zora* into the slip, Flagg climbed out of the boat onto the dock.

"I'll be in touch," he said. "Your bad guys are on ice. Mine are still looking for trouble. My team is on its way. They may already be in place."

"What should I do?"

"Keep your head down."

I dropped Alyssa off at the gallery and said I'd come by later after she was rested. Then I went back to the *Zora*. The old tub had been through a lot lately and deserved some TLC.

After I made sure everything was ship-shape, I climbed

back onto the wharf and glanced around at the people taking photos and doing things tourists do. That's when I saw two men in loud flowered shirts, who were standing in front of the pirate museum. The pair matched the description of Mike and Rick, my supposed old friends who'd asked the bartender if I came into the Bradford. I watched them peek in the museum windows, look around, then peek again.

I'm a natural troublemaker, I guess. I walked slowly in their direction to see what would happen. I was around a hundred feet away when one of them did his peek thing, and stared at me longer than is normally considered polite.

He tapped his buddy's shoulder and said something to him, then they started in my direction, walking with purpose in their step.

Mike and Rick looked as if they had something in mind. Maybe I should have been worried, but Flagg said he'd have his people in place. When they got closer and no one rushed in to make an intercept, I dug out the phone Flagg had given me and called him.

"Where's your team?" I said.

"They got stuck in traffic at the canal. They'll be there soon."

The Hawaiian twins had seen me talking on the phone and had slowed their walk, but they were still moving in my direction.

"How soon is soon?" I asked Flagg.

"I'll check and see. You sound worried. What's up?"

"I'm at the wharf. Two goons are moving in on me and nobody's stopping them. Tell your guys I'm heading toward Commercial Street. I'll try to duck down an alley."

I hung up and started toward town, thinking I could buy

time by blending in with the crowd, but a second pair of muscular guys dressed for a Don Ho convention were walking toward me from the direction of Commercial Street. From the way they sauntered, as if they had all the time in the world, they may have known about the deadly encounter with Flagg that their pals had on Martha's Vineyard and were not about to make the same mistake.

I was no Flagg. I was a middle-aged, unarmed private gumshoe. Once they figured that I was a lightweight, they could gather around and tickle my ribs with the point of a knife. Maybe they'd herd me to a car. Or they could jab a poison pellet into my skin. Either way, the outcome would be the same.

I paused near the whale watch boat docks and scanned the wharf for any sign of Flagg's team. The pleasant-faced woman in the ticket booth saw me loitering and must have noticed the indecisive expression on my face.

"Want to go on a whale watch?" she said. "Still some tickets left."

"Thanks. Maybe another time."

She smiled. "Lots of whales out there. Normally we'd be full, but things are slow this time of year."

The Hawaiian shirt gang was closing in. I dug my wallet out, plunked down the proper amount of cash, and grabbed a ticket.

"Have a nice afternoon," the ticket seller said.

I walked down the ramp to the floating dock and joined the last dozen or so passengers waiting to board.

"How long is the trip?" I asked the ticket taker.

"About four hours," he said. "You'll enjoy every minute of it."

"I know I will," I said as I climbed on board.

I blended into the crowd milling around on the stern deck and congratulated myself on my cleverness. The trip would take a few hours of my life but might extend it by a lot more. Heck, I might even see some whales. I had to put thoughts of breaching humpbacks aside. The flower shirt quartet was coming down the ramp, tickets in hand.

Being out at sea with a team of killers didn't seem like a prescription for good health. Here's how it works on a whale watch. The boat goes around the tip of Cape Cod into the open ocean. On the trip to Stellwagen Bank, the spotter keeps a running commentary over the public address system, telling the passengers about whale habits and talking about previous sightings.

Some of the whales have been given cute names. When the spotter sees a whale spouting or breaching, the boat speeds in that direction. Ginned up by the spotter, the passengers crowd the deck on the side closest to the whale and the boat tilts at an angle from the shift in weight.

I could find safety in the crowd for a while, but with passengers moving from one side to the other, and fore and aft, the Hawaiian guys could eventually close in on me. While everyone's attention was on the whale, I'd be easy pickings for that poison pellet I was worried about. It wouldn't be the first time someone had a fatal heart attack while out at sea. When the boat docked, the killers could simply walk off in the midst of the inevitable confusion.

All four men had boarded the boat. They huddled for a few seconds, then split into pairs. Two men headed for the bow. The others worked their way in my direction.

I moved to the starboard side, then went through a door into the large cabin that takes up most of the center part of the boat. The space has tables and chairs where passengers can eat and drink while the boat travels between the town and the whale grounds. I lined up with some of the passengers at the snack bar. When the pair on the port side deck passed, I stepped out of line so that I was behind them.

By then, the shore crew had untied the dock lines. The boat was backing out of its slip. Once it was clear of the dock and in open water, the boat would spin around and head out of the harbor. I peered around the corner of a doorway. The two pincers of the Hawaiian quartet had come together on the starboard deck.

I only had a few seconds before they split up again and came in the doors on both sides of the cabin. I stepped out of the cabin and made my way along the deck.

Unless I wanted to spend the next four hours playing whack a mole with the killers, I had seconds to make a move.

"Excuse me," I said to a young couple blocking the rail. "I think I forgot something."

They moved aside and I put two hands on the rail, swung one leg over, then the other. I was standing on the narrow metal ledge that runs around the boat. I twisted my body around to face away from the boat, with my arms stretched out at angles. My hands were holding tightly onto the rail, and they didn't want to let go. The launch didn't worry me. It was the landing.

If I didn't jump soon, I'd be carried along by the momentum of the moving boat. I'd either hit the edge of the dock or land in the water.

I jumped.

Desperation had honed my muscles and mind. The soles of my sneakers came down about a foot from the edge of the dock. The boat had been pulling me sideways at the same time, and I landed at an angle. My aging joints buckled from the twisting impact. I might have rolled off the end of the dock into the water if one of the whale watch crew hadn't grabbed my arm.

"Hey man, are you crazy? You coulda been killed."

"That's what I was trying to avoid," I said. "Thanks."

I pushed myself halfway up and he helped me to my feet. My elbow was on fire where it had slammed against the deck.

The whale watch boat had pulled entirely free of the slip and was starting its pivot. Four men in bright shirts stood with the other passengers close to where I had climbed over the rail. I waved. None of them waved back.

I staggered along the dock, then climbed up the ramp. I was hobbling past the ticket booths when I saw a woman whose face was familiar. My park ranger friend Beth Williams was walking in my direction. She was out of uniform, dressed casually in white shorts and a turquoise shirt. She wore a straw hat instead of her Smokey the Bear chapeau.

She came up and said, "Flagg said some guys were chasing you."

I nodded. "Four of them."

She noticed me trying to rub the pain out of my elbow. "Are you all right?"

"I'm a little banged up, but I'll be fine," I said.

She scanned the wharf and put her hand on the bulge that was visible under her shirt at the hip.

"Where are those guys now?"

The whale watch boat was making its way along the breakwater. "They decided to watch whales."

"Is that something like sleeping with the fishes?"

"Whales are mammals."

She furrowed her brow. "Flagg said you could be hard to understand some time. I don't have a clue what you're talking about."

I pointed at a bench near the whale watch booths. "Have a seat and I'll tell you about it."

We sat down, and when I finished telling her how I had lured four killers onto the whale watch boat and jumped onto the dock, she laughed so hard she had tears in her eyes.

"Flagg also said you were a funny guy," she said. "I didn't know what he meant until now. That was brilliant."

"This was more a case of desperation than brilliance, Beth."

"Whatever. Sorry we were late. Some of the team flew in from Washington."

"Traffic at the canal bridges can be a killer in more ways than one. "

"We should have accounted for that, but we didn't expect you to get into trouble so soon."

"Neither did I. What comes next?"

"That's up to you."

"Unless those guys are strong swimmers, they're stuck watching whales on Stellwagen Bank. They could call in reinforcements to chase me down, I guess."

"That probably won't happen. I doubt they'd want their bosses to know you slipped through their fingers in such a humiliating fashion."

"We've got four hours to figure it out."

"We'll have an alphabet soup welcome party waiting for them. FBI. CIA. ICE. DEA. We'll find a reason to detain them. Once they get off the boat and get clear of the crowds, we'll move. Maybe you should make yourself scarce for four hours until the action starts."

"Good idea."

We shook hands, then she walked off and disappeared into the crowd. I decided to go back to the dune shack and hunker down. But as I started walking to my truck I glanced off at the harbor and discovered that the action the ranger predicted was more likely to start in four minutes than four hours.

Chapter Forty-One

THE WHALE WATCH BOAT had stopped by the breakwater, turned around and was heading back to the dock. I guessed that the Hawaiian guys weren't interested in breaching humpbacks and had conveyed their feelings to the captain.

The boat came into the inner harbor and prepared to tuck into its slip. The Hawaiians were lined up at the rail waiting to leap onto the dock. Tourists strolled along the wharf and shopped at gift kiosks. Some of them might be part of Flagg's team, and they wouldn't be expecting action so soon. If they had to improvise, the wharf could become a shooting gallery the second the Hawaiian gang got off the boat. I had to draw them away from the crowds. I stood at the top of the dock ramp to make sure they saw me. One of them said something to his friends and pointed in my direction.

The boat pulled into its slip. Seconds later, the gangway was down, and the Hawaiians vaulted off the boat and sprinted up the ramp. I trotted toward the other side of the wharf, thinking that if I got to Joe's boat I could escape in the inflatable. I stopped once to look back. The Hawaiians were at the top of the ramp. I waved at them to get their attention and they started walking in my direction. That's when things started to go wrong for them.

Several people detached themselves from the crowd of

whale watch spectators. They walked briskly, with purpose, not in the aimless manner people on vacation tend to meander. Flagg's team culled the Hawaiians like cowboys and herded them to a seafood truck parked nearby. The truck doors opened, more people jumped out and cuffed their catch's hands behind their backs.

A couple of big guys persuaded the four men to get into the back of the truck. The doors were closed, and the truck drove off the wharf sandwiched between black Tahoe SUV escorts. The roll-up had been done quickly and quietly. No one except me noticed that a quartet of potential assassins had been whisked away.

I'd been keeping out of sight behind a ticket booth. When I stepped back into the open, ranger Williams came over and said, "Hope you enjoyed the show."

"I especially liked the curtain closer," I said.

She surveyed the tourists strolling along the dock. "It might not have gone as smoothly if you hadn't drawn those guys into the open where we could pick them off."

"Attracting bad guys is my specialty. What's next for the reluctant whale-watchers?"

"Federal jail in Boston for questioning."

"Will Flagg be there?"

She gave a quick shake of her head. "No one can ever say for sure where Flagg will show up. That's probably why he's survived so long in this business. Here's my ride. See you out on the dunes."

Another black Tahoe pulled up and she got in. I was feeling pretty good as I watched it drive away. With Fowler and his gang on ice and Flagg's bad guys out of the way, I could concentrate on my own business. I started back to my truck. My thoughts were on what lay ahead, not behind. I didn't notice the man trailing me. He stepped behind me and stuck something in my ribs as I put my hand on the truck's door handle.

"Get in," he said. Speaking in an undefinable accent, he said, "Open the door real slow, and keep your hands on the steering wheel."

I did what he said. He walked around the front of the truck, hand in a shoulder bag. He was big, maybe a couple of inches taller than me. He wore shorts and a surf shop T-shirt that went with the rest of his appearance, long hair over his ears, and a scruffy beard.

He got in on the passenger side. He was grinning, but I would have bet that if I could see the eyes behind the bamboo frame sunglasses, they would be hard and cruel.

"Drive," he said.

"Where to?"

He pulled his hand out of the bag and pointed the way with a shiny pistol. "Out of the parking lot. I'll tell you where to go."

I drove toward the exit, keeping watch for my park ranger friend. It was a futile gesture. She and her crew were on their way to Boston with their catch of Hawaiians. I went left onto Commercial Street toward the West End, past the Provincetown Inn, then around the traffic circle.

He told me to pull over and park. He pulled a wig off his head and ripped the beard from his chin. His black hair was cut close to his scalp military style and his chin was clean-cut, revealing a face that was as hard as the knuckles of a clenched fist.

"Where's Flagg?" he said.

"You know Flagg. He could be on the other side of the world."

"Bad luck for you if he is. Call him."

I told him I was going to reach into my jacket pocket for a phone. He raised the muzzle of the pistol up to my head.

"Carefully," he said. "Put the phone on speaker so I can hear."

I eased the phone out of the pocket using the tips of my fingers and my thumb and punched the call button. Flagg's voice came on.

"I heard the operation went off like clockwork," he said.

"Not quite. The hit men team had five guys, not four."

"How did you find out?"

"The fifth is sitting next to me with a gun pointed at my head."

After a brief pause, Flagg said, "Sorry I miscounted."

"Me too."

"Where are you?"

"Tell him," the gunman said.

"We're at the breakwater near the Provincetown Inn."

"On my way," Flagg said.

A couple of people were coming back to shore along the top of the breakwater. The gunman waited until they came off the jetty and watched them drive away in their car. He got out of the truck, came around and opened the door on my side. Pointing to the deserted breakwater, he said, "Get out and start walking."

We had only taken a few steps before I answered the chirping cell phone. Flagg said, "What do you want me to do when I get there?"

The gunman answered, "I want you to know that you're about to meet the brother you didn't kill."

"I know who you are. Still think I'll come?"

"I think you'll try to save your pal."

"Maybe we're not the pals you think we are."

"That's why I've taken out some insurance. I've got a ship with three hundred units of my choicest product on the way to the Middle East. The ship is loaded with explosives. I have only to make a quick call to send them to the bottom."

"By units you mean women."

"A few children. They get swept up in the harvest at times. There is a market for them as well."

If he was trying to unnerve Flagg, it didn't work. "I'll see you on the jetty," Flagg said in a calm voice.

We started to walk out onto the rocks. It was slow going because of the gaps and crevices between the big boulders. After a couple of hundred yards the breakwater makes a sharp bend to the right. We were at the turn when Flagg called again and told me to put the phone on speaker.

"Can he hear me?" he said.

"I hear you," the gunman said. "What do you have to say?"

"One word. Trifecta."

Flagg hung up. The gunman laughed. "He must think he's at the racetrack."

Flagg knew exactly where he was because I heard a soft thud and a wet gargle. The gunman dropped his gun and crumpled onto the rocks.

Flagg called seconds later. "Did I get him?"

"He's lying dead on the breakwater. So yeah, I'd say you got him."

"Stay where you are."

A figure was moving fast on the breakwater. Then Flagg was at the scene, carrying a long canvas case. A dark stain was spreading over the gunman's shirt.

"You've been practicing your marksmanship," I said.

Flagg raised the case he was carrying. "Compact sniper rifle with a scope and sound suppressor. Guess he won't be making that phone call."

"What do we do with him?" I asked.

Flagg looked around to make sure we were still alone, then got some transparent plastic envelopes out of his pocket and tucked them into the gunman's pockets. "Heroin," he said. "They'll think it's a drug deal. Don't forget, this is Helltown."

"You think of everything, Flagg."

"If you don't, the other guy will, and that could be fatal with my job. Let's tuck this guy in a hole. Some tourists will find him. Hope it doesn't ruin their vacation."

We rolled the body into a gap between two large rocks and started the long walk off the jetty.

"What next?" I said.

"Without the three brothers, their organization will crumble. Cops in a bunch of countries will stomp on the pieces."

"What about the ship full of women and children?"

"We've been keeping an eye on the guys in charge. They won't act without that phone call. Teams can move in now. Seems like most of my loose ends are tied up."

"Wish I could say the same."

"Anything I can do to help with your case?"

I thought about it for a minute. When we reached the end of the breakwater I said, "I think there might be."

Chapter Forty-Two

FLAGG GRUMBLED ABOUT the limits of what he could get out of the government bureaucracy, but after making a few phone calls, he came up with a time and place the next day. He gave me a ride to my truck and told me to keep the cell phone so I could let him know how everything worked out.

"Where are you off to next?" I said.

"Back to quiet ol' Aquinnah for a few days before my next assignment," he said. "Drop by some time."

"Thanks. I'll call ahead to make sure you're not having company in quiet ol' Aquinnah."

"Sorry about the mess-up, Soc. Can't see something like that happening again." He paused in thought, then said, "On the other hand, you never know."

"That's right. You never do," I said. "Give me a call when you want to go fishing."

We shook hands, and he drove off in his Crown Vic, leaving me alone in the parking lot. I watched his car disappear around a corner, wondering as I did whenever we said goodbye, if I would ever see him again.

Maybe Flagg was rejuvenated by the prospect of going back to his family home, or maybe he's simply the super-human I've always suspected him of being. He hardly seemed tired after the day's adventures. I was ready to crash, on the other hand, but before I headed back to Tink's apartment I swung by the gallery to see how Alyssa was doing.

She and Diana were in the showroom, drinking tea and enjoying the calming ocean light that poured off the wall paintings. Alyssa appeared rested after her nap. Diana went into the kitchen to get me a teacup. Alyssa picked up on my weary expression. "It's not over yet, is it?"

"Some of it is. I still don't know who killed Joe, or why. I intend to find out."

When she came back to the showroom, Diana asked me to stay for dinner. Since I didn't have any other plans, I accepted. We moved to the dining room and sat down to a meal of baked cod and potatoes done Portuguese style, washed down with copious amounts of mind-numbing wine.

After dinner I sat on the sofa, leaned back, and closed my eyes. When I opened them, I was stretched out on the couch, covered by a blanket, and morning sunlight was streaming through the windows. Diana was setting a coffee pot and cups on a table.

I sat up. "Sorry, I must have dozed off."

"I guess you did," she said.

I lifted off the blanket. "Hope I wasn't a bother."

"You can never be a bother. You're welcome to stay any time you'd like."

I checked my watch. I had an hour before I had to leave, long enough to wake up with a couple of cups of coffee and scrambled eggs with sliced linguica and sweet bread toast.

I polished off breakfast and I thanked Diana, who asked me to wait while she packed some fresh-baked cookies for the road. While she was in the kitchen, Alyssa managed to whisper a warning. "Remember what Father Nick said.

Please be careful."

Her warning echoed in my head as I drove to the Race Point lot and parked near the Coast Guard station. The helicopter arrived exactly on time, landing in the same spot as when it delivered Flagg's goodies. The chopper lifted off almost as soon as I got on board and strapped myself in.

I told the pilot where I wanted to go. The helicopter flew in a straight line across Cape Cod Bay to the South Shore, made a single pass over Fowler's mansion, and set down in the center of the circular drive. I said I'd only be a few minutes, then got out of the chopper and walked up to the front door. As I went to ring the doorbell, a voice came out of a hidden speaker.

"Come right in," Fowler said.

The lock made a soft click and the door opened silently. I stepped inside. There was no one in the veranda of the Immortals, but the voice from another speaker told me to follow the hallway to my right. The passageway led to the porch where I'd talked to Fowler the first time. He was in his wheelchair obviously waiting for me. On the table was a decanter and two snifters.

He motioned for me to sit down.

"You should have let me know you were coming for a visit, Mr. Socarides. I would have had a snack prepared."

"It was a last-minute decision," I said.

"So much of life is. I never expected I'd see a helicopter land on my front lawn, and I was even more surprised when you stepped out. The best I could do with a few minutes' notice is cognac."

"Thanks. I've had breakfast."

He poured a couple of fingers of amber liquor into one snifter, swished it around, and raised the glass in toast. "To history," he said.

When I didn't touch my glass, he put his snifter back on the table without taking a sip. "I'd forgotten that you like to get right down to business. I like that. Tell me what brings you here."

"I need some questions answered."

He chuckled softly. "I thought you were going to tell me the Coast Guard has impounded my yacht and arrested the crew. Well, I've already been notified. My lawyers are working on getting it back. Apparently, the crew was using the vessel without permission."

"Funny, you told me the yacht was loaded with cameras that allowed you to see everything that was going on."

"You must have misunderstood."

"There's something else I don't understand. Why your crewman didn't use his rocket launcher when he had us in his sights."

"You're assuming that he was following my orders."

"Yeah, that's a big problem with me. I make assumptions based on the evidence."

He gave me a sly look. "You're not wired with a recording device, are you?"

"You probably scanned me with an X-ray and metal detector the second I stepped through the front door, so you know I'm clean. Why was no order given to fire the rocket-launcher? Attack of conscience?"

"Hardly. More likely the order was given, but it didn't go through."

"Technical glitch?"

"You'll have to talk to someone more knowledgeable. The connection was broken at a crucial time. The cameras went blank and voice communication ceased."

"Good thing. If the Coast Guard arrived after you blew us out of the water, it could have been awkward for you."

He dismissed me with a wave of his hand. "A rocket launcher would have made mincemeat out of their helicopter and cutter."

I searched his cold eyes for a trace of irony, but all I saw was madness.

"You'd go that far?"

"In for a dime, in for a dollar, as the old saying goes. Any more questions I can answer?"

"Yeah. Who murdered my friend Joe?"

"What makes you think I'd know the identity of the killer?"

"From what I've seen, you'll do anything to get your hands on that hunk of bronze sitting on the sea bottom. Maybe Joe got in the way."

"That argument falls apart in the face of logic. Why would I kill the only person who could give me what I want?"

"If it wasn't you, who was it?"

"Let me answer that with a question of my own. What happens now with the Alexander Poseidon?"

"I didn't know it had a name."

"It's got a name and a fabled history that says it will make the man who owns it rich beyond his dreams."

"You think the statue is filled with treasure?"

"Professor Braddock leaned in that direction, and I respect his scholarship."

"So do I. But my guess is that it will take years to resolve the ownership issue. Greece will make a claim. So will the country that calls itself Macedonia. Even if they haul it out of the sea, no one will be able to lay a hand on the statue. If you're lucky, you may find out what's inside about the time you're getting out of jail."

"We'll have to see about that, won't we? I will tell you what you want to know about your friend's murder. In return, I want you to do me a favor. Tell Alyssa that I'm sorry about her uncle. We were friends and colleagues. I enjoyed his company."

"Not enough to prevent you from killing him."

"A difficult but clear-cut decision. With Braddock gone, Bonega would come back to me."

"But that didn't happen, did it? He brought me in."

"That's right. I never expected he would throw his lot in with an old comrade in arms."

"And I never expected that the wheelhouse had been bugged and that someone was listening to every word of our conversation."

"Planting a listening device turned out to be a good investment in time and money."

"Wilma visited Joe on his boat to convey your offer. Is that when the bug was planted?"

"It seemed like an opportunity not to be missed."

"Why didn't you plant a locator beacon at the same time?"

"There was no need. Joe had indicated that he was going to make a deal with me. Seems I underestimated him."

"A lot of people have learned about Joe the hard way."

"And I underestimated you as well. I accepted the popular stereotype of the private detective as a loner. I never dreamed you would have armed back-up on board. Who was that impressive gentleman?"

"Joe wasn't the only one who could call in an old comrade in arms."

"Band of brothers."

"Something like that. You've got a deal. I'll relay your heartfelt apology to Alyssa," I lied. "What have I got to lose?"

"Your innocence."

"I lost that a long time ago, Mr. Fowler."

He smiled, then took a cell phone from his pocket, and tapped the screen. He put the phone down on the table. I listened to the recorded message.

"Are you sure you don't want to have a shot of cognac?" he said. "The color seems to have drained from your face."

I could have used a stiff drink, but instead, I got out of my chair.

"We'll be in touch," I said. "I can find my way out."

I must have been in a daze because I got lost in the labyrinth of rooms and hallways. I found myself in the room Wilma called the rogues gallery, trying to decide which exit was the right one, when a female voice said:

"Do you have a favorite?"

I turned and saw Wilma in a doorway with her arms crossed and a bemused smile on her lips.

"It's hard to pick one. They're all so charming. What about you?"

She pointed to the marble statue of a woman flanked by a couple of hogs.

"I've always admired Circe's power to turn men into swine."

"Some men are pretty swinish to begin with."

She nodded. "Speaking of swine. Did you have a nice chat with Mr. Fowler?"

"I wouldn't describe it as nice. He's not a nice man, but

you'd know that. You work for him."

"Not anymore."

"When did you quit?"

"I was never really working for him. I have other employers."

"Anyone I know?"

"Probably not. I'm with the Macedonian security services, on loan to Greek security on a joint operation."

"I wasn't aware they worked together."

"Sometimes, when there's a common need."

"What was the common need in this case?"

"They wanted to infiltrate Fowler's organization and dig out information on his illegal trade in Greek and Macedonian antiquities. In the long run, to foster cooperation between the two countries."

"You told me things aren't always the way they seem. Fowler trusted you?"

"Enough to send me to see your friend Joe with an offer to give him a split of any revenue from the Alexander Poseidon in return for its location."

"An offer he declined."

"Unfortunately."

"How do I know you're telling the truth? That you're not part of Fowler's organization."

"Think about it. Had I not been there, Fowler's men would have carried out his orders concerning your large friend to the letter."

"What were those orders?"

"Find the information with the location of the statue. At all costs."

"Maybe there's something else you can explain. Tink heard a woman's voice say the word *duster*. What was that about?"

"*Dosta!* It's Macedonian for *enough.* The big man would have been killed if I hadn't stopped them. And you and your friends would have been blown to pieces at sea if I hadn't sabotaged the rocket launch."

"Fowler told me he lost communication because of a technical glitch."

She raised her hand. "Meet the *glitchee.*"

"You broke the connection?"

"Fowler runs his international operation from a room filled with sophisticated communication systems. Its complexity means it is easy to disrupt."

"I guess I owe you an apology."

"Over the Ruth Wonderly accusation. Yes. I looked it up. Not entirely flattering. I suppose I could be the reverse Ruth. She was bad posing as good. I'm good posing as bad."

"Sam Spade would have liked that. I think he really had a thing for Brigid O'Shaughnessy."

A smile danced on her perfect lips. "My job here is done. I'll be heading back to Skopje to file a report that will implicate Fowler."

"Will your report say what's inside the statue?"

"You should know what the Alexander Poseidon contains, Mr. Socarides," she said, a sly expression in her green eyes.

I gave her a lopsided grin. "You'll have to help me out. I'm a little slow at times."

"I don't think you're slow at all," she said with a smile. "If I'm Ruth or Brigid, you'd be Sam."

Before I could ask her what she was talking about, Wilma led the way to the front door and gave me a warm handshake. Then I walked back across the lawn to the helicopter. A few minutes later we retraced our route across the bay to Provincetown.

I didn't want to do what I had to do. I wanted to tell the helicopter pilot to turn around and fly away from Provincetown, as far as the fuel in his tank would take him. Instead, I watched as the long sandy arm of Cape Cod grew closer, curled in an uppercut, arm cocked to with a clenched fist positioned to give me a punch right in the gut.

Chapter Forty-Three

THE HELICOPTER SET DOWN on the parking lot at Race Point about where it had lifted off. I thanked the pilot, told him to keep what was left of the cookies, and drove back to the office at Diva's to use the phone. I called the number on the dune taxi poster that was tacked to the wall. Manny's recorded voice came on the line.

"Hi, you've reached M and M dune taxi. Manny is probably out leading a tour of the spectacular Province Lands, but if you'd like to make a reservation, please leave a message with your name and number."

"This is Soc," I said. "Call me."

Seconds after I hung up the phone chirped. "Hi Soc," Manny said. "Great to hear from you. What's going on?"

"Something important has come up," I said.

"This have to do with Joe?"

"Yup. There's been a development in his case."

"I'm out on the dunes. Remember the hill I said was my favorite place in the world?"

"Sure. I said it would be easy for it to be my favorite place too."

"That's right. I'll wait for you."

A few minutes later I was retracing my route back to Race Point. I followed the tracks through the Province Lands and drove to the top of the hill Manny had shown me on our dunes ride. Parked on the summit was a Chevy

Suburban like the SUVs Manny uses as a dune taxi. But unlike his taxi, there were no pictures of dunes on the exterior, which was painted in dark gray primer.

Manny got out of the taxi as I pulled up next to it. Speaking as if he owed me an explanation, he said, "Just came out to clear my head."

"Is it all clear now?"

He gave me a sad smile. "Not hardly, but it sure is pretty out here."

We gazed at the distant blue of the Atlantic Ocean. Neither one of us spoke until he turned and said, "You got something you want to say to me?"

I nodded. "I just came back from Fowler's house. I had a long talk with him."

"What did you talk about?"

"Everything," I said in a dead voice.

He opened his mouth without speaking, then glanced up at the sky as if he were following the flight of an imaginary gull. "So you know."

"Yeah, I already knew about the electronic bug on the *Zora*. I didn't know it recorded you killing Joe."

He filled his lungs a few times as if he were getting ready to make a deep free dive, and said, "It wasn't supposed to happen that way."

"How was it supposed to happen?"

"After Joe found the statue, we talked about what he should do with it. When Fowler said he wanted the statue and would pay to know where it was, the offer seemed like a dream come true. Joe said he could quit fishing, pay off Mary, and put money in my business to buy some new dune taxis."

"The professor talked him out of it."

Manny chuckled. "Yeah, the guy told Joe about the treasure legend. Our deal went up in the air. Poof."

"Then the professor went poof."

He nodded. "Too bad. I met him once. Nice guy, but I wasn't sad with him dead. I thought Joe would get back on track with Fowler. That didn't happen. Joe was going to salvage the wreck without Fowler, and he was cutting me out after he learned Fowler had hired me as a 'consultant' to talk him into a deal."

"How'd he figure you were working for Fowler?"

"Joe could size people up. I was pushing him hard to go with Fowler. He came right out and asked me. I told him the truth, said it shouldn't change his mind about Fowler. He said he was done with me."

"That must have been tough."

"I went crazy, Soc. Everything I dreamed up was turning to crap. He told me to get off his boat, pointed the trident at me. I twisted the thing away from him. It was easy with him holding it in one hand. He grabbed a section of net off the deck. Threw it over me like a fight in the Roman Coliseum. I jabbed with the trident, trying to punch my way through it, just as he lunged. It was an accident. I swear it was, Soc."

"Like gut-blocking me and stealing the GPS from Joe's boat were accidents?"

"That wasn't supposed to happen either. I panicked when you came on board."

I didn't know whether killing Joe was an accident or whether Manny's panic was real or imagined. It didn't matter. What mattered was what he did afterwards.

"Why did you call Fowler after killing Joe?"

"He was the only one I could think of. He wasn't

shocked like I expected. Real calm. He asked me where I was and how I killed Joe."

"He already knew what you did from the bug. He was getting your confession down on the record."

"I know that now. I had to do what he said. He told me to get Joe's body into the wheelhouse out of sight. Then he told me to wrap up the trident and take it to the airport. He said he would send a plane in to pick it up. Once I had done that, I called him like he asked me to."

"What did he want?"

"Said I had caused him a great deal of trouble and owed him. He played the recording. He said I would work for him to find out where the statue was, or he would turn the recording in to the police. He wanted me to tell him everything that was going on as soon as it happened."

"That's how Fowler always seemed to be a step ahead of me. Anything else?"

"Yeah. He told me he would send some people to Provincetown, and I was going to do what they wanted."

"Like chasing me through the dunes."

"They grabbed my new taxi. It was in the garage, all primed for a paint job. They made me hand over the keys."

"They knew where to wait, Joe. That was more than handing over the keys to your truck. They beat up Tink and would have killed him. You told them to meet him at his workshop."

"They didn't say anything about killing someone. They wanted some stuff you had. Pictures and a video. What could I do? Damnit Soc, I didn't want Mary to know I had killed her brother. Put yourself in my shoes."

"They wouldn't fit me, Joe."

He seemed to shrink. "Wait a second," he said.

He went to his taxi, opened the door, and reached inside for something. When he turned, I saw that he had a pistol in his hand.

"Don't be stupid, Manny. I'm not the only one who knows about what you did," I said. "The truth is bound to come out."

A look of surprise came to his face. "Hell, Soc. I'm not going to hurt you. I'm thinking what this will do to Mary. It's better I'm out of her life when she finds out I killed Joe."

"She's not going to find out," I said.

"What do you mean? What are you going to do?"

"Nothing."

"You're not going to tell the cops? Or Mary?"

I shook my head.

"You'd get arrested and thrown into jail, dragged into court, and sent to prison for the rest of your life. Mary would be in the cell with you every day. She doesn't deserve that. This way, you live out your sentence with the secret eating away at you. That's the kind of punishment money can't buy. So, you can take that gun and blow your brains out and make her miserable. Or you can take this as a gift you don't deserve. I don't give a rat's ass about you, but I care about Mary."

I got back in my truck and as I drove off the hill, I checked the rear-view mirror. Manny was still standing upright, the hand with the gun hanging down by his leg. I guess that was good. I didn't really care.

I drove off the dunes and back to the office. I phoned Frank Martin, my pal in the district attorney's office, and got right to the subject of my call.

"Have you solved the Provincetown murder case?"

"I know the victim is dead, and that's about it," Frank

said. "Why, what's up?"

"I've got a lead for you."

"I'm listening."

"Talk to a guy named Avery Fowler. Real estate mogul on the South Shore who has a side business dealing in Greek and Roman antiquities. He was very interested in the trident Joe pulled out of the bay."

"How do I approach this?"

"Ask him if his company chartered a plane to fly to Provincetown the night Joe was killed. He'll probably lie and say he knows nothing about it. In that case, pull the FAA flight records and track down the charter company. You can use his lie as leverage to swear out a search warrant for his house."

"What if he doesn't lie?"

"He will. It's what he does. But if he doesn't, I'll bet you can come up with another excuse to get into his house."

"I'll bet I can. What am I looking for?"

"The trident used to murder Joe."

"That would be sweet! You're not blowing smoke up my flue?"

"Wouldn't dream of it."

Chapter Forty-Four

MARY WAS ON THE deck built out onto the beach from behind the club. She was in a bathing suit, lying in a lounge chair, her face in the shade of a wide-brimmed straw hat.

"One of your staff people said you were out here," I said."

"I'm trying to clear the bar fumes out of my lungs." She sat up, instantly alert, adjusted the back of her chair into a vertical position, and slipped the hat off her head. "Why were you looking for me? Something to do with Joe's case?"

I settled into a nearby deck chair. "I don't think I'll be able to find Joe's murderer. The case is too complicated for a single investigator. We'll have to let the police do their work. There's a chance they'll turn up something I missed. Sorry."

She reached over and put her hand on mine. "It was too much to ask of anyone. Don't forget, you weren't even supposed to be working the case."

"Maybe it's a good thing I kept poking around. I think the man behind Joe's murder was Fowler, the rich guy who wanted Joe to tell him where he found the trident."

"What reason would Fowler have to kill Joe?"

"It made Fowler angry when Joe refused his offer and went to the professor. I think Fowler had the professor killed. Then he took care of Joe somehow after he decided to go out on his own."

"It's so hard to believe that Fowler would go that far."

"We'll both believe it when the police charge Fowler in the professor's murder. He had motivation, method, and opportunity. He'll go away for life. It won't be for killing Joe, but Braddock's murder will put him in jail."

"It's not the ending I wanted, but it's a good one. I don't know how I can thank you for all you've done."

"No need. We'll always have memories of Joe, no matter what."

"I'll take it even further. Diana called me to talk about Joe's artwork. She wants to schedule a one-man show and would like me to help. I said I'd do it."

"That's ambitious, especially with the summer season coming up."

"I'm taking a break from Diva's. I want to help Manny build up his taxi business. Tink will run the club. Maybe with an option to buy me out."

"What are you going to do with Joe's boat?"

"Is there any hope for it?"

"Not much," I said.

"Maybe I'll just scrap it."

I told Mary that was a good idea, and said I'd be clearing out of Provincetown and heading home. She said she would let me know about the gallery opening for Joe's show. She'd probably combine it with a memorial celebration. Then she gave me a long hug that made me want to stay longer. But I had a Maine coon cat to tend to and the pieces of my life to put back together. She unwrapped her arms finally and gave me a kiss on each cheek.

I was still bathing in what a poet would call the warmth of her embrace as I walked along the beach to the wharf and stopped for a last sad gaze at the *Zora*. Then I got in my truck and drove to the art gallery.

Alyssa was sitting at the garden table typing on her laptop. She looked up and smiled. "I hoped you'd be coming by."

"I'm on my way out of town and wanted to see how you're doing," I said.

"I'm doing fine, thanks to you and your friend. I don't want to think what would have happened if you hadn't arrived on the scene. Please tell him how much I appreciate his help."

I wasn't sure when I'd see Flagg again. But I said I'd pass along his message.

"When will you be going back to Central America?" I said.

"I've postponed my return and put my Mesoamerican research aside for now. I want to continue Uncle Emory's work on Alexander. I never dreamed that ancient Greek studies could be so exciting!"

She would be working at the MFA and said to call if I was going to be in Boston. I said I would let her know when I was in town and apologized again for jumping on her from the roof. She gave me a hug, and I got another one from Diana on the way out of the gallery.

I said I would come back for Joe's show.

"You can stay here," she said. "I'd love to have you. I like having company. Alyssa is leaving soon. With Joe gone, this will be a big old lonely house."

I'd been so busy tending to the lives of other people I'd neglected my own. It had been a long time since I'd had female companionship. Diana was intelligent, interesting, and pretty, and I looked forward to seeing her again.

"I'd like that," I said. "I'd like that a lot."

I stopped at the Bradford on the way out of town to thank the bartender for his help. He offered me a beer on the house, which I refused, partly because I was anxious to get home, and partly because Jerry McGuire, the *Globe* reporter, was waving me over from down the bar.

"I was hoping to see you," he said. "Got some good news. As a result of our story, I've got an advance from a publisher to do a book on the story of Joe and the statue."

"Congratulations. Call me when you're ready and I'll fill you in on what I know."

"I'll do that. Wait." He reached under his computer and pulled out a white business envelope which he handed to me. I looked inside and saw a check with lots of numbers.

"What's this all about?"

"It's payment in advance for the time you're going to spend talking to me."

"Are you sure?" I said.

"Very sure. I wouldn't have the story or the book without you."

We shook hands and said we'd talk soon. I stepped away from the table, only to stop and turn.

"Do you have a title for the book?"

"My working title is The God in the Sea."

"I like it," I said.

On the way home I swung by the neighbor's house to fetch Kojak. She said he'd been the perfect gentleman and was welcome to stay any time. He'd just had something to eat, but when I got back to the boathouse, I gave him his favorite kitty treats.

Then I picked him up and went out on the deck where I sat in an Adirondack chair with my old buddy on my lap. We watched the sailboats cutting wakes across the bay, and

I apologized for abandoning him so soon after we got back from Florida. Kojak broke into a wheezy purr that must have cost him some energy at his advanced age, but it told me everything between us was all right. I patted his boney head, and started to tell him about the River Styx, but the purr changed into a snore.

As I gazed out over the bay, I couldn't help thinking about that old saying that you can choose your friends, but you can't choose family. Your friends choose you, too. Kojak chose me when he scratched at my door as a lost kitten, almost as if he knew I wouldn't take him to the animal rescue shelter. Flagg could have picked a different bar stool when he sat next to me at that joint in Vietnam. My old fishing partner Sam didn't have to say "Finestkind," when I asked him for a job on his boat. And Joe never regretted his choice to put himself in the way of a load of hot shrapnel.

Your family has choices too. My mother chose not to give up on her eldest son who'd disappointed her so many times. Sister Chloe would walk to the moon for me. George was right about me using my guilt over leaving the family as a crutch, but he won't let me forget we're brothers. None of them has stopped loving me.

When I drifted away from the family orbit, it was inevitable that as my parents aged, the scales would tilt off balance. If family harmony hadn't been disturbed by the disagreement over the boat loan, it would have been something else. I should have seen that.

It's never too late to learn, I guess.

I got up slowly and put the sleeping pile of fur down on the chair. Then I went into the house, grabbed the phone, and made two calls. The first was to Jim to tell him *Thalassa* was no longer on the market. The second was to the number penciled on the wall.

The phone rang a couple of times before someone said hello.

"Hi, Ma," I said. "It's Aristotle."

July

It's amazing what a difference a month makes.

The Cape Cod spring had ended abruptly just before the Fourth of July. The weather changed from cool to hot and humid. The busy weekends had spilled over into the weekdays. The roads were clogged with SUVs carrying families from Boston, Connecticut, and New York, and the bustling restaurants and clam shacks were filled with sunburned and tanned beach goers,

I pointed the truck into the driveway of St. George's Greek Orthodox church and was directed to a parking space that had been blocked off with orange plastic cones. The space next to me was occupied by a very long Mercedes sedan with a vanity license plate that read PIZZA.

I could hear the insistent notes from a bouzouki going head-to-head with a clarinet from the band in the parking lot, where a bunch of teenagers in native costume were doing a circle dance. I went into the big tent and scanned the rows of folding chairs and tables. Chloe waved me over to a table occupied by my brother George, my mother, and my father. George's wife was there and so were his college-aged kids.

Pop has his good days and bad days, but he must have felt well enough to ride down in my brother's Mercedes with the rest of the family. The last time I saw him was a few months ago, and he barely knew me. I wasn't expecting any miracles, but this was a church after all. With help from my brother and sister, he got unsteadily to his feet, held his arms out, and said, "Aristotle."

That was the beginning of a round of multiple hugs that demonstrated without a doubt that no one can hug like the Socarides family. I might have been hugged to death if Father Nick hadn't shown up with trays of *psari plaki* made with some of the fish I had donated.

We were digging into the feast when I could sense from the way brother George picked at his plate that he was less interested in his food than he was in me. I put my knife and fork down and thanked him for pulling together the family reunion.

"You're welcome," he said. "You got something else to tell me?"

"Yup. I'm buying the baklava for the whole table."

"You got to be kidding me," he said. "That's it?"

"Not at all. I'm also rejecting Ma's offer to make me a director. You're right about me helping other people. I can still do that, but I should be more than a token member of the family. You and Chloe can run the company just fine without me."

My brother isn't big on hugs, but he gave me a real crusher. He isn't great about picking up the tab, so I was surprised when he added, "The baklava is on me."

"That's very generous of you, George."

"We've still got the issue of the late boat payments."

"Not anymore."

I took the payment for editorial consulting services and held the check under George's nose. He looked at the numbers in the payment space and said, "About the baklava."

"Yes, George."

"I think the older brother should pay for dessert."

Epilogue

Four Months Later

I DROVE FROM THE boathouse to Boston on a cool, crisp day in late fall. Alyssa met me in the special room at the Boston Museum of Fine Arts that had been set aside in the Greek and Roman art department for the Alexander Poseidon. The statue had been attracting steady crowds since McGuire's series in the *Boston Globe* in anticipation of his book. Alyssa had used her position at the Museum of Fine Arts to arrange a special fifteen-minute showing for just the two of us.

The belt loops that had been built into the design of the statue had allowed for its extraction from the sea once the government of Greece had signed off on the salvage. Seems that no one wanted it to remain on the bottom where it would be a target of poachers or simply fall apart.

The deal was that the statue would not be cracked open. Nor would it be X-rayed until all the parties that claimed ownership agreed. It could be years before anyone knew whether the statue held gems or rocks.

The mystery about the contents whipped up even more interest. People waiting in long lines to get into the exhibit could only imagine the riches that might be behind the green patina. The exhibit's clever visual displays played up the question of whether the statue contained treasure or trash, and visitors ate it up.

Joe and the professor figured prominently in the credits for the archaeological discovery. The museum was doing a brisk business selling T-shirts and coffee mugs with old Posy's image on them. McGuire's book was on a rush publishing schedule so it would be out in time for Christmas.

Poseidon was submerged in the greenish water of a glass tank, where he was protected from the corrosive effects of air. The statue was illuminated by low level lights. When I'd seen Poseidon at the bottom of the bay through the electronic eye of the ROV, he'd been dwarfed by the sea that was his domain. But in the confined space of the gallery, from a few feet away, Poseidon was an imposing figure.

He was more than eight feet tall as I'd estimated, broad-shouldered, with powerful biceps. The marine growth had been cleaned away from his face, revealing features that were more human than god-like. He didn't have a long, curly beard, nor did his eyes project anger and violence, like those in the pictures Father Nick had shown me in his office.

The elevated chin and determined set of the lips projected an expression of supreme confidence. It was the face not of a cruel god, but of a mortal, someone who wouldn't hesitate to set out on a campaign to conquer the world before he was thirty. Someone like Alexander the Great.

It was kind of gutsy for old Alex to stick his head on the body of a grumpy god like Poseidon. The Immortals squashed mere mortals who behaved like gods, but maybe Alexander thought Posy would be pleased by the magnitude of what was inside the statue. Or maybe Poseidon had the last laugh when Alexander died before he could begin the conquest of India.

Alex was a showman to the very end. He couldn't resist the chance to have his personal sculptor show Poseidon with the trident points angled down. It was the position Alexander's spear would have been in when he waded into the surf and plunged it into the beach to claim Asia. The original trident was still being held as evidence by the police, and the statue held a replica made of composite material made to look like ancient bronze.

"Well? What's your guess?" Alyssa said.

I'd been thinking that maybe it had been a good thing when I'd poured whiskey into the harbor as a gift to Poseidon before we left for our sea battle with Fowler's thugs.

"Pardon me?" I said.

"The statue. Any opinion what's inside?"

"Sure, I know exactly what's in the statue."

"You *do?* Then please tell me."

I remembered what Cindy the librarian had said about the story line of *The Maltese Falcon*, and Wilma's comment that if she were Brigid, I'd be Sam. Switching to my best Humphrey Bogart accent, I growled, "It's the stuff dreams are made of."

The End

Acknowledgments

I'D LIKE TO THANK Daniel Scherl, host of *Memories of a Moonbird*, and Lew Taylor, proprietor of I Cannot Live Without Books, who gave the first draft of this book the benefit of their sharp eye and keen ear, and Barbara Clark, whose editing pencil smoothed out the rough spots in the manuscript.

Special thanks to Christi, my wife and research assistant, who knows from personal experience that living with the mood swings and insecurities of a fiction writer at work is not for the faint of heart.

About the Author

PAUL KEMPRECOS IS the author of nine novels in the Cape Cod-based Aristotle "Soc" Socarides private detective series. His debut book, *Cool Blue Tomb*, was awarded a Shamus by the Private Eye Writers of America for best original paperback. *Shark Bait*, the eighth book in the series, was nominated for the same award. He was the first series co-author to work with Clive Cussler and wrote eight best-selling NUMA Files novels in collaboration with the "Grandmaster of Adventure."

He also wrote a stand-alone thriller entitled *Killing Icarus* and two adventure novels featuring Matinicus "Matt" Hawkins, including *The Minoan Cipher*, nominated for a Thriller award by the International Thriller Writers. His short story, "The Sixth Decoy," appeared in two anthologies, *Nothing Good Happens After Midnight* and *Best Mystery Stories of the Year, 2021*, which was edited by Lee Child, along with literary luminaries Stephen King and Joyce Carol Oates.

He and his wife, Christi, a financial planner, live on Cape Cod.